THE MINX

Set in the tumultuous times of the early 14th Century,

A Historical Novel by

Janet Cameron

It may not have happened *exactly* like this - but it could have...

Janet Cameron asserts the moral right to be identified as author of this work. No part of this book may be produced in any form, except for the quotation of brief passages in criticism, without written permission. All rights reserved.

Copyright: © Janet Cameron (2019)

CONTENTS

CHAPTER 1 ~ The French Court, Spring 1307 ~ 7

CHAPTER 2 ~ News and Gossip ~ 20

CHAPTER 3~ Gossip is Juicy but Dangerous ~ 25

CHAPTER 4 ~ To Boulogne for the Royal Wedding~ 34

CHAPTER 5 ~ To England ~ 46

CHAPTER 6 ~ Out of Favour ~ 51

CHAPTER 7 ~ The King's Infatuation ~ 62

CHAPTER 8 ~ The Love Potion ~ 69

CHAPTER 9 ~ A Meeting with Guy ~ 77

CHAPTER 10 ~ Ellie the Schemer ~ 79

CHAPTER 11~ A Forced Separation ~ 88

CHAPTER 12 ~ Where Did All the Love Go? ~ 93

CHAPTER 13 ~ Gaveston is Back ~ 102

CHAPTER 14~ Gaveston is Undone ~ 116

CHAPTER 15 ~ Placating the Pregnant Queen ~ 132

CHAPTER 16 ~ Battles at Home and Abroad ~ 141

CHAPTER 17 ~ Charlotte's Wedding ~156

CHAPTER 18~ The Dreaded Despensers ~ 171

CHAPTER 19 ~ Trouble with the Barons ~ 183

CHAPTER 20~ Roger Mortimer Escapes ~198

CHAPTER 21~ Vengeance in Mind ~ 214

CHAPTER 22 ~ Death to the Traitors ~ 230

CHAPTER 23 ~ The Execution ~ 244

CHAPTER 24 ~ The Trials of Being King ~ 254

CHAPTER 25 ~ Sisterly Concerns ~ 263

CHAPTER 26 ~ A Well-Deserved Death ~ 277

CHAPTER 27~ Queen Isabella in Exile ~ 287

CHAPTER 28 ~ Ellie's Fate ~ 296

CHAPTER 1

The French Court Spring 1307

I'm fourteen years old. I have the face of an angel and the heart of a devil. So says my father, and I suppose he knows me best. I told my father: 'I think it's better that way around, Father. Imagine, having the face of a devil and the heart of an angel! That would do a young girl no good at all, since she'd be both ugly, and unable to look after herself.' Father frowned, but said nothing.

I pity my sisters. Whenever I'm asked who is my favourite sister I find it impossible to say. As far as it goes, if asked what is my favourite disease I'd be just as confused. The truth is my sisters aren't in the least like me and this makes me special.

There are three of us.

Like puppies or kittens, we grew together in our mother's womb and that was where our conflicts began. Naturally, I struck out first, thrusting into the world with a lusty bawl two hours before my sister, Charlotte. I was the first one. As Charlotte fought through the bloody pathway of our mama's birth canal, her face was ugly with fury at being out-manoeuvred by me. Painful moments later little Mathilde slid waif-like from between Mama's trembling thighs.

Fourteen years on, Papa still refers to Mathilde as 'The Runt.' This may be cruel but it's still true. Mathilde pretends not to mind. As a child, she had a little doll made from rags and she punished it, not in play, but in revenge. I remember her clearly, smashing its little flat head against the hard, stone walls and screaming like a dervish till father took a rod to her. Poor, angry Mathilde! But such are the compulsions of many children's games.

It was little wonder my mama's soul flew her weakened body even before her afterbirth was expelled. She went with barely a whimper, while I lay howling my lungs out. So here we are, three of us, three motherless daughters with no prospect of a brother to support us if we fail to make good marriages. In my case, this will not be a problem. But first, I intend to live my life.

'Ellie,' says Princess Isabella. 'Ellie, are you quite sure he'll fancy me?' Her question disturbs my happy daydreams.

It's an effort, but I steel myself to give Isabella, my mistress, all my attention. This is not for altruistic reasons. My sweetness has earned me many glorious gowns, (only one previous owner and hardly worn) and a riot of precious gemstones and necklaces of fine quality and infinite sparkle. These, for some obscure reason, no longer please Isabella. Grateful for my services, she enjoys playing Lady Bountiful. It gives her a sense of power. But it's helpful in another way. If a lover gives me some little trinket to show his adoration, I don't need to explain it to my father or sisters.

'Will he?' she repeats, 'Will he love me?'

'How can he help himself?' I murmur, stroking her long, silken hair, a sensuous moment which she enjoys. She tilts back her head and closes her eyes, so her lashes cast shadows on her cheeks. 'I'm sure he'll admire your beauty. But you know he's not as other men. This could be a difficulty. You do understand, don't you, Isabella, dear?'

I blush at the euphemism, 'not as other men.' One needs a better expression to describe Edward's sexuality, an expression that resorts neither to outright avoidance nor insulting metaphor.

'Of course,' her response is a little too abrupt, too sharp and, anyway, I know her too well. She's mad with anxiety. Stories have reached the French Court about this ambiguous English Prince. She has his likeness and he's a fine-looking young man with golden curls. Often, I catch her gazing upon this likeness when she thinks she's alone, her lower lip trembling and moist with the worrying of her tongue.

'He may change,' says Isabella. 'Sometimes people do change. Especially if I'm very sweet and docile and accommodate his needs. That's how to persuade a man to fancy you, isn't it Ellie?'

Oh dear! How the myths of the elders are passed down to the innocent youth of our day! I can see them now, all those old women with their wagging, twisted fingers and their fat, smelly shawls, spitting out their so-called words of wisdom to credulous daughters and grand-daughters. A bottle of scent and a pair of red lips and young ladies think their fortune is about to be made. Not me. Oh no, I was born with more intelligence than that.

Gravely, I shake my head. 'You have a soft nature and we ladies always believe we can change our men. The truth is men can only change themselves. But they don't. Not ever. They believe they're already perfect, so why should they change?'

'Ellie, you're being very hard on them.'

'Do you think so? But, don't you see that I'm right?'

'I haven't your experience, Ellie.' This admission brings a lump to my throat. It's so true and one has only to look at Isabella's hunted little face to know it.

'Are you scared?' I ask her, this time, more softly.

'I'm not scared,' Isabella retorts with spirit. 'It's not the business of the future Queen of England to be scared.'

'But I hear trembling in your voice. Anyone would be mad with anxiety with all the stories we hear at court of this English Prince. After all, he's your future husband.'

She doesn't answer. She sits silently, with her head down and I begin to comb and braid her hair for sleep, just as she likes it. It's natural that she should choose me for her chief Lady-in-Waiting. I'm reddish blonde rather like her, while my sisters are darker. As I've said, they're not in the least like me, but look extraordinarily like each other. Charlotte is dark, sallow and stocky, Mathilde dark, sallow and puny. While Charlotte is a course sort of pea, hard, inedible, Mathilde is the pea you miss because it's stuck like a tiny bead in the point of the pod. Whereas I, well, I am a different kind of pea altogether, luscious, juicy and ready to burst.

'I have his likeness, you know and he's a fine-looking young man. Such golden curls! Look Ellie.'

She shows me the picture. The English Prince is delightful to look at. It's hard to believe all the bizarre stories we hear about him. It would be a pity if all this luscious masculine beauty were wasted.

'How's your father?' asks Isabella. It's to her credit that she takes an interest in me and in my affairs.

'He's well.'

'And your sisters?'

'Ah! So you yearn for some gossip, dear Isabella! You need to hear about the unfortunates so that your own problems will seem less demeaning.'

'Ellie, you're impertinent. Never forget who's Mistress and who's merely a servant. Now tell me news of your sisters.'

I continue to braid Isabella's hair and oblige with some exaggerated tales about Charlotte and her histrionics and about The Runt and how she lets us both control her. Isabella listens, enthralled. I become more and more enthusiastic with each telling.

'So I say to Charlotte, Leave me alone. Go bully The Runt, Mistress. Go bully someone weaker than yourself, for I have your measure.' To reassure Isabella I use the silky, confidential tone I reserve especially for her. It's a trick I've perfected.

'I think your sister foolish to try to better you. She must know she can't rise to your exacting level of intellect and beauty. You'd think she'd see that.'

Inwardly I agree, but remain mute, allowing the silence to speak for itself. It's unseemly for a woman to display excessive pride.

'It's strange how my sisters don't look like me, even though we're triplets. I'm berry-blonde and they're dark and displeasing to look at.'

But Isabella can't concentrate for too long on me or my problems.

'Ellie, are you sure he won't fancy me?'

'I didn't say that, Isabella. As you said, if you're very sweet and docile and accommodating, he may be transformed into the prince of your dreams.' I almost choke on 'the prince of your dreams.' She doesn't see me crossing my fingers inside the folds of my kirtle. Even so, she's not so easily fooled.

'Ellie, I love you but I don't think you're always truthful. I think you're sweet to me for the sake of the presents I give you.'

'I'm deeply hurt you should think so.' My hand begins to shake. It's true. I am hurt. Nobody likes to be misjudged. Of course, presents do help a person to feel affectionate towards the giver, and I'm just as prone to temptation as anyone else, but that doesn't mean... What doesn't it mean? I try to think of how I'd feel about Isabella if she didn't give me presents. Would I still love her? I think I would, for whatever happens to either of us, I hate to see her in despair. But Isabella is still talking in that accusing voice.

'I heard you tell your father that I gave you that sapphire pin you got from your lover.'

With assumed innocence, I raise my eyebrows. 'A lover! What lover?'

'Oh, never mind, Ellie. Your reputation is no mystery to me.'

Finally, as the last, fat braid is tucked safely into the sleeping cap, I murmur in my silkiest voice, 'Madame, I know there will be trials ahead. But, how wonderful life will be when you are joined in marriage to the fair Edward and one day you become England's true Queen?'

'I shall love him. He has passion in his eyes. It will be good for us all, Ellie.'

She allows me to indulge her. Both of us ignore the fact that this is to be a political marriage, a means to prevent two warring nations from destroying each other in a bloody riot of severed limbs and heads and worse. That it's been planned throughout the duration of both our lives. Isabella asks if the Prince of Wales will love her. It doesn't occur to her to question whether she'll love him. This is a curiosity to me.

My full name is Eleanora. Ellie to my Lady, the eldest of three sisters, the favourite, the confidante of the Princess Isabella, soon to be Queen in England's licentious Court. Our closeness permits me many familiarities, such as speaking to her and using her name as an equal. And as her pet, I shall be at her side. She's promised. The possibilities stretch before me, above the trees, beyond the stars, beyond the blackest night, the most gloriously-golden day. Oh, I'm ready for a change.

Isabella has hoisted up her skirts. She's squatting on her chamber pot, her night gown falling demurely around her. She expects one more thing of me before I retire to bed. But this particular duty is not to my liking.

'Dear Isabella! You're on your pot and you have no handmaiden to attend you,' I cry.

'Then conceal your distaste, Ellie, and don't consider yourself too grand to attend to me in this matter. You should know it is the highest privilege to be Mistress of the Stool.'

It rankles that she'll not allow a handmaid to attend to her in this delicate matter. We've had cross words about this before. Concentrating on my many beautiful gowns, I keep revulsion within. I wait till she's finished, holding my breath till I almost faint right away. She rises and turns her back to me. I keep my distaste to myself. Finally, she adjusts her clothing. I lift the pot, managing not to pinch my nose within Isabella's sight, and slip from her chambers. My footsteps echo in the silence.

'Mathilde!' I bellow as soon as I am out of my Lady's earshot. 'Mathilde, I want you.'

Along the corridor towards me, Mathilde is scurrying, dun-coloured like a mouse, her hair let down ready for bed, but not yet combed. I thrust the chamber pot at her.

'Take this to the garderobe and be quick about it or I shall empty the contents over your silly head.'

Mathilde's puny arms encircle its circumference and she clutches it to her concave belly.

'Thank you, sister,' she says, as if I am doing her a great favour. She half-smiles, then sets off in the direction of the nearest garderobe to discharge the proceeds of my Lady's emissions onto the castle walls.

I stretch my arms towards the great, stone roof. It's been a satisfying day. Quickly, I re-enter my Lady's chamber and snuff out the candles. She has left her gown across the carved oaken chest in the corner, perilously close to the last flickering candle. As I move it away, I see she has dropped the small likeness of her betrothed.

He is, indeed, fair. Blue eyes sparkle at me, as though in life. Golden curls erupt from beneath the precious stones in his crown. Gently, I lift the painting and press my lips against the sensuous mouth and imagine him in my own bed, pleasuring me. Oh, blissful thought! It has been some time since I had a man; at least two weeks.

Guiltily, I replace the painting on the chest, snuff out the last candle. I must be careful, or I shall find myself in the dungeons!

Next morning, I'm late rising. Lady Mortimer

is already up and sitting on a stool, silently sewing a dull tapestry. She does this to make me look bad. She has a low spirit and somehow I can't help but be mean to her. She's working on a raven's cruel beak, so she's enjoying herself as far as she is capable. Hawk-like herself, with small eyes and hooked nose and little pinched mouth, she's no beauty. Brown flaps of skin under her cheeks dribble onto her jaw as if trying to escape; they shrink from admitting they are part of her face. Bored, I wander over to her and watch her labours over her shoulder.

'Lady Mortimer,' I say. 'May I see the tapestry you're sewing? Oh, what's that? A raven! And such a cruel beak. It reminds me of somebody. Somebody with teeny-weeny eyes and a hooked nose.'

'Your insults don't impress me,' says Lady Mortimer.

'It has no nose holes,' I insist, leaning over her shoulder. 'How can it breathe? And what's more, it has insufficient claws. It would fall off that tree and break its beak. That's if it didn't suffocate first.'

Lady Mortimer fixes me with her meanest stare, but I stare back at her just as meanly. Eventually, she says: 'It will not fall as fast and as fatally as you, my dear Eleanora, if you don't mind your manners.'

I laugh and walk away. Then I hear Isabella crying out. 'Ellie, where's Ellie?' She bursts into the room, her face red and she slaps the back of her hand against her forehead. When she sees me, she flings herself on my shoulder. 'Ellie! Oh, Ellie!

Sometimes I cannot help but think she should join the travelling players!

'Please leave us,' I tell Lady Mortimer in my most imperious manner. She begins to object and I give Isabella a little pinch.

'Please leave us,' says Isabella, so a shrinking Lady Mortimer must helplessly gather up her sewing and remove herself.

Isabella turns to me. 'Ellie, there are drops of moisture running down your cheeks. You, too, weep for me, dearest Ellie.' She brushes my face with her fingertips. 'You feel what I feel. My pain is your pain. You're not just my friend, but my devoted sister.'

'I'll get you some physic,' I murmur. Although I don't like to see Isabella miserable, I cannot help but think how arduous it is, being Chief Lady-in-Waiting. It's such a huge responsibility. Perhaps I should resign in favour of Lady Mortimer. But that I would never do. I must keep a cool head. It's my cool head that's got me where I am.

'Hurry, Ellie, I'm dying,' cries Isabella.

'I'm coming. Here, take this. I hope it'll soothe you. I can't see you like this without weeping.'

Trustingly, she drinks the physic. 'Ah, my head's full of misgivings.'

And so are mine. If the rumours are true and Isabella is misused, what will be my prospects for advancement? Yet, it's unwise to listen to rumours. They're often false and malicious. Edward is probably a charming, affectionate fellow. Forgetting Isabella, I wander to the window and gaze out.

I, too, am the object of rumours. I think they're all jealous of me because I'm Isabella's favourite. And also because she's had her seamstress sew me five new kirtles for the adventure. If the English Court is as dull as they say, then I shall shine like a single star. Isabella will be married and no competition at all.

'Ellie, I'm expiring. Come and talk to me.'

I join her and try to think of some cheerful talk. 'Shall I tell you about my new gown? I shall wear it when I wait upon you at your marriage. The crimson velvet will cling to my body, showing my little waist and the curve of my hips.' I spin around to show her.

'Ellie!'

'Gold embroidery on my bodice will shimmer as though the sun is setting into the cleave of my milky breasts.' I can't believe I said that! It's beautiful. Almost like poetry. I run my hand across the top of my full breasts. 'My sleeves,' I continue, 'will swing tantalisingly around my fragile wrists. I shall wear all of my necklaces and bracelets and rings. Fine jewels shall glint in my hair.' I smile at Isabella. She doesn't smile back.

'You speak out of turn, Ellie, for it is I who shall be the centre of attention. Don't forget your manners.'

But I'm on a flight of fancy. 'Everyone will notice me,' I declare. 'Who's that lady, they'll ask, with the beautiful face and the aristocratic air? She must be a lady of great importance.'

Isabella is almost bouncing up and down on her stool. 'I'll be wearing a gown of azure,' she says. I smile my approval. 'But what about my hair?' she continues, panic-stricken. 'Who's going to dress my hair?'

'Lady Mortimer will arrange mine,' I explain. 'She has great skill and although she'll resent doing this, she has pride in her work. I can rely on that.'

'My royal hair is of greater importance than your common tresses.'

Surprised, I stare at Isabella, wondering what has got into her? 'Your royal hair is of little consequence,' I tell her. 'You'll have your crown to cover it up, after all.'

She sticks out her bottom lip, then slowly turns aside. 'I shall have a tiny rest now,' she says, in the tone of someone who has finally given up.

I pick up my cloak. 'It's such a fine day. I think I shall walk the dogs.' Seizing a royal dog under each arm and, with a brief curtsey to Isabella, I set off.

'Gundulph, Odo, my little mutts. Be good dogs and we shall walk outside in the bailey. Gundulph, Odo, stop yapping so! Isabella was clever to name you for two English bishops. Like them, you act fierce, but one can get around you with presents.'

CHAPTER 2

News and Gossip

While Isabella is napping, I love to wander around the far side of the bailey. Today, there is hardly anyone around and the grass smells fresh from a recent shower. I find this time alone very precious, for I love to dream. I yearn to be a serf, or, even better, a gypsy. More romantic to be a roving gypsy girl, free to sing and love and dance and make merry. Ah, to be outside these oppressive, stone walls! The weather is mild for this time of year and I enjoy the fresh air, well away from the sour castle smells.

The Princess' little dogs follow me, yapping at my heels. When I see my father, a skulking shadow in the distance, but distinctive for all that, I'm surprised, for I thought he was still abroad on business of the King. Beneath his dark breeches, his knees are bony and his head is uncovered, although he wears a warm cloak. He's walking slowly towards me, musing.

As he comes closer, I see he looks drawn and there is a grey pallor to his skin, which puts me in mind of a cadaver. This frightens me. I draw my light shawl tightly around my shoulders, almost dislodging my head-dress.

At present, my father is preoccupied, for the King has promised him lands for services in respect of the dispute between the Monarchy and the tempestuous Pope. Something to do with taxes, I believe. Father says the Pope is greedy. The dispute has been settled now and the surly Pope despatched, but King Philip is so engrossed in his political affairs and foreign exploits, he just doesn't get around to rewarding my father. I never found out exactly what father did for the King. It's strange how my father's so loud and pompous and stuck-up, but as soon as he's in King Philip's presence, he collapses like a dying daddy-long-legs.

It doesn't matter to me whether Father gets his lands or not. I shall be well married by then and have lands of my own, for I intend my husband shall be rich and eager-to-please. Handsome, too!

'Father, what news?'

'Little news that's good. The King still hasn't compensated me for mediating in the tax dispute between the monarchy and the greedy Pope. Whatever I say, the King is unmoved.'

'Father, you should confront the King and demand your reward. You should stand up for yourself.'

Then my father says something that always makes me feel murderous.

'Don't you bother your pretty head about such things.'

It seems to me that whenever they are feeling tetchy, men must speak to women as though we are children?

'You're insulting me, Father, by quoting such

a thoughtless maxim,' I tell him. My father merely shrugs, which is the closest he can get to showing regret.

'I wish it were better news, Daughter,' says he, in a gentler voice. I grimace. It seems appropriate. Father grimaces back.

'Your sweet Mistress will need all the support and love you and the Good Lord can bestow upon her. Gaveston's a rascal, a scoundrel. His is a perversion of the most foul persuasion.' He lowers his voice to a whisper. 'It is unconscionable that our young prince is so easily influenced by this man. I dread to think how he will suffer in Hell's Fiery Furnace.'

My father always speaks thus, like a pompous jackass. But some people are impressed by his affectations. Right now, I am a little concerned. Father really doesn't realise how loudly he speaks and how the voice carries in this open space and how ears hover all around, behind a bush, a tree, a wall. How careless words are twisted and used against the unwary. Under this very sod on which we stand, for all I know. In this way, reputations and lives are destroyed, for the Court is hot with intrigue and scandal.

'Hush, Father. Someone'll hear you. You don't realise how dangerous it is to have such strong opinions.'

'Daughter, you exaggerate.'

'I do not. A gentleman out of favour today may be your master tomorrow. If you're taken, then

I'll have no one to protect me.' He lifts his bearded chin so high, I can see the course, black hairs thrusting from his nose and his little eyes glint each side of the flaring nostrils. He looks as though he is about to engulf me with a great breath of fire, like a dragon.

'You only think of yourself. Your sisters would have no one to protect them either, and they are not as cunning as you, my dear.'

I feel a rush of anger at this admonishment. It's unfair. Who would even notice Charlotte or the Runt? Whereas I…

'It's a shaming matter, but there's nothing to be done to protect Isabella from this outrage. You must help her to bear it, Eleanora, as best you can.'

'Yes, Father.' I drop a small curtsey, like a submissive child. We don't embrace. After a long, lingering look that I can't read, my father leaves me with my thoughts. I call the dogs, who are chasing a squirrel. 'Come Gundulph! Come Odo!'

Mad squealing of a pig about to be butchered sets off the dogs, so I follow them wearily. The butcher plies his trade on the edge of the bailey, so that rubbish and offal can be tossed over the wall to the scrambling fists and snatching jowls of the poor. It keeps down the mess in the bailey and makes the poor grateful. A jovial man, the butcher rewards the Princess' dogs with an ear each.

'There's a treat for you my pets,' I cry.

How proud they look as they trot before me, each sporting his prize aloft like victors in a joust.

24

How simple life is for dogs. How easily they take their pleasure and what little gives them joy.

CHAPTER 3

Gossip is Juicy but Dangerous

I love feasts. Feasts are my very favourite way of spending my all too few leisure hours. And this very evening, there's to be a feast. Margaret and I are beside ourselves with excitement, trying out different clothes and testing pretty colours on our cheeks and lips.

Do you like this, Ellie?' squeals Margaret. 'And do you like this? And this? And this?

Female company is great fun when one is planning such events. Although, sadly, Isabella seems listless. She lies around, uninterested in sewing or music, hardly bothering with her toilette. We leave her to her misery, not because we are unkind, but there isn't enough excitement in our lives as it is. We can't bear to miss a moment of it. All the handsomest young men, the most desirable young women, the prettiest children, the funniest jesters, the grandest old dowagers, will be there. There will be saucy adventures for the most daring. This, of course, includes me, as you will have guessed.

The feast is in honour of my father's return and ordered by the King as a sop to his envoy's injured feelings. If a small favour is bestowed with pomp and ceremony, it's impossible, except for the most sturdy of characters, to ask for the larger one already promised but withheld. My father is foiled and checkmated by the wily King.

In the Great Hall, a number of oaken trestles have been set up around the perimeter and covered in fine, white linen. They are laden high with venison, veal, mutton, cured bacon and goose in huge, silver platters. Enormous slices of bread rest in their trenchers. Already mulled wine is flowing freely, for men roar with laughter and their faces are red, their noses riddled with veins. Two midgets dance a drunken reel to a Genoese fiddler, and a noble tries to trip them, encouraged by his fellow revellers. The pig, bereft of ears and dignity, roasts slowly on a spit over the great fire and I can smell its delicious aroma already. And it is hot, so hot.

Lady Mortimer is sitting as near to the King as she can get and she's mopping her brow. The King's playing chess, although he doesn't pay much attention to it. After all, he well knows his partner has to let him win. Only one foolhardy knight ignored this essential court protocol and I can't repeat what happened to him. It's far, far too gross. I have little sympathy for the King as I wouldn't enjoy such a victory myself.

Lady Mortimer is watching something going on in the far corner. She catches my eye and casts her beady eyes skywards, a sneer bending her mouth. I follow her gaze. I see my sisters are already here.

Charlotte is stuffing herself and I watch her stomach and hips bloat beneath her gown as the various meats chase each other down her gullet, and the greasy dripping runs down her chin and breasts. The Runt wears a voluminous gown. No, I lie! She wears an enormous piece of sacking, dyed ochre.

'Such a trial to you, those sisters of yours, Lady Eleanora,' says Mortimer, sounding more cheerful than she has all day.

'You shouldn't talk so freely, Lady Mortimer. You, who manage to be unpleasant without even trying. You're a sour old boot and I shan't allow you to make me miserable.'

'Are you looking for your father?'

'Do you know where he is?'

'Behind that pillar, talking to a young noble. I swear his voice is loud. His recklessness borders on the suicidal.'

'Who is the young noble,' I ask.

'His name's Guy de Clare,' she replies.

'Aah, he looks as though he would taste very nice,' I murmur and Mortimer humphs and re-arranges her kirtle.

Intrigued, I draw closer.

'So you say the English Prince is out of favour with his father?' remarks the handsome young noble, Guy de Clare, in that polite way people have when listening to news that doesn't much concern them.

'Indeed, for he is already plotting the return of the banished Gaveston,' continues my father. 'That fop! That bane of the French Court and devil of the English Court! That underhand nincompoop! That strutting scoundrel! I shouldn't be surprised if

Prince Edward doesn't bestow an Earldom upon his arrogant favourite when his father, the King, is dead.' It's clear to everyone Father doesn't much care for Prince Edward and even less for his lover, the cunning Piers Gaveston.

'An Earldom! I think not,' declares Guy de Clare, tweaking his hat and managing to look fascinating even though he is clearly bored.

'It's said the old King is tired and sickly already and cannot last for long. Then young Edward will have his way. It's an enduring shame that he's so unruly and has failed so miserably to make a man of himself in the Campaigns against the Scots. Needless to say, the Prince's attitude has enraged the powerful Earl of Lancaster, not to mention the influential Mortimers, and these are not men to be trifled with.'

'Indeed…'

'But what is it to me?' continues Father, enjoying the effects of his strong voice. 'Why should I interest myself when I am denied my dues as a loyal Frenchman and Courtier?'

Apart from my fascination with this comely noble, I'm also drawn by this tirade against my mistress' intended husband and his troubles with the Earl of Lancaster and the Mortimers. I quite forget to interrupt and detract my father from his careless talk. Gossip is so very juicy and it get juicier with repetition. So, I stand silently listening, idly contemplating de Clare's handsome face, as my father continues to rail against Prince Edward of

England's favourite.

Charlotte notices me and rises to her feet, her bosoms spilling from the slack top of her gown and a large goose leg dripping from her fist.

'Ellie!' she shrills, as if she hasn't seen me for several months. I groan. Her mouse-skin hair hangs forward, hiding her face. That, at least, is an improvement. Then she rushes past me and confronts our father, holding the goose leg behind her back like a tiny girl, so that it drips gobs of grease onto her hem.

'Dear Father,' she drops a small curtsey. 'Dear Father, I've been looking for you ever since I had word of your arrival. What of dear Piers? Piers Gaveston, Father? What of him?'

I perk up my inquisitive ears, for Piers Gaveston, said to be Prince Edward's lover, is a constant subject of court gossip. I can hardly believe the decadent stories are true and neither can poor Isabella, who is expected to marry this gender-confused heir to the English throne. They must marry even though he wastefully scatters his seed upon his own sex.

Father almost chokes and is clearly at a loss to reply to Charlotte's entreaty. I feel sorry for him. Eventually, he recovers and tells her, 'Gaveston is not at the English Court. He's displeased the King and is in exile.'

From this, it's clear that Edward's old papa is not so old and unwary as he looks!

'In exile!' cries Charlotte. 'You say he's in

exile? Then, can he possibly be in France? Oh, why hasn't he come to see me?' Charlotte's face crumples and she covers it with her free hand, mixing goose-fat with the soot that has settled on her skin from standing too close to the roasting spit. This, combined with the thick layer of powder she always wears, has created a heavy dough. Were it not for the soot, one could scrape it off her face and make tolerable buns.

Poor Father. He's struggling. How can he explain to his empty-headed, ignorant daughter just why she should not harbour a passion for Gaveston?

'Come, Charlotte,' I say. 'Don't bother our father at this moment, for he has important matters on his mind.' Protesting, she nevertheless allows me to draw her aside. 'Piers Gaveston is not for you, dear Charlotte. You must forget him.'

'What's wrong with you, Ellie? Are you jealous of my undying love for dear Gaveston?'

'No.' I keep my voice low and reasonable. 'I'm not jealous, Charlotte, but I know more than you do about this particular...worthy.'

Charlotte sticks out her fat lower lip. 'Gaveston was always good to me when he was here at Court. He made a great fuss of me and brought me sweetmeats and charming gifts of ribbon and bracelets. And he kissed me for saying thank you so prettily.'

'Charlotte, you were eight years old!'

'And now I am fourteen. His interest will grow.'

31

I stare at her, her chin wet with goose-fat, her face mucky, the flesh of her bosom spilling over the stained material of her gown and I sigh. There is nothing to be done with Charlotte. She flashes me a coquettish glance and saunters back into the thick of the celebrations. I watch her, half-fascinated yet ashamed that she makes such a spectacle of herself. An ageing, would-be lover grabs her around the waist. I am surprised he can find it! He tosses her into the air so her raiments swing wide and her shift billows, and Charlotte shrieks. Thank God there are no plans for her to travel to England with us. But, in France, I cannot pretend she is nothing to do with me.

'Ellie!' My father is standing before me, rocking on his heels. 'Ellie, there is no point in lecturing your sisters, for they have no common sense. But surely you must realise, even in your privileged position, how grave the situation has become.'

I have no idea what my father is talking about, but I dislike the emphasis he puts on 'grave'. Uneasily, I study him under my lashes. Certainly it's a pity for my poor Lady that her future husband is not as suitable as once we hoped. But there is no use in fretting over what cannot be altered and I am so looking forward to broadening my experience and savouring the delights that the English Court will provide.

'Ellie!'

'Father?' I lower my eyes and try to look

daughterly.

'Ellie, there has been great unrest in our country. Our King is curbing the Knights Templar, those heroes of the Crusades, by the most heinous means. Indeed, atrocities are being committed in both town and countryside. Toolmakers everywhere are growing richer, devising new instruments of torture, whose terrible machinations I would not impart to the ears of a young woman.' I glance at my father, intrigued. Does he think I am made of china? My father sighs, as he continues:

"The rack and the gibbet, the scalding iron and the strappado have become both the slaves and masters of men and they are utilised without moderation or mercy. Many have confessed to crimes they have not committed and some have gone to their deaths protesting their innocence and the honour of their Order. I dread to speculate how it will end, or, indeed, if it will ever end.'

'What is a strappado, father?'

'It is a most dreadful instrument of torture, where the victim's wrists are tied behind his back by a rope, and he is then dropped from a great height and halted by a sudden jerk…You cannot imagine the awful agonies of fire and pain that course through the human body as the arms are forced back and wrenched from their sockets, the…'

'Please father, we shall be eating soon.'

'And that is merely the Templars. Do not forget the poor maidens accused of witchcraft and those unfortunate moneylenders, the Jews.'

33

It confuses me that my father is telling me this, for what can I, a mere woman, do about it all? I shrug and turn away. I am ready to flounce and flirt and dislike talking of desperate matters at such a jolly time. It is such extremely bad form. But my father grabs my arm so hard, hauling me around to face him again, that I almost lose my balance. I stand before him, tucking my head down tight to my chest, making a barrier between us. I await his wrath for my rebelliousness.

'Be careful, Ellie,' says my father. I am amazed by the softness of his voice, for I never knew he was able to temper that mighty organ. 'Be very, very careful, my dear Ellie.'

'I will Father,' I tell him. Already my eyes are darting around to see if there are any new faces to enthral me, any new adventures to experience, or any new opportunities to explore.

CHAPTER 4

To Boulogne for the Wedding

The last leg of our journey to Boulogne is gruelling. I dislike the discomfort of such long journeys. Isabella isn't strong and is soon wilting like a dying rose, which is a dreadful anxiety to me. I must watch her constantly, make sure she doesn't get too hot or too cold or too unhappy.

As we draw closer to our destination, one of the escort's horses steps into a pothole and goes lame and we rein in our mounts. To our horror, there's an ugly scene unfolding on the outskirts of the small village we are passing. Isabella clutches her hand over her mouth, while Ladies Margaret and Joan, who are travelling in the cart, fall into each other's arms, with eyes scrunched tight. I glare at them in scorn, for they seem to crumple at the slightest thing.

But now I, too, look out on the scene. What are they doing? What in God's Holy Name are they doing to that poor girl?' As I take in the scene, I almost wet myself for the horror of it. A huge pile of logs and kindling has been propped around a heavy stake, to which is tied a very young girl, probably no more than ten or eleven years old. Surrounding the pyre, a rowdy crowd of rough, yelling men and screeching hags with greasy hair strike fear into our very souls.

35

While the man attends to the ailing beast, we are forced to sit upon our mounts and witness this distressing scene. A sudden deluge of rain has soaked the kindling, so it is impossible for the men to ignite a fire. They shout at each other, blaming and cursing in their rage at being denied the spectacle of the young girl's agony. One springs forward with fresh, dry kindling, another with a blazing torch.

'Oh! Oh! Oh!' cries Isabella, rocking to and fro. I ride my mount close to hers and try to pull her back into the trees. She's too tender-hearted for her own good and must be protected from such sights. 'Don't look, Isabella. Look away.'

'Witch! Witch! Filthy witch! Burn! Burn!' scream the peasant women. The young girl secured to the stake is screaming too, screaming wildly and shaking her neck as though to tumble off her head. Frenziedly, she strains against the cruel ropes which bind her and cut into her flesh. Her cries pierce my very soul, for she is so young and doesn't look in the least like a witch to me.

Princess Isabella begins to cry too, standing up in her stirrups and holding out her arms towards the scene. No one notices her. Such is the power of the bloodlust in men and women that they don't even know their royal mistress while in the grip of it. After what seems like forever, a few twigs of kindling begin to smoulder. The young girl becomes exhausted and her chin drops forward onto her chest, from which her clothes have been ripped to expose her innocent breasts. Long, brown tresses ripple down her writhing body as though weeping.

'Ellie, we must stop them.'

'Believe me, Isabella, there's nothing we can do. They outnumber us twenty to one and they're mad with the bloodlust. We'll all be thrown into the flames if we interfere. Come away!' I almost shout the last two words, for it's impossible to get through to Isabella in this mood.

I pray for the kindling to catch alight quickly, for the ordeal to be over, for the poor girl's pains to be stilled. Isabella starts forward, 'I must help her. They must listen to me, for she's so young, she's surely innocent.' I urge my horse forward and push Isabella down into her saddle; the first time I have ever treated her so roughly. 'Isabella, they won't know you. They're so fired up, they'll surely kill you. Then what will happen to the union between France and England? There will be even less control and more will die.'

I see she doesn't like this, but, at that moment, the escort remounts, the cart lurches forward and begins to roll again and I breathe a deep sigh. I don't look back. Isabella weeps softly until I persuade her to pray to the Blessed Virgin instead of ruining her complexion with weeping. 'Isabella, this will also be easier on your spirit,' I tell her. She complies and tears roll down her cheeks as she whispers to the Holy Mother.

While I cannot help but pity her, I also envy her soft heart. For I never experience the release of tears. I suffer sadness for the burned girl, but leave guilt and sorrow where it belongs - with the priests and the martyrs. To dwell upon common injustice increases grief and is for idle natures, an indulgence to be mastered. I shall say no more about the remainder of the journey, for I don't care to think upon it, except to mention that my knuckles are chapped and raw with the cold.

When we arrive at the great Manor House, the King of France is waiting there for his daughter. Isabella is now as ready as she will ever be for marriage to Edward, which will take place tomorrow in Boulogne. She will be accompanied by her usual retinue, the protectors and the servants and the two favourite dogs and the Chief Lady-in-Waiting. And me.

You see, I lied. I'm not, and never have been, my Lady's 'Chief Lady'. Oh no... and this is thanks to my Lady's father, King Philip, who always regards me with a beady eye as if he is thinks I exert a bad influence over his precious progeny. Who stamped his foot and almost pulled out his beard with frustration. Who spoke loudly for Lady Mortimer because his wayward Isabella wanted to promote me. Such foolishness! For all of these Mortimers are equally dreadful and there are so many of them.

No, I'm not Chief Lady, but because I say I am, and behave like I am, people treat me as such, except for the King and my family. Even Charlotte puts in her small offering, despite being none too honest herself.

'You're a sly little slut,' she says, 'acting as

though you are the most important female next to your Mistress.'

Once, the King heard I had told some lies and he said to me that I must be contrite. He forced me, on pain of a whipping, to beg forgiveness. This is unreasonable, for to say you are sorry in order not to be whipped is no apology at all. Rather than be whipped, I begged forgiveness, but didn't mean a word of it, so crossed my fingers behind my back.

'You should not tell lies,'" my own Father says to me whenever his sharp eyes detect some tiny deceit. 'You must say sorry at once.' Thus he insists that I tell yet another lie, under the pretext of being penitent. This seems to me illogical and yet my father apparently prides himself on his sense of reason.

My father has always told me that lying is my worst fault. At least, as I righteously point out, it is my only fault. In every other respect I'm perfect. See how charming I am, how beautiful, how intelligent, how learned and how gracious. If I did not lie, I would be an angel and he, my father, would be deprived of his most desirable daughter. Besides, I only lie when it is of gravest importance when not to lie would cause me personal inconvenience.

If one is good at deception, why, then, it is a talent. The Bible says we should use our talents to the best of our ability. And, it was only a tiny lie, hardly a lie at all, for Isabella confides only in me, trusts only my counsel.

'I love you most among my Ladies,' she says,

gently. 'You must not forget this, ever, my dearest. Why, Lady Mortimer, indeed! That old witch! How can you doubt my sincerity, Ellie?'

At this moment, Isabella is conferring with her father, the King. She has grave reservations about this marriage. We, the Ladies of her Household, are gathered together in one of the huge, reception rooms. The room is grand and dark and thick with ancient tapestries and everything creaks as though it were a thousand years old. Even lively little Joan seems intimidated by our surroundings and chews on her knuckles like a frightened child.

'Well, Ellie, it won't be long now,' says Margaret.

It's a colourful gathering and I'm glad my gown and my robe are red, for red stands out in the throng. I am aware that all eyes are upon me and I revel in the glow of approval from the gallants and the disapproval from their ladies. Yet, disappointingly, I become separated from my Mistress, for she is borne forth by her royal father who manages to force me aside with his elbow, yet subtly as if by accident. I'm all too aware this slight is deliberate, so I make an impertinent face at him. One of his minions spots this insubordination and glowers at me and I turn my head away. After the ceremony, I will make sure I am at Isabella's side.

Inside the cathedral, the ceilings are so high I am sure the angels live in them. All is rich with crimson and purple velvets and gold trappings. Great swathes of flowers fill the air with pungent aroma. I am so excited, that I hardly hear the young couple made their marriage vows.

Isabella looks a little anxious. Yet her bridegroom is a fine, young man, even more handsome than his likeness. Confidence surrounds him like a saintly aura, as tangible as the golden curls beneath his illustrious crown. A cloak of rich, tawny velvet hangs in deep folds from his shoulders. He's twenty-three, almost twenty-four years old. She's just twelve. Childlike, and strangely trusting under the circumstances, she keeps glancing up at him from under her favourite head-dress. He remains upright, upstanding. I'm glad I'm not in her shoes, for she's a virgin. If he were to be my husband, the dreadful Gaveston would have little chance of infiltration into our marriage. But Isabella is inexperienced in the ways of the world, and won't be a match for him, or for Gaveston. Sometimes, her fragility disgusts me.
Either she will learn this important lesson with indecent speed or all will be lost.

After the ceremony, I watch Prince Edward carefully, to see how he responds to her beauty and trust. He's charm itself, radiating approval, taking care she does not step into a puddle or trip over an uneven stone along her path. He introduces her, with polished ease, to his friends and counsellors and brushes the back of her hand with his lips. His lying lips!

While Edward is talking with his new father-in-law, Isabella impatiently weaves her way through the wedding party towards me. We fall upon each other's necks.

'Ellie! I am so happy. He is fine! Oh, he is handsome! How could I believe the scandals that abound in the French Court? They were all lies, perpetrated by my father's enemies. I shall never be such a goose again. I am now Queen of England, Ellie. King Edward and Queen Isabella. What do you think of that?'

'And Lady of Ireland,' I remind her.

'And Duchess of Aquitaine,' she continues, and seems about to do a girlish spin, but remembers her dignity just in time. Her infectious giggle make me laugh too.

'Now you will be far too grand to talk to me, my Lady,' I jest.

'Ellie, how can you say such a thing? That never can be.' Yet, it seems to me Isabella is counting her Treasure Trove while her ship is still far out to sea. But I cannot bring myself to tell her about my reservations. Affectionately, she presses me to her breast, so I curve my arms around her neck, then over her shoulder I find myself gazing into the eyes of her fine, new husband. It is like drowning in exotic spiced wine. I feel a fleeting stab of envy for Piers Gaveston.

If Isabella is wrong, if the rumours are true, it's a shameful waste, that mouth, those eyes, that roguish look. I've heard that Edward is comfortable with common people and once I thought that naïve, but now... now I understand, as he turns to the gathering crowds, shaking hands, allowing his palms to rest on the flaxen heads of grubby little children. It's charming, if a little reckless. I would want to be sure they were free from nits or any other dreadful disease that afflicts the poor before I let them venture near me!

As we separate from our embrace, Isabella turns and sees her Prince and with a little whinny of delight, she prances over to him. He has turned away from her to talk to the King of Navarre. The interruption makes his eyes dart daggers of annoyance over his shoulder at his wife. Disconcerted, she withdraws and her shoulders stoop. Why doesn't she make a great fuss and demand his attention? If he treats her like this on her wedding day, how will it be when he's used to her? She should fight fire with fire and earn his respect, if not his love.

I've left Gaveston behind as my Regent,' he's telling the King of Navarre. 'I know I can rely on him to take care of my dear country.'

'Surely one of your illustrious landowners, like Lancaster, would have served your purpose more fitting,' says the King of Navarre.

'No, indeed, I have every faith that dear Piers will be dutiful in his role as Guardian of the Kingdom,' laughs Edward.

Isabella hovers behind him till he moves on, ignoring her, to jest with Charles of Valois, who has three marriageable daughters. The poor man... he will never get them married off despite their dowries, for they are far from fair and lacking in charm. The daughters gaze upon Edwards' proud face with some sadness, he now being taken and beyond them, even in their wildest dreams.

Isabella draws back, almost shrinking. The Prince has spent as much of his affection on her as he can spare. She sidles close to me and grips my arm.

'I know what you are thinking, Ellie. If the rumours are true, it's a shameful waste, for he's comely.'

'You're right, Isabella. Those eyes, that mouth, that roguish look! See how he talks with peasant and with king exactly the same.'

'Charming, if a little reckless. I think I must go to him. I must be by his side.'

Taking a deep breath, Isabella marches towards her husband, who is now reeling drunkenly against Navarre. 'My Lord,' cries Isabella. 'My Lord, lean on me.'

'What! Ho, ho, what! Dear Lady, you're treading on my cloak. My, such huge feet! Oh, it's you! Hah!' He gives Isabella a playful slap on the behind and her eyebrows shoot up and disappear into her hairline.

She withdraws from him, turns to me, clings to my sleeve.

'Ellie, he didn't even recognise me,' she cries.

'He recognised your feet!'

For the remainder of the day, Edward remains aloof. Now Isabella, hurt and rejected, is making an enormous effort to linger in conversation with the dowager Queen Marguerite, who appears to be doing most of the talking. Then the King of Sicily makes a great fuss of her and she responds prettily. No longer does she pursue her husband. I'm glad Isabella has her pride, although I damn her for her lack of spirit.

I allow my eyes to rove with casual interest over the attending English Lords and Earls. I wonder if I'm setting my standards too low and should try for a royal sibling or two. But I cannot rouse within my breast any excitement over the attending royalty, who are either elderly or dull. So a Lord or Earl it shall be. At least the Barons are invariably young and rakish. As for me, occasionally, I have been described as a hot piece, but, in truth, I prefer to bide my time, to see how they behave, these men who attract me. To see how they deport themselves, how they converse, whether they command attention sufficient to make them worthy of mine.

Oh, I am a great looker-on. But once I have made up my mind - well, I have made up my mind and nothing will change it.

Now Isabella is in deep conversation with her father. Offering him her upturned palms, beseeching him with her wide, blue eyes, she's an object of pity. It is not difficult to imagine the content of her pleas. Not to send her to England with this difficult, distant-hearted husband. To grant her an annulment. To take her home, back to the safety of the people who love her and care about her welfare. Now she's crying in earnest and people are staring. I can barely bring myself to gaze upon her shame.

King Philip is shaking his head. He seizes her hands, squeezing them as she speaks, but still he is shaking his head.

'My daughter, your impatience doesn't become you,' I hear him mutter. 'Don't make such an intolerable fuss.'

She persists, but he's implacable. I feel a little twinge of relief. Margaret approaches. She scolds me for looking at the men and there's a jealous gleam in her eye.

'You value too highly what lies beneath your kirtle, Ellie.'

'Stop fussing, Margaret. I've never seen any of these people before.'

'But you had that burly groom at the inn in France. And you'd never seen him before.'

I laugh. 'I shall never see him again,' I tell her, 'so what does it matter?'

Oh, how I long for Dover's white cliffs and the delights of a new city, a new Court, a new life. The great change I have promised myself is now upon me.

CHAPTER 5

To England

Banquets, banquets, banquets! I'm sorely tired of banquets. This one is a farewell banquet for soon the Queen and I will set sail for England.

And I'm so sick that I am of little use to my mistress in her distress. This malady has been caused by the forced jollity we had to endure after the wedding, prior to our setting out for England. Banquets, banquets, banquets, so many banquets, so many visits, so many polite conversations, so many false compliments, and all the while the necessity of behaving with perfect decorum.

'Oh, my Lord, I am so pleased you could take wine with me!'

'Oh, my Lady, this psalter is exquisite, such fine stitches.'

'Oh, your Grace, what fine porcelain!'

'Oh, your Holiness, I so admired your sermon!'

'Oh, your Worship, may I pay homage to your Big Toe?

'It's all exceedingly tedious and I don't know how I manage to control myself during all this ceremony. I long to bat my eyes at a devilish earl or two. But how can I begin any discreet adventures with my Mistress' father, the King, watching my every move, ready to pounce upon me like a fox upon a hare? It is a good simile, for his beard is like a brush and I'm trembling like prey. He waits for the moment when he can pronounce me unworthy as my Lady's counsellor and prevent me from sailing to England, where his power to control me will cease.

I have a dream one night, to which he pays a visit. (Truly, one just cannot get rid of him!)

'Whore!' he bellows. 'Cheap strumpet! Begone. You're not fit for your station and you shall not sully my royal daughter with your strumpet wiles.' It is so real that when I awaken I believe my dream and I am sweating a cold, cold sweat. One day, I swear, I shall drip poison into his kingly tankard!

But thankfully, King Philip will not accompany us to England. He and Isabella are lances locked for the first three days, but when she realises he will not be persuaded to take her home, she withdraws into herself. I can do nothing to cheer her. Her father decides the best strategy is to ignore her, thinking, no doubt, that she will become used to the idea. She doesn't. She observes the proprieties with her husband, but she is miserable beyond misery.

And so am I, as I lean over the bows of our sailing vessel and spew my dinner into the sea.

'Dear Madame, you are clearly ill. May I help?'

I can't turn around, although I am stirred by that low, masculine voice. I cling to the rail, mortified. For the bile rejected by my belly has blown back into my face on the wind. This kind of incident is supposed to happen to Charlotte, not to me. I drag my cloak across my mouth and pray the crossing may be speedy. Sensing the sour smell of my breath, I wish my benefactor would go away. Already the white cliffs of Dover loom large before me.

'Madame, allow me to wipe your face clean.'

He does, drawing me towards him with gentleness, using a moistened cloth of silk. He removes my soiled cloak from my shoulders and wraps his own around me. He fetches some small beer for me to wash out my mouth. It smells stale and I take care not to swallow, but it is better than nothing.

It touches me to be treated kindly when I am weak and overcome with humiliation. He's not of noble blood, but a mere underling, someone's servant. The 'someone' whose servant he is - is probably not of any particular importance either. This is a rough man, but a manly man and broad of chest. I have a penchant for rough men, although, of course, one cannot be seen with them in public. Oh yes, a fine specimen, coarse as a mariner, yet such an invitation in his laughing eyes! And he does not fawn upon me as some nobles do, with coy entreaties.

Truly, I despise men who grovel.

By the time we drop anchor I'm lost. I forget all about the troubles of my Royal Mistress, but how can it be helped? Impatiently, I wait for the men to carry ashore the giant crates that contain the royal couple's heavy store of wedding presents and Isabella's personal possessions. I can feel the excitement squeezing tight my innards and I am breathless with the very idea of what is to come.

Dusk is falling and everyone is busy with the Reception of the future Queen. Nobody notices that we slip away. The packing crates lie forgotten for the moment, with just a sleepy guard lolling against the largest to deter potential robbers. The man slips his hands inside my clothing, pinching my breasts. I can feel them rigid beneath his calloused fingers and I shiver with longing. For it is *ever so long* since I had a man, at least three weeks and five days.

Of one accord, we sink into comparative anonymity amidst the sundry collection of wedding gifts and possessions stacked high on deck, and he has me over a crate and is pleasuring me under my kirtle and I, too, am pleasuring him. We pleasure each other for as long as it takes, and it takes a pleasingly long time, for he is an experienced lover. To enjoy such fine passion in fear of one's whimpers being overheard by the guard is exquisite terror. It is such a fine release after so much torment and I no longer feel sick to the stomach or sad. After we are done, I wish I could know what he looks like naked. It's now much too dark to see. If only I had a candle. I nestle into his arms and we drift into pleasant slumber.

Suddenly, he is shaking me awake. 'I must go,' he says, 'I shall be missed.' Already most of the packages and crates have been transferred ashore. Our secret hideaway will be a secret no longer.

I realise with a start that Isabella, deprived of her husband's attentions, will be searching for me, too, although she has the company of Margaret and Joan. I pray that necessary duties have distracted her and will protect me from her wrath. With due haste, I adjust my garments and dash around the deck, in a panic, searching for the Queen and her entourage. But they're not there any longer. All is silent apart from the cries of gulls and the sounds of the sea. The royal party has moved on and are *en route* for the homecoming banquet and dancing. I have to get ready. I have to dress Isabelle, she so prefers me to Margaret or Joan. I also need to rest, for I am exhausted. There is a tight, hard feeling in my breast.

I shall be so so late! And what is worse, I may have to make my entrance alone.

'Where have you been, Lady Eleanora? I've been looking for you everywhere?'

CHAPTER 6

Out of Favour

It's clear I am severely out-of-favour, for it is seldom my Lady addresses me as Lady Eleanora.

'My Lady, I was unavoidably detained and then... then I got lost... I was so frightened... and it was only when a kind gentleman put his cart at my disposal and... I told him to drive his horses hard, for I had to be at your side... and...'

'Don't lie, Ellie. It's your worst fault and I'm not deceived by you.'

I have to hide a smile. My Lady is learning. Life is teaching her that things are seldom as they seem - something I've always known. As though to hide a tear, I hang my head and sniff and pull my hair across my face.

'My Lady, I am overcome with remorse. Please forgive me.'

'What was his name?'

'My Lady, you misunderstand.'

If I'd known I would not have told her. Only I had no idea. Nor need I know, for I do not intend to further this acquaintance. Only, I hope my lover will be discreet. If he shows any signs of betraying me, I shall have to deal with him.

'It wasn't as you assume,' I add, hopefully.

'What was it, Ellie? What was it? You have something to hide. Maybe a rushed fumble down a dark alley?'

'Oh no,' I say with conviction. For it had been far from rushed and far from a fumble and not quite a dark alley. The truth shone from my eyes, for Princess Isabella relaxed and held out her arms to me.

'Ellie, I am not angry with you. I needed you and I missed you. And you were not here. But I don't understand. Why have they done this to me? What have I done to deserve such despicable treatment? And I hate this dreary old Castle. It's draughty and dirty and uncomfortable.' She falters and her gaze sweeps to take in the scene before her. 'Oh, Ellie, just look at them. I cannot believe what a fool I was to believe he might be attentive to me; to think that he might at least try to fall in love with me.'

My eyes follow her gaze. I recognise Gaveston, a well-known and notorious figure at both the English and French Courts. At his side, hip-to-hip, Isabella's new husband. The two of them have eyes only for each other. They indulge in the gentle foolery that men do to show that they are fond of each other, an elbow crooked around a neck, a hearty shove, a slap on the arm; attentions that might appear harmless to an innocent eye. Yet, there is definitely something more… Isabella's right. It's a look, a touch that lingers a moment too long.

They all were right who spoke doom of this English and French alliance. For Gaveston's dark, broody expression, Edward's fair and adoring gaze, tell me everything I need to know. These two have long been lovers. Isabella is simply a pawn in a game of such complexity she cannot hope to win. For Gaveston the Wily, will slide swiftly across the diagonal like a cruel bishop and sweep her from the board.

It is too much for my Lady. She can hardly fathom how to conduct herself, for nothing in her training has prepared her for this.

'Where were you, Ellie?' Her voice is now high with frenzy and those around stop talking in order to listen. 'Where were you when I needed you? It's outrageous that you should abandon me to face this alone. I don't think I want you as my special Lady any longer. Indeed I do not, for you are a false friend. Today is the saddest day of my life, for the magnitude of falsehood it contains. You'll get out of my sight, Ellie.'

She's never spoken to me like this before. She's so beside herself with grief, so needful of expressing her anger. I'm the only one of any consequence upon whom she can vent her fury without reprisal. Already I can hear a rush of intaken breath, a low murmur of gossip. I can't afford to invoke her anger, nor to become an object of scandal. I can see myself speedily on a ship back to France, where the wrath of my father and my King will fall like a thunderbolt upon my shoulders. The disgrace would be more than I could bear.

'Madame, you do me wrong. I didn't wish to tell you the truth because I wanted to protect you, your innocence, your goodness. It wasn't my fault I couldn't reach your side. I'm hurt and sorely distressed, thinking only of my precious Isabella. Oh Madame, you do me great wrong.' I whimper into my kerchief, amazed at my own inventiveness.

I have her attention. She is rigid, staring at me, not knowing what to believe. 'Ellie?' she says wonderingly. Then, 'Ellie, you must tell me. We must have no secrets.'

'I cannot tell you now, for we might be overheard.' I lower my voice to a whisper, compelling her to lean forward and align her ear to my mouth. 'Later. Later. When all this is over. Then I shall tell you, for it is a most personal matter…'

Isabella's short upper lip is quivering.

I have bought myself a little time to think upon a fabrication, to vindicate myself and move back into Isabella's good grace. It's of desperate importance that she believes me. I steer her gently in the direction of some elderly dowagers and princesses, who will keep her busy and give me time to think. 'You must behave as your country would want you to behave. You must be proud and make me proud of you. Don't allow anyone to find you wanting in dignity. My heart is with you, remember that.'

This has the desired effect. Isabella always responds to an authoritarian stance. She trusts me again. She lifts her little chin high and gathers the long folds of her robe and trips across the floor. With cries of delight and open arms, the Ladies receive her.

Tomorrow, they will be picking her to pieces.

Bleakly I eye the scene. It is a poor show, for a welcome feast. Little of the food has been eaten, for it is of inferior quality and the tables are not covered. But lovemaking has made me ravenous, so I take a little bread and fowl meat, which is all I can stomach and nibble, trying to ignore its blandness. I take no wine, despite being pressed by several male members of the party, for I need my wits about me. As soon as I have assuaged my hunger, I withdraw and find myself a dark corner to sit in and ponder.

I must concoct a story so complex, so incredible, that it simply must be true. Such is the art of convincing deception. Experience has taught me this. Experience has also taught me that a lady needs a good memory to employ such a deception successfully. I must be meticulous in the details I choose to commit to memory.

Is this how men feel when they are jousting or setting off to battle? If so, I understand the rush of excitement that consumes them. For the second time since I arrived in England, I feel alive, truly alive. Passion and Danger! Without them, what is a woman?

Quickly, I find Margaret and tell her to inform my Lady that I am ill and have retired. As I climb the dark narrow stairs that lead to the upper quarters where my room is situated adjacent to my Lady's chamber, I hear footsteps following behind. At the top, I turn to see who it is.

Gaveston! He bounds over several stairs with

deer-like grace to land nimbly beside me, inclining his head to acknowledge me. Staring at him, I decide I do not find him attractive and that I would feel this way even if he were a normal man. This is strange, for he is certainly handsome, in a dark, mischievous way. Yet, there is something about him that I cannot explain.

'Mistress, we have met before, I am quite certain.'

'Indeed,' I say briefly. 'My name is Eleanora. Lady Eleanora.'

He takes my hand in his long fingers and raises it to his lips, in traditional gallant fashion, although I have the uncomfortable feeling he is mocking me. As his full lips touch my hand, I freeze. For as his fingers curl around mine, I perceive something familiar sparkling on his middle digit. I snatch back my hand as though it is burned.

'Sir, that ring! It does not belong to you!'

'Indeed it does, fair Eleanora. It was given to me by my sovereign to mark his gratitude in respect of my acting as Regent while he was in Bolougne to be wed to your esteemed Mistress.'

'I recognise that ring. It is part of my Lady's Dowry.'

'I think you might be mistaken.'

'I know I'm not.'

'Nevertheless, it's now mine.' He holds out his hand, his long fingers extended so that we might both admire the sparkling, ruby gem, in its fine setting of heavy gold. I turn away, but in another of his exuberant leaps, he blocks my passage.

'I do know you.'

'In passing. I think you are better acquainted with my sister, Lady Charlotte.'

'Charlotte! Of course. Indeed, I remember. Charlotte. Charlotte the Harlot! Little Charlotte the Harlot with the bouncing tits!''

Now, I might call my indiscreet sister anything I please, but when another person insults my relatives, it is a different matter. With unladylike efficiency, I fling my right arm across my breast, then, with a forward thrust, I smash the smirk off his face with the knuckles of my hand. A deft flick of my wrist causes the emeralds of my largest ring to gouge that hated cheek. Before he has a chance to comprehend what has happened, I have thrust my face close to his. I can see the blood oozing from the wound and running down his chin. We are eye-to-eye, for although he is tall, so am I. I am too angry to be afraid of him.

'You will take that back, Sir,' I snarl.

I can tell he is taken by surprise, but his breeding is such that quickly he recovers. To his credit, he does not hit me back, although I can tell by the manner in which he clenches and unclenches his fists he is itching to do so.

'You will take that back,' I repeat.

'Madame, I will not. It will not change the truth.'

You might remember there are other truths that cannot be changed by the wearing of my Lady's ring,' I retort and I push him aside and hurry on.

Panting with rage, I enter my Lady's chamber and prepare her bed. It's not long before she slips through the door, clearly defeated. Ladies Margaret and Joan are with her.

'When will your Lord be joining you?' I enquire.

'I cannot tell you, Ellie, for I do not have the powers of a seer,' she replies, dejectedly. 'But if he does, I shall not allow him to enter. If he breaks down the door, I shall kill myself before he shall touch me.'

Impressed, I stare at her. She has changed so, this pliable girl, this sweet innocent who once lived in a world of dreams.

'Are you sure that would be for the best, to reject your Lord?'

'He wears his lover's likeness around his throat in a pendant. Did you know that, Ellie? And what is worse, he has given his own likeness to Gaveston. They cannot bear to be apart, such is their corruption of each other. And so my honour is compromised.'

'What will you do, Isabella?'

'I shall write to my father now and I shall upbraid him in strong terms for agreeing to marry me to… such as he.'

I'm relieved she seems to have forgotten to ask me to recount the story of my ordeal. It's difficult to choose between three or four convincing tales I've dreamed up, just which would be most effective and evoke most sympathy. Now I shall have a little extra time to decide. Nor does it seem the best time to acquaint her with the extent of her husband's betrayal by using her precious ring as currency. Although I suppose it would be better that she heard it from me than from someone else.

Isabella sits down to her writing bureau, places the parchment before her and picks the quill from the stand. For two hours she laboriously writes, dipping the pen, stopping to think, changing her mind and crossing something out, her light hair resting on the parchment, like a curtain masking a dark and sinister tale. Eventually, she takes up her seal and the task is done.

'Now I shall go to bed, Ellie,' she says.

I send Margaret for the chamber pot. I am instructing her so that she may assume some of my less agreeable duties. With more pressing matters on her mind, my Lady is unlikely to protest at being attended by Margaret. Kissing Isabella goodnight, I am almost winded by the vehemence with which she embraces me. Then I retire to my own room. I lie awake all night, listening for the sound of the Edward's' footsteps outside Princess Isabella's bedroom door, but I wait in vain. My Mistress spends another night alone and she has only been married a few days.

This leads my mind into philosophical questions, especially on the nature of Temptation, and the words of St. Matthew. 'Watch and pray, that ye enter not into temptation: the spirit indeed is willing but the flesh is weak.' If Isabella (passionate Isabella!) is denied the pleasures of the flesh as sanctified by marriage, whatever will she do? St. Matthew does not seem to take account of this. We are, after all, creatures of instinct and it is to deny our true nature if we deny this. Perhaps her royal spouse will do his duty, for the sake of an heir...but that is not a satisfactory solution.

The flesh is weak. I must say, I would not have my flesh any other way. Oh, delicious, plump breasts that stick out like fat, white geese, waiting to be stroked and kissed. For, doesn't the Bible also say, 'Hope deferred maketh the heart sick: but when the desire cometh, it is the tree of life'?

That's what I most admire about the Bible. You can choose the parts which are the most accommodating. So long as you are discreet, for I have noticed that, almost without exception, the official line is usually the least attractive!

And there is a young man who takes my eye in the English entourage. Contrary to my usual rule, I do not intend to waste too much time observing him in society and shall have him as soon as we are safely established at Court.

Charlotte once said to me, 'You're quite mad, Ellie. You say it's prudent to observe a man before you demonstrate your willingness to take him for a lover. But you had that burly groom and you had never seen him before.'

Charlotte misunderstands the argument sometimes. The groom was indeed burly, but fair of face. In addition, he was due to be hanged the following day for some minor offence. It was an act of charity to steal down to his cell while the guard was sleeping and take the key from his belt. How my heart pounded in my breast! How I gave my all! How I must have lightened the step of the doomed felon on his walk to the gibbet. How I must have filled his heart with the joy that, although he would die young, he would most truly have lived.

Besides which, he couldn't destroy my reputation, for anything he said would be dismissed as delirious ramblings and soon forgotten. I didn't attend the execution, for I have no stomach for such squalid carryings-on.

Because I cannot sleep I pick up my Bible and turn to the psalms. 'I will give thanks unto thee, for I am fearfully and wonderfully made.' Psalm 139. There is, indeed, much wisdom in the Bible. So, I put down the Holy Book, caress my large, brown nipples into rigidity and I am comforted.

Now to drift into a soft, floating dream, in which the face of my next intended hovers with welcoming gaze. I hope he is as well-endowed as he looks. I must seek out some gossip that might indicate his qualities, for such a disappointment will ruin my life.

CHAPTER 7

The King's Infatuation

It's April, the Year of Our Lord, 1308. Two months we have been here, in this dreary, draughty old Tower. The only bright things to be seen are my Lady's priceless rings and golden chains and gem-studded brooches which grace the person of the hated Gaveston. Gaveston, who glories in the title, Earl of Cornwall, given to him last summer by Edward on the death of the old King.

Edward's cousin, the Earl of Lancaster has been wild with fury ever since and eloquent in his fury. He demands that Gaveston be banished. Most of the Earls are sympathetic to the Queen, for example, Pembroke, Warwick, the Mortimers. Of one accord, they detest the strutting Gaveston. All the same, they are impotent against the intensity of the new King's infatuation with his favourite.

The new King Edward II was crowned this year, in February. In some respects, the Coronation was glorious, and everywhere was like Fairyland.

Gaveston had the most illustrious time! Carrying Edward's glittering Crown and dressed fine as a peacock, everyone else, including the King, was eclipsed. The Barons were incensed and muttered mutinously between themselves. It was also Gaveston who made all the arrangements, and there was the rub. He mismanaged the seating plan for the Abbey, everything took far too long, the food was poor, the service slow. Isabella's sparkle slowly died, for no one paid her any attention while Gaveston reigned supreme. He seemed oblivious to the pig's ear he had made of everything.

There were one or two more minor incidents; a knight was trampled underfoot in the Abbey and we could hear him howling although no one could fight off the crowds to help him. I don't think anyone actually tried, such was the chaos. The poor man's cries were pitiful to hear, as they grew fainter and fainter, then ceased. The affair was hushed up at the time so as not to mar the Coronation; we only heard about his funeral after the event.

Just one thing is certain, that every man, woman and child is in love with my Mistress, who despite her trials, composes herself, slips on her mask and charms the entire city of London.

I know better, for I see her often, listless, withdrawn, as though she longs only for obscurity, perhaps even death. Secretly, she hates England and its filth. Nor is she impressed by the crudity of the English Court. She has little energy, except when she is writing to her father.

At these times, she spares no effort. I watch her in profile, with head bent, small chin rounding as it sinks tight into her neck, thick, fair eyelashes brushing her cheeks. She labours at her writing desk for many hours, seeking to compose a letter which will evoke her father's pity and make him relent. When she has finished, spoiled and heavily blotted sheets of parchment litter the floor, enough to cover the walls of her chamber. It is difficult to revive her spirits, although I try.

'It's said that Gaveston dabbles in witchcraft,' I tell her. 'How long, do you think, before he's burned?' She doesn't reply, so I press on. 'His mother was burned for witchcraft, you know.'

'I know.'

'No doubt she taught him all her best spells before they burned her.'

'No doubt.'

'You know, Gaveston makes himself most unpopular with the nobles. He calls them names and the Earl of Lincoln is incensed with the nickname, Burst-belly, for it has caught on. Yesterday he heard one of the kitchen wenches describing him as such. She's been whipped to within an inch of her life. And he has other names, which I would not repeat. What do you think of that, Isabella?'

'He is a rude and vulgar creature. A trumped up clown. A minion.'

'Cousin Lancaster has been complaining again about Gaveston. He says your Royal Master should send him away forthwith. Perhaps Lancaster can have him executed. He could be hanged, drawn and quartered, for he's not a true noble. I'm sure Lancaster could arrange it.'

This realisation lifts my spirits, for those of noble blood are merely beheaded, and are usually dead within two or three blows of an axe to the neck. Far too painless and speedy an end for Piers

Gaveston!

'Ellie, you are in error. Gaveston is of noble blood.'

This irks me so much I won't accept it. 'But, my Lady, that's not possible. Everyone says…'

'These are wishful thoughts. Besides, Ellie, you shouldn't contradict me.'

'I beg pardon, my Lady. I suppose I'll have to be content with the axe.'

'Either way, it is of no consequence, Ellie. My husband will do as he wishes. He's the King,' she replies simply. There's really no easy answer to such an obvious truth. I persevere.

'Hereford, Warwick and Arundel refuse to be in his presence. And he's wearing your very best chain around his neck. And your gold brooch set with precious rubies secures his cloak. And what's more, my Lady…'

'Ellie, dearest, you are making my head hurt.'

I'm in despair. Isabella is no fun…and the little adventure I had planned with the young cousin of the new King's nephew has not borne fruit. This young cousin's name is Guy de Clare whom I saw speaking with my father not long ago, and he's indeed comely. In addition, he's distantly related to the King's young widow, Margaret de Clare. What greater name than 'de Clare'? 'The Lady Isabella de Clare.' What an elevation, to be a relative by marriage of the Dowager Queen! How I should strut and preen and talk down to those I despise. There is no gossip about this young man; it seems he keeps to himself, apart from the crowd and he is uninvolved in gossip and scandal. This worries me slightly, but I am sure he is not…like Gaveston.

Always I smile at him and he is courteous, doffing his hat and carrying for me if I am straining with a large burden. Despite making every effort to carry large burdens in his presence, he simply deposits them back in my arms when the errand is complete, doffs his hat and strides away. This is a great frustration for me. Foolish girl, I tell myself. Perhaps he thinks you're just a minion. How I admire his long, smooth beard, so striking in one so young.

Greater effort must be made to inform Guy of my exalted status and I shall not be carrying any more burdens, for the strain is beginning to show on my face. On the other hand, perhaps he is simply afraid to pursue me, is intimidated by my hauteur, thinks he is not good enough for me. That I could understand. He cannot be so dense as not to notice my efforts on his behalf. Surely he cannot be immune to my appeal. A tingle of fear courses up my spine at the very thought of losing my power to do with men as I wish.

Once more, I shall try to make fortune smile upon my love. For I'm sure Margaret has a spell to make a man fall in love with a maid. We must be secret about this. There are some who would be pleased to accuse me of pagan beliefs or even to brand me a witch. How Gaveston would howl with laughter to see me burn! I wouldn't give him the satisfaction. Margaret will be frightened to help me, but this won't prove an impediment. I know something about her she would prefer I kept to myself. I save up little treasures like this, for one never knows when they might come in useful.

I decide to find Margaret immediately and ask her to help me with the love recipe.

The old King died in July of last year, six months before my Lady's marriage and just a short time after his young Queen, Margaret, gave birth to a new little daughter. This child he speedily promised in marriage to the son of the Duchess of Burgundy. So life goes on. What are female daughters (especially royal female daughters) but pawns in the politics of men? Women have to make the best of whatever has been arranged. That is, most women. Not me, for I shall make my own arrangements.

The old King Edward became tired, people say; he became weak with his ordeals. Yet, in spite of all that, he fathered a child! Such a lustful old gentleman, one cannot help but admire him.

They call the old King the Warrior King because he fought to the end to quell the indignities the fearsome Scots tried to foist upon him. Such was his will, he requested his bones be wrapped up and carried before his army, so that, even in death, he might lead them to victory. In my opinion, having your bones rattling about before an army is unlikely to inspire great courage in the soldiers. Especially with the flesh still attached and rotting, for the smell would be putrid and you would probably fall off your horse in a faint.

When I point this out to Lady Mortimer, she sniffs and says, 'He wanted his flesh boiled off first.'

'And a fine, nourishing soup that would make,' I reply. After I have made this joke, a twinge of anxiety twists my heart for allowing my tongue to run off with me. Lady Mortimer grunts and swishes out of the room. I hope she will not repeat what I said. My careless wit has caused me trouble before. Unfortunately, I do not know anything about Lady Mortimer to guarantee her silence. This is an obstacle I intend to remove at the earliest opportunity, for everyone has something to conceal.

CHAPTER 8

The Love Potion

'Oh Mistress!' says Margaret, 'I cannot. Oh, really, I cannot!'

'Of course you can, Margaret. I'll help you.'

'But we would need to go outside the walls to seek the ingredients for the potion,' says Margaret. 'And that will be dangerous without a chaperone.'

'I shall be your chaperone.'

'But who will be yours?'

'You will.'

'Oh. But Mistress Ellie...'

'It's decided then. I'll bribe the guard to let us out secretly through the river gate. And you shall be handsomely rewarded. You know that kirtle of Indian silk the Queen gave me? The one you almost fainted over? Well, Margaret, it shall be yours. We can sneak off in a small boat under cover of dusk. But, we will need to see a little if we are to find what we are looking for. It'll be a full moon tonight and the sky is clear. It'll be an exciting adventure. Who knows what will happen?'

'Oh Mistress!' cries Margaret. 'I cannot.' I sigh. Margaret is becoming tedious.

'You know what that will mean, Margaret?'

'Mistress Ellie, you wouldn't...?'

'Mistress Margaret, I would...' I mock her.

'But...' continues Margaret, excruciatingly caught between fear of saying yes and fear of saying no, which must be the worst kind of fear imaginable.

I give her one of my long, lingering, meaningful looks.

'I'll be ready,' she whispers.

I knew that she would.

The little boat cuts noiselessly through the inky waters and I can hear Margaret panting with fear. She sits opposite me, huddled into her dark robe like a cornered rabbit. I row carefully, not splashing too much with the oars, but making due speed so we will not be spotted by one of the guards. Torches lit by the banks of the river cast their glow and I try to avoid them, not only to elude possible capture, but also to mask the painful sight of abject terror on Margaret's pale face. Her little nose twitches so and she looks more like a terrified rabbit every minute.

'Oh, Ellie, I'm so scared,' whispers Margaret.

'So am I but I do not complain.'

'This was your idea. Not mine.'

'Silence! I must concentrate.'

By now, we are gaining, for the tide is with us and the torches gradually grow fainter and disappear. Reeds and willows line the banks and provide us with light cover. 'Here,' I mutter and push an oar into the mud, so we are propelled into thick reeds and the wooden hull bumps against the bank. I have to jump to avoid being soaked, which is difficult constrained as I am by my kirtle. With due speed, I tie the boat to the trunk of a willow. The night air is crisp, but not chilly and we can hear the sounds of tiny night creatures scurrying and squeaking in the undergrowth.

'Come, Margaret. I'm certain we shall find what we need right here.'

I give her my hand and she scrambles to the bank beside me although her hem drags in the mud. 'Never mind, you will have a new kirtle soon,' I tell her before she can begin to complain. There is no path, so travelling is difficult, but there is the full moon to light our way and I have hidden a sharp knife in my raiments to make our progress less irksome. Valiantly I slash at the undergrowth till we have cleared our way beyond the brambles and vines that cling to us like serpents. Like a man, I ignore the scratches on my arms and shins.

'Have you done this before, Ellie?' asks Margaret.

'You would be surprised at the things I have done when required,' I answer briefly.

'Who…who is the man you wish to enchant?'

I wish she would stop her mouth and allow me to set my mind fully on my task. 'Now, what do we need first?' I ask.

'Frog-spawn.'

I stare at her pale face in the moonlight. 'Frog-spawn? Then we need to find some water.'

'We've just left the water.'

'Do frogs spawn in the river or the sea?'

'They certainly spawn in the small pond the other side of the woods.'

'So, we need not worry about frog-spawn at this moment. What else?'

'Red berries.'

'It's the wrong time of the year.'

'There might be some early berries.'

'What else?'

'Lichen.'

'That shouldn't be too difficult. Here.' Relieved, I grasp a fistful from a damp stone and stow it in the cloth bag I have brought for the purpose. 'What else?'

'Two dead mice. For their tails and eyes. But we can get them from the traps in the cellars.'

I groan, for I shall commit murder before the night is through. 'Margaret, let us think about things we cannot get in the cellars.'

'Purple flowers and the droppings of a female hare.'

I grip Margaret by the shoulders and begin to shake her soundly. 'In God's name, if you cannot tell a male hare from a female hare, and I'm sure you cannot, how will you tell the sex of their dropping? Margaret, you useless creature, why did you fail to warn me that the ingredients would be so difficult?'

'You didn't ask me,' she whimpers.

She's right. Nor did I ask her what was to be done with these revolting ingredients after they have been made into the love potion. Surely I am not expected to eat them, or smear them on my person, or slip them in my intended's tankard.

'Margaret…' I begin.

She sees the look in my eyes and quickly replies. 'We must mix them up and chant a spell over them.'

'Are you sure that's all?'

In the moonlight I see her pale chin jerking up and down in desperate confirmation. 'You mustn't mind the ingredients, Ellie. It is a powerful spell and many have found happiness through it. It's not my fault about the female hare droppings.' Convinced she's lying, I start towards her and I cannot predict what would have happened next, for a hearty groan freezes me and strikes fear into both our hearts. There's a pair of horses tethered in the distance. With Margaret stumbling at my heels I draw closer and the sight that meets my eyes draws all the breath from my body. I am fair faint with shock.

I have never in my life seen an orgy take place with just two people in it. But if it were possible, then this is an orgy of two, as defined by an excess of utter abandonment and pleasure. How I envy them for it.

'Many waters cannot quench love, neither can the floods drown it,' I murmur.

'My Lady?' questions Margaret. She is behind me and sees nothing.

'Song of Solomon,' I tell her. She frowns. I am proud of my learning. My father spent many hours tutoring me as a child, for I was the only one of his daughters with the ability both to assimilate and to apply myself to a task. I can find a Bible quotation to fit any event and people are always impressed by my book-learning. It is a great advantage, for it sets one apart from the herd and one can appear uncommonly clever even when one does not know what the Lucifer one is talking about.

'What are you looking at, Ellie?'

'Never mind. It is not fit for your eyes. Cover them at once. Face towards the river and stay right here.' In Margaret's place, I would surely have peeped, but she is not made of such strong stuff as I am. I wait a moment to see she does not succumb to the temptation to peep between her plump fingers, and then I steal through the trees to get a closer look.

I cannot believe it!

All my life my eyes have been open to the ways of the world. All my life, I have witnessed life and birth and death and love in all of their many shades of dark and light. Never have I shut myself away from any manner of knowledge.

But I have never seen anything so outrageous and so utterly beautiful as these two young men cavorting in a forest glade at dusk. A golden head against a darker head, bodies touching, exploring and delighting. Believing themselves alone and safe, they are unselfconscious, oblivious to the world around them. The golden-haired one embraces the darker one from behind and I think how the backsides of young men are so delicious... For a moment, I forget to hate Gaveston, and I am further aroused as my gaze wanders over the strong curves of the King's long, masculine thighs.

The low murmur of their voices carries through the still, night air.

'I should die a thousand deaths than be parted from you, sweet Gaveston,' murmurs the King.

'I should walk through fire, I should brave a pit of snakes than leave your side,' replies Gaveston.

Oh, such glorious chatter!

They continue in this vein and my ears are flapping so hard, I feel I might fly like a bird. Yet I cannot stay, although I wish to. I must leave Edward and Gaveston to their frolics, lest Margaret becomes frightened and forgets my warnings. She is so clumsy, she would be sure to expose us by squealing or crying.

Nor must I let them observe me observing them, for my life would be as dust. I shrink back, watching where I put my feet that I should not crack a twig or step in a hole and twist my ankle.

'Margaret, come, it is time for us to go. Never fret about the ingredients. I shall find another way.'

Margaret is only too willing, so we make our way back to the little boat and soon we are cast off and wending our silent way back. Margaret is glum but my mind is in a turmoil.

The Earl of Lancaster is already tearing out his meagre hair with rage and will soon be quite bald once acquainted with a detailed account of what I have seen. I shiver with anticipation at the thought of what he will do next. I shall await the perfect moment for a chat with my Lord.

I have not been pleasured by a man for two

months, two weeks, five days, several hours and many minutes.The last thirty minutes have seemed the longest. Peering in the looking-glass I can see the effects of all this on my face. I have a spot. Two spots, one of which is particularly ugly, for it sits on the end of my nose and weeps copiously. This is unconscionable and cannot continue.

CHAPTER 9

A Meeting with Guy de Clare

My Lady rings for me. Margaret is not available at the moment, so I must do my duty with the chamber pot, except I have no Runt of a sister to perform the onerous emptying chore. And Dame Fortune frowns upon me, for as I trot along the main passageway leading to the cut-off stairway to the garderobes, there he is! Guy de Clare!

I feel my chest tighten that he should see me thus, with a pot full of piss between my pert breasts. Horror swamps me and I scurry, making myself small. The recognition dawns on his handsome face. I pray he will, at least, affect not to recognise me, for I feel unbearably humiliated carrying this particular burden.

'Mistress! May I?'

Dumbly, I shake my head and hurry on, although my knees are so weak, I am afraid I will tumble.

'Mistress, I insist.'

He makes as though to seize the pot from me and I am filled with dread that if I resist and cling on, there might be an unseemly accident with the contents. This may not augur well for any future romantic entanglement.

'My Lord is too kind,' I murmur, and feeling

bound to explain, I continue: 'You see, the maid who serves my Lady is unwell, for this is not my usual duty. I am Second-in-Chief Lady-in-Waiting.' (I feel I should be honest about this, as he knows Lady Mortimer well.)

'Mistress, you are ill-used,' he replies. He shakes his head in wonderment that I should be expected to demean myself in this way. 'You must be a saint to bend your will to such a task. Please, wait for me here, for I cannot allow you… in the name of Heaven… such a sweet and noble Lady!' Boldly, he strides off, stiff-legged, the pot held at arm's length in front of him, which looks so funny that I stifle a giggle behind my fist.

I'm enchanted and wait until he returns. We linger and he kisses me and I kiss him back and the wetness of his tongue is on my cheeks and chin and the very marrow of my bones is on fire.

He pushes me into the full, soft drapes and he is pulling up my kirtle and, with his other hand, exposing my breasts, and I wonder if I am mating with a man or one of those strange creatures of many tentacles that live in the ocean. Oh, fortunate, fortunate creatures of the ocean. Not for one moment do I worry that someone might pass by and hear the crazed pantings and gruntings or remark upon the suggestive billowings of the drapes. Let them gossip if they must, for it will be nothing but jealousy.

Holy Mother of God, I do not need the love potion with the female hare droppings after all! All I need is my own Precious Treasure.

CHAPTER 10

Ellie the Schemer

The Earl of Lancaster is a fearsome creature, quick of temper and passionately self-righteous. That's why he is the very one to whom I must impart my news. He's Gaveston's worst enemy and is not fond of King Edward either, whom he blames for wicked extravagance towards the favourite, as well as for his poor show on the Scottish campaigns.

'The Scots triumph because their leaders command the loyalty of their armies,' Lancaster is fond of saying. 'Our King must be persuaded to do the same if we are to hold our heads high as Englishmen.'

It's a shame for poor Edward, who is a gentle soul and fond of the common people, and who would be a tolerably good King were it not for the stupid wars with the arrogant Scots and the stuck-up Welsh. Besides, if Gaveston were not around, Edward might treat his Queen with more respect.

I'm attached to Isabella and growing increasingly fond of her as she begins, with maturity, to show more spirit. I cannot abide women who have to be wet-nursed and treated like porcelain china lest they crack into a thousand pieces. I will do this for brave Isabella. Besides, if she is happier, we will have more fun and I will get more presents.

So, next day, I am bursting with goodwill towards the world. For this I have Guy de Clare to thank. It was the most delightful tumble I have known in ages, even better than the incident with the rough man who took me on the crate at Dover. Of course, one should not compare. Yet, there is something so intense about pleasuring a man while you are both standing and your knees are shaking like ducks' arses.

I send a servant to inform Lancaster I must see him urgently. The man returns immediately and says he will conduct me to my Lord. My heart begins to pump inside my breast and I take many deep breaths as I follow the servant to Lancaster's quarters.

'Mistress Eleanora,' booms Lancaster, his defiant brown beard bristling. I offer him my hand to kiss and he slobbers over it. I have to pretend I enjoy his slobbering, but it is worth it.

'My Lord, as you may know, I'm Chief Confidante and Lady-in-Waiting to the Queen. I'm aware you have her interests close to your heart, and so I wish to confide in you something that may…that is… affecting her health and happiness.'

My Lord invites me to sit. He offers me some pale yellow sweetmeats from Turkey, but I decline, thinking of my spots, which are still visible. It is a pity that sweet treats give ladies spots and I don't know why that should be, but it is an observable phenomenon.

'Please state your business, my Lady.'

'It's a matter of the most delicate nature.'

'You may be sure I shall treat it with respect.'

'It's about Gaveston, the King's favourite.'

'I'm well aware of the Gascon's standing with the King,' growls Lancaster.

After that, it is not so difficult. Somehow, enthusiasm increases with another's absorption in your narrative, so I am able to find all the right words to expand on Piers Gaveston's perversions and his wily influence over the King. Even to embellish a little. For good measure I throw in a quotation or two from the Bible. I am pleased with myself. I can see the Earl is mightily impressed.

'What's more, my Lord,' I add, 'it's said he uses sorcery to influence the King. He may have learned much from his mother, who was burned for a witch.'

Lancaster's response is true to character. He roars. He rages. He tugs at his beard and strikes his temple three times, almost knocking himself unconscious. At the same time, he stamps around the room in a highly theatrical manner. A servant slips in to see if I am murdering him by slow torture, but is summarily dismissed.

'I must speak to Henry de Lacy of Lincoln about this. Parliament will sit upon this and pronounce a resolution.'

'But, Sir!' I cry, alarmed, 'I don't seek publicity, merely justice.'

'Do not fear, my Lady. I shall not allow your name to be revealed. Only in the Earl of Lincoln shall I confide and you can rely upon his utter discretion. It will be another sword to drive into the heart of Gaveston, but it will be the sharpest sword of all because it is honed by the word of a Lady.'

'I trust my Lord Lincoln knows that Gaveston calls him Burst-belly because of his heavy middle region.' I fancy I see a faint smirk on Lancaster's lips, for who does not feel a tinge of quiet satisfaction at the comeuppance of a fellow-peer, even an ally. Encouraged, I continue, 'And what's more, my Lord, he is most disrespectful to your own elevated person. You he calls...'

'The Fiddler!' roars Lancaster. 'I know what he calls me. That's because he's jealous of my fine clothes. But, I do not care to be reminded, my Lady Eleanora, for I set myself above such trivial nonsense.'

I desist from pointing out to my Lord that it is his ludicrous dress sense, his desire for finery made ridiculous by total lack of good taste that incites Gaveston to parody. It is difficult not to enlighten him, but I judge that such a painful home-truth will scarce improve his temper.

'Please accept my apologies for my clumsiness. I only meant... And, anyway, he calls others far worse than that. For instance...'

'Your gabbling does not please me, Mistress.'

I see I need to change my battle strategy forthwith before I'm banished. This is really a most intemperate Lord.

'My Lord, I thank you from the depths of my

tender feminine heart for myself and for my Mistress. She suffers mightily and cries into her pillow every night.' The change that these words bring about is amazing. Lancaster's face drops at the image and he looks so forlorn - like a droop-eared dog - that I want to laugh. I manage to re-arrange the laugh into a dazzling smile which I hope he will construe as a compliment to his brilliance. Immediately, his anger is forgotten and he almost grovels.

'My dear Lady, this Gaveston, is he… very well-endowed? Forgive me! I am clumsy to speak thus to a lady.'

'My Lord,' I place my forefinger across my lips to hide the mischief there. 'He's…huge. Utterly, unbelievably *enormous!'*

'Indeed…' murmurs Lancaster, wincing.

'Like a bull,' I assure him. 'Few women could accommodate his hugeness without extreme fortitude.'

(It will do no harm to add jealousy to the many reasons that Lancaster has for hating Piers Gaveston.)

'Are you certain you wouldn't like one of these? They're very good,' says Lancaster, pushing the plate of sweetmeats under my nose. It's too much. I take one and pop it into my mouth.

Before I leave, he insists I take the entire platterful. Dropping a curtsey, I depart. It pains me mightily, but I steel myself and throw them down the garderobe chute before I return to my chamber. What a creature of steely resolve I am! Then, I take some physic for my spots.

It has been a good day's work. Perhaps what I have set into motion will culminate in Gaveston's end. Never again will he frolic with my Mistress' husband or wear her glorious jewels or call my sister Charlotte the Harlot in such an impertinent manner. Remembering Charlotte makes me suddenly homesick and I find myself wondering how she is and what she is doing and whether the Runt is growing breasts yet.

I do not have to wait too long to find out. A messenger comes to my room to tell me my father is on his way to visit me.

'I do not see a Bible on your table,' says my father. 'Aren't you observing your religious duties?'

'I've recently made a pilgrimage to Canterbury with the Queen to pray over the tomb of brave Thomas a Becket,' I reply. 'I prayed for over an hour, much longer even than my Lady.' This does not answer Father's question, but deflects his curiosity. He may disapprove of my using The Holy Book to dry out some deadly nightshade, which Margaret swears will give Lady Mortimer severe stomach cramps if I crumble it and slip it into her gruel. I felt it more discreet to hide my Bible, with the incriminating evidence, at the bottom of my raiments' chest.

'A grand Cathedral,' says Father approvingly, 'with a proud history. Oh, the stories those ancient walls could tell. I am glad you have seen it in all its Holy Glory. And did you pray for me, Daughter?'

'How can you ask that, Father?'

'I won't ask again and impel you to lie,' says my father, who is the most cynical creature I have ever met.

'How are my sisters?' I ask quickly.

'Charlotte is well and sends you her tender love. The most exciting news is about the Runt. Suddenly, she has grown tall and firm-breasted and blossomed into one of the most beautiful young ladies in the French Court. She has grown graceful in manner and temperate in all of her actions. All the nobles are in love with her and she has received three proposals of marriage. What is more, they are from young men with excellent prospects. We must not call her the Runt any longer, for she flies into the most fearful temper. Ellie, do close your mouth. You look like a fish.'

I have to sit down. It takes some time to even begin to understand what my father means. But he is not prone to making jests so he must be serious.

'You mean...someone wants to marry the Runt?'

'Mathilde, Ellie, Mathilde. Three young men are in competition for your sister's hand. I have told her to wait, for she must choose carefully.'

'Choose!' My amazement is so great, it bites deep into my heart.

'Yes, choose the best of the bunch. Or wait a little longer, for something even more suitable to present itself.'

'Something more *suitable*?'

'Ellie, you sound like a parrot from the tropics.'

'I look like a fish and sound like a parrot. I am beginning to feel insulted by you, my father. Not least, because you would consider marrying the youngest daughter before the eldest two are spoken for.'

My father laughs and slaps his thigh. 'Will you be so particular about two hours, Ellie? You are a comical child.' Then his voice takes on a more serious tone. 'I have heard there is a feast in the Great Hall. Will you be there, Ellie? For I know your Mistress, the Queen will be attending. I must talk to her about Mathilde.'

'Why must you talk to my Lady about Mathilde?' I ask slowly, apprehension gnawing at my stomach.

'Mathilde might benefit from a short, educational visit to the English Court. And it would be company for you,' says my father carelessly. 'I must go and prepare myself now, Ellie. Put on your highest head-dress for the feast tonight, for I am so proud of all my daughters.'

After he has gone, I am breathing fast and shallow, barely able to contain myself. With a terrible cry of rage, I throw myself onto my bed and pound at my pillows, weeping noisily. Everything was so utterly perfect. My lusty new lover! My brilliant plan to discredit Gaveston! Even my spots are slowly fading.And now! Now I have been assigned to chaperone the Runt. To introduce her to all the people who matter in the English Court. Probably even to share her with Isabella. It's bad enough keeping the surly Lady Mortimer in her place.

And the Runt…the most beautiful young lady in the French Court! Could it be…could it be that my father is merely teasing me?

It's so terribly hard to imagine that this particular scrawny nymph has become a glorious damselfly.

I thought I found a white hair in one of my ringlets yesterday morning.

CHAPTER 11

A Forced Separation

The Queen is in a foul temper. For she has just heard that three of Gaveston's ill-gotten properties have been beautifully renovated and laid end-to-end with fine-glazed floor tiles and every one encapsulates his proud Coat-of-Arms.

'It's disgraceful. When have I had anything new to please my eye? How I hate this dull, dusty old place!' The Queen dismisses the entire Royal Dwelling with a sweep of her slender arm.

'My Lady, such ostentation is not seemly. It shows vulgarity of taste. You do not need that kind of display to prove your worth,'

'I think you are saying that to improve my temper, Ellie, for you enjoy ostentation as much as anyone. Besides, these floors are dull with age and one can scarcely see the pattern. It doesn't lift the spirit. And it is the same with the walls and the ceilings and the furnishings. Dull, dull, dull.

She sends for her seamstress and orders twenty new gowns with which to console herself. I rub my hands with glee. The Queen can wear only one gown at a time and space is running out to store the mountains of raiments she possesses. This is bound to vex her and there is a black velvet that would look well on me. I happen to have noticed it is too small for her.

So much happens in the next two weeks that I can hardly believe it. Gaveston is banished. Banished! He must be gone by 15 June or it will be the worst for him. The Queen and I are overcome with joy. The meeting of the Barons must have been a heated affair, for I am told that one nobleman stood up strongly to speak in favour of the King and his lover. The Court is buzzing with the news. His name is Hugh le Despenser.

When I speak to Isabella about him, she said, 'No doubt he seeks to ingratiate himself with the King. He's a fool.'

'It's fortunate he was overturned. Guy tells me that he has been dismissed from his position on the council.'

'Any person who supports Gaveston is my enemy,' says Isabella. 'No punishment is too severe for such a traitor.'

These are strong words and a cold shiver runs down my spine. I would not be in Hugh le Despenser's shoes for the world.

Many matters have taken place in secret that I cannot get to the root of. Many have been striving for some time against the King's favourite, but I suspect it was my special audience with the Earl of Lancaster that settled the matter. I hug myself tightly, and dance around my room, delighting in the knowledge my efforts have borne such rich cherries. Only the two Earls and I will ever know of the part I have played in the Gascon's downfall.

Ah…'Stolen waters are sweet, and bread eaten in secret is pleasant'.

Of course, an execution would have been preferable, but I have not given up hope. For the present time, I will settle for banishment. As well as a Noble Lady, Chief Confidante and Lady-in-Waiting, I am also a Politician and a Mistress of Intrigue. My little chat with Lancaster was my first sortie into politics and now I am an expert in such matters. The sense of power fair goes to my head.

My liaison with the beautiful Guy de Clare continues. We love each other wherever we can, whenever we can, for as long as we can. He is sensitive to my needs and I shall probably never grow another pustule. The Queen looks aslant at my dewy bloom, and I can tell that she knows all there is to know about me. She has her spies. In normal circumstances I believe she would be happy for me, but it must be hard for her with the burdens she has to bear. I hope her life might be better soon.

My father has returned to France, but he has left me a note and I now hear to my horror that Charlotte, too, is to accompany The Runt.

Charlotte is bereft that she might be excluded from her sisters,' writes my father. 'So I have told her she may join you at Court. I rely on you to ensure she behaves herself as a lady should.'

The date of Gaveston's departure from England and my sisters' proposed arrival here coincides. As the month progresses, my Lady suggests she and I, with Margaret and Joan and the customary escort, should make a journey to Wiltshire to stay with her distant cousin. I'm delighted. She says it will be good for her to be away, while the awful fuss dies down and her husband recovers from his grief at losing Gaveston. We leave two days before my sisters arrive. Although I sometimes find it tedious to be forever travelling from Castle to Castle and back again, this time it is expedient. In truth, it is almost perfect. But, as always, there is a pig's eye in the pig gruel. If the Runt is all that my father says she is, I won't be there to prevent her from encroaching on my territory. My eyes scrunch tight at the thought.

'I don't think we have enough manly protection,' I say to Isabella, as casually as possible. 'Why don't we ask Guy de Clare to accompany us? He's strong and brave and would not allow any harm to befall us, for he is a god among men.'

She gives me a black look. 'We have our escort, which is chosen for its training and experience. I don't think an extra man would be a good idea, Ellie. Besides, I would like your attention and your company for a change with no distractions from gods.'

Perhaps it was my last statement that gave me away.

Sometimes, I wish my Lady were not so suspicious. I think on it long and hard. Finally, I have a little chat with Guy, naked on his knee, my perfumed breasts pressed against his mouth. Then I take them away and cover them, for I am afraid my highly-aroused lover is not thinking on my words while my tits distract him. He makes a soulful face as I push his hand away from my inside thigh.

'My youngest sister is quite attractive,' I say, 'but I'm sorry for any man who fancies her, for she's a scold of the worst kind. What's more, she has venereal disease and the most horrid pox marks under her powder. I try not to get too close to her, for fear I might catch something.'

He smiles. 'I promise I will stay away from her and be faithful to you,' he says. 'But don't be away too long.'

I give him a night to remember me by and I reckon it is worth at least six weeks. After that who knows what will happen, for men have such short memories?

CHAPTER 12

Where Did All the Love Go?

The thing about journeying abroad is that one realises how blessed one is. It is late summer and already the leaves have transformed themselves into hues of gold and chestnut. While in the soft peace of this idyllic landscape, one may feel that the world is a gentle place. But in towns and villages it is different. Often we pass poor villages of dwellings of wattle and daub and people in dun-coloured ragged clothing. They look dirty and worn out. They are out in all weather, rain or shine, doing all the things that poor people do. Most of which is tedious in the extreme. I remind myself it is their destiny. We are all born to our station in life and that is the way of the world.

We pass a leper colony and I ask the first horseman to stop so we may look, but to be ready to gallop away fast if they approach us. We do not have long to stare at them, for they come running almost immediately, their ungainly stumps at peculiar angles to their wasted bodies. I notice one has only half a head. If a body has only half a head, can a body think only half a thought? I wonder.

We stop at an inn and nearby sheep are being shorn, for the wool trade is one of England's prime exports. Isabella is fascinated and I can see she would like to try, but I pull her away. It is my sworn duty to remind my lady she is a Queen, should she ever forget.

'You make too much fuss, Ellie,' she complains. 'My husband is happy to talk with the common people and to work with them thatching and planting and ditching.'

'Indeed, my Lady. And see what trouble he has got into because of it,' I reply. 'The common people prefer their Kings and Queens to partake of royal pastimes, like hunting and horseracing and jousting, or in the case of a Lady, sewing psalters, having babies and being charming.' As I lecture my Lady, I think how like Lady Mortimer I sound. Poor Isabella, for who wants to sew and have babies?

Isabella pulls an unqueenly face. 'It's not the common people who get upset. It's the stuffy old Barons.'

'All more reason to take care. You have the Barons on your side, my Lady and we are all safer for that.'

'Sometimes, I wish I were an ordinary person.'

'I am sure you do not, my Lady. Who wants to starve in times of famine and be left to rot in times of pestilence? And till the soil, day in, day out. Besides, the people need you. We all need you.' This pacifies her and she allows herself to be led into the inn.

Our stay in Wiltshire is pleasant but tedious and the boredom wears me down. The cousin is elderly and prone to forgetfulness and the food is disgustingly English. Isabella and I take walks on our own and she unburdens her heart to me. She hopes that when we return, Edward will be ready for her, might even have missed her, once he has adjusted to the exile of his favourite.

'You know, Ellie,' she says, 'my husband had a difficult childhood. He was left alone for many years as a small child, while the King and Queen went away to do homage to King Philip, my father, for their French acquisitions. He hardly saw his parents for the first five years of his life. When children are not properly loved, they grow up lacking much valuable experience.'

This is quite a new viewpoint for me, and I think upon it. Is my Lady unduly wise, or is she making excuses?

'Do you love him?' I ask wonderingly.

'I wish to love him,' she says. That is not at all the same thing and I feel sorry for her as I think of my own lover, the passionate Guy. When you have to try so hard, it is not love, can never be love.

'It is so beautiful here,' muses Isabella and bends down to pick some wild flowers. Soon she has a huge bunch of yellow and purple blooms and she sniffs at them as though she believes they will impart new life into her body. I smile, and pick out some out of the bunch and weave them into the long, golden ringlets that escape from her head-dress.

'You are the most beautiful lady in the land.'

'Am I? Sweet Ellie. Wish that I were. Then

maybe my Lord would love me.'

And maybe the Ravens would leave the Tower! But this, we know, they will never do. Each thing to its own nature must be true. My Lady will learn and I hope, in the learning, she will not lose her reason.

But I can tell her none of this. It is something she must understand for herself.

On our return, we learn that Gaveston is banished to Ireland of all places. And that the King is taking great care to ensure his comfort, safety and pleasure. The cunning knight has been presented with a bundle of Open Charters, if you please, to do with as he wishes. The Barons are furious that he has taken the Great Seal with him to use as he desires. This takes much of the joy out of it for the Queen and me.

I'm noticing, increasingly, that the Queen is becoming sharper with me. Before, I could guide her and she sought my advice about almost everything, never questioning the wisdom I possess from being almost three years older than she is. But now it's different. Once, she regarded my gentle rebukes as sisterly concern for her welfare. Now, she is apt to turn upon me and accuse me of impertinence or obstinacy. Me... impertinent!

'It makes me sad to see you so irked, my Lady,' I murmur. 'You're not well.'

With a snort of annoyance, my Lady shoves Gundulph off her lap and the little dog slinks into a corner in confusion. 'I'm perfectly fine and you know it, Ellie. You just like to have your own way and you use your clever tongue to get it. I swear your head is becoming so swollen, your hair will grow thin. It is time for you to realise that you are merely my servant.'

This is too much! That I should be dismissed as a servant, even by my Mistress, the Queen. Indeed, I should not accept such slight from the King himself.

'My Lady, you're not yourself.' Gently, I take up the comb to groom her hair. She knocks it clean out of my hand and the small face she turns towards me is ravaged and there are dark shadows beneath her eyes. As she speaks, she twists at her rings with her free hand, pulling and twisting till her knuckles are sore.

'Don't patronise me, Lady. Even your title, Lady, you would not sport were it not for my good favour. You're no Lady. Your father is a humble envoy. And your mother was little more than a serf. You, Ellie, are a Lady in my service simply because I once liked you.'

I begin to tremble. Her cruelty has cut me to the very bone and I can barely stand for the shock of it. To my shame, I can feel fat tears welling from my eyes and dripping down my cheeks. Tears of anger and humiliation, for I never cry from self-pity. Through the blur, I see my Lady's face still turned towards me and I expect her to shed tears too, to clutch at my hand and beg my forgiveness for hasty words.

'Get from my sight, Ellie,' she whispers.

It's so unexpected!

I try my best to flounce, but it is not a very successful flounce for I trip over my hem, slip on a rug and sprawl heavily across the floor. I bang my head hard and bright lights dance before my eyes.

'Joan! Joan! Help Ellie to her feet and take her back to her own room where she can think upon her transgressions.

'Don't touch me,' I hiss.

Unsurprisingly, Lady Joan is confused, staring first at me and then at the Queen. Joan starts weeping too and then Lady Margaret joins in. The alarmed dogs begin to yap in sympathy. There's such a noise of female wailing and canine howling, it's enough to awaken the dead in their tombs in the vaults.

'Stop! Stop!' I yell as I scramble to my feet.

'No one would believe,' Isabella announces, 'that I'm the injured party in all these proceedings. All of you shall leave me at once. I've had quite enough of you for one day.' Then, horrifyingly, 'Never forget I am still your Queen and I can send you to the White Tower whenever I wish to.'

The young ladies run out screaming fit to burst their lungs. I follow them, with murder in my heart. What use words of wisdom? 'A soft answer turneth away wrath.' Can it be that even my Bible can no longer be relied upon?

I hide myself away in my top of the Tower chamber. Perhaps if I were to suggest my Lady coax her Lord into taking a trip to Kings Langley, it might improve their relations. The King is known to love his sojourns in Kings Langley, where he has often frolicked with Gaveston, even before they became men. Kings Langley supplies his needs in the way no other castle can, for there he can indulge his love of country pursuits without criticism. If my Lady were successful in persuading him thus, she would be so happy she would allow Guy to accompany us.

Guy must know I am home. He must be beside himself with joy and will long for the comfort of my bed. Soon he'll come knocking on my door. I need something to take my mind away from my worries. I wonder why he's so long. I won't search for him, won't give him the satisfaction of knowing that I'm bereft with yearning for him. No. He must come to me. Why doesn't he come? He must be ill, in prison or dead! Oh please, not dead, not Guy, for who could replace him?

Time is passing. All is quiet.

Where is Guy?

I slip to my door and peer up and down. Delicately, I trot barefoot to the nearest stairway, shivering from the cold. I peer up and down. No Guy. All is quiet, all is still, except for the draught which plays with my light shift and causes tiny bumps to rise on my arms. I run down the stairs. I pass a room to my left and from it I can hear sounds which I recognise.

Sounds of passion. Sounds of unbridled passion and a sort of grunting that happens when

Guy discharges his seed inside my loins. And after that, a loud, long wail. Guy has a particular wail that comes from deep inside and grows much louder before it abates. It is like the deep-throated howl of a wolf, with a whimper of surprise at the end as though the wolf is shot mid-thrust, and cannot quite believe it.

Trembling, I stand beside the door and push it carefully. It's not locked. A little more, and I can see inside, for a candle burns on the table. My timidity is not justified. They are so passionately engaged that they would not see me were I to dance a jig at the foot of the bed and howl like Gundulph and Odo.

My whole body starts to convulse. I am dreaming. I must be dreaming. I see Guy, his fine head thrown back in agony of passion, his mouth open, and resting between his naked, hairy arms, I see…myself. I am outside my own body, for there it is on that rumpled bed, soaking up Guy's spurting juices, throwing its red-golden head from side to side and begging for more with total absence of inhibition. Its legs are thrust out, long and slender and inviting. Surrendered to abandonment, it's most certainly me.

Yet I'm here. I look down. These are my arms and those are my feet, peeping from under the hem of my shift. I press my palms against my cheeks to be certain my face is still there.

The jolt of sudden recognition causes my eyes to roll behind my temple and I tumble in a dead faint into the room. All is blackness. All is nothingness. Slowly, as my consciousness is aroused, I feel damp cloths pressed on my face. I open my eyes. Distractedly, I try to rise on my elbow, staring around the room.

There's no sign of Guy.

But there's something else. 'It's you! The Runt!' I scream as my tall, full-bodied sister leans over me. The compassion on her lovely face turns to bewilderment. 'Runt! Runt! Runt!' I scream. Demented, I tear at my hair, but she pushes me back with a roughness that belies her appearance.

'No one calls me that any more, Ellie,' she informs me icily. 'My name is Mathilde and you had best remember that for the rest of your days.'

CHAPTER 13

Gaveston is Back

It has all gone so terribly wrong.

My Lady has lost respect for me, my sister has betrayed me and my lover has abandoned me. And I have not had a man for seven weeks and two days and fifteen hours. Counting the minutes is irksome, for these are the hardest to bear and I do not wish to dwell upon them.

I cannot accept it, yet I must.

'Nothing happens to anybody which he is not fitted by nature to bear.'

This is not from the Bible, for I am disenchanted with the Holy Teachings. This is Marcus Aurellus, from his Meditations, which I am reading to send myself to sleep each night. I must be strong, for my reading teaches me that how I conduct myself in my moment of darkest despair will affect my entire future.

I need some time alone, some time to think. Some time to conceive a means to change what seems impossible to change. For Plotting Time is never wasted. But when I return to my chamber, someone is waiting for me.

'Charlotte!'

'Ellie, dear Ellie. It is good to see you.'

'When did you arrive?'

'Mathilde and I have been here for fourteen nights.'

Reluctantly, I offer my cheek for Charlotte to kiss and manage not to rub it free of grease when she removes her wet lips.

'It's late. I'm surprised you come to call upon me this hour of the night.'

'Sleep doesn't come easily in this awful, draughty place. I heard you were back from your Wiltshire sojourn and I'm surprised you didn't seek out your sisters immediately. And then, the cold, Ellie, the biting cold! I hoped to creep into your bed with you for warmth and comfort.'

I shudder at the thought. 'Our sister had no difficulty in finding warmth for herself,' I mutter bitterly.

Charlotte laughs. 'Ah, indeed, she didn't. The delightful Guy de Clare! She set her eye upon his fair person the moment she saw him. A fine dandy, he is, and very much in fashion for this backward English Court. How well he looks in his stylish short doublet, with his pretty rear end so clearly defined in his hose.'

'Really…!' With pretend nonchalance I swish my skirts and sink into a chair. Charlotte sits opposite me, her plump knees lazily apart. Her thighs spill over the sides of the stool most unbecomingly. I avert my gaze and wait for her to speak. I know she is trying to work out just how affected I have been by my lover's betrayal.

'Oh, yes. I would not have minded a go at

him myself, but he had eyes only for Mathilda.'

'Did he...Did he resist her at all?' I'm alarmed at the way my voice is starting to crack.

Charlotte doesn't answer me in words, but her peals of raucous laughter tell me all I need to know. I feel sick to my stomach. Changing the subject before I humiliate myself, I ask, 'And you, Charlotte, have you been enjoying Court society?'

'Not much.' She wrinkles her nose, which is red and studded with blackheads from her over-indulgence of wine and sweet things. 'I saw dear Gaveston. The King is clearly very taken with him.'

Poor, ignorant Charlotte! Hasn't she worked out yet that they're lovers? That Gaveston is not as other men? Is she still living in hope that he might one day pay some attention to her? Perhaps it is time she was acquainted with what he thinks of her.

'He's not a gentleman, Charlotte, but a rogue and of the rudest persuasion. You should know he has a name for you.'

'Does he? I hope it is a more complimentary name than the one he has for you.'

This is too much to take sitting down, so I leap to my feet with my hands on my hips. 'I demand that you tell me immediately what it is.'

'Of course I shall tell you, Ellie. He calls you Chief-Lady-in-Mating. From which I presume you have been spreading your favours around.'

Incensed, I start towards her, my fists clenched tightly and she shrinks back in the chair with her forearms across her bosom. 'Ellie, whatever is wrong with you? It's not I who am at fault.'

'Hateful man! Cruel, despicable Gaveston. It's a filthy lie. There's been only one man for me since I arrived here and I've been true only to him.'

'Maybe it is the quality of the mating to which Gaveston alludes rather than the quantity,' suggests Charlotte with a wicked gleam in her eyes. I'm so upset, I completely forget to counter my sister with Gaveston's 'Charlotte the Harlot' nickname, an omission for which I scold myself after she's gone.

'Charlotte, I'm tired. Please forgive me if I don't invite you to share my bed. If you are cold, here's an extra coverlet.' I thrust a spare horsehair blanket at her. 'Please leave me now.'

'Well, that's not much of a welcome for sisters who have been apart for so long. But you were always a strange and rather awkward maid. I often wonder what goes on in that devious head of yours.'

I don't bother to answer, but push her out of my room with due haste. But I'm not ready for sleep. A letter must be written and it must be written now, while I am on fire, for it will serve two purposes. To help remove the canker from my heart and to ensure my father recalls his two youngest daughters before they have completely ruined my life.

I take up my quill.

'Dear Father, there is a matter of great importance that I must bring to your attention in respect of the Runt.' I tear up the sheet of parchment and quickly grasp another, onto which I inscribe the same sentence, substituting 'Mathilda' for 'the Runt.'

Knowing my father as I do, the letter must not appear to have been written in a violence of anguish, but rationally, almost distantly. I continue:

'Be assured that if you do not immediately recall my sisters to France, the reputation of Mathilde will forever destroy her chance of making an appropriate marriage with one of the three suitors of your choice. At this very moment, Mathilde is frolicking in the bedchamber of one of the most dissolute young knights of this Court. Their wails and howls can be heard all over the Tower, even so far as the Great Hall. I beseech you, Father, do not disregard my abject plea, for I fear that I too will be contaminated by her depraved and disgusting behaviour.'

I realise I must be careful, for my father might recall Mathilde and leave Charlotte, which will curtail my activities to an unacceptable degree. So, for good measure, I add:

'As far as I can tell, Charlotte's behaviour has been fairly moderate, for her, but she is growing enormous with the mountains of excellent cuisine at the Court. (I cross the fingers of my left hand as I write this).'She will not find a husband at all if her appetite is not curbed by your own wise counsel. You will be left with her on your hands forever. Therefore, she too, should return.

'Trusting this finds you in good health, your loving, affectionate and respectful daughter, Ellie.'

I feel better now. That should scare my pompous father half to death. I re-read my letter several times, and then, satisfied, I fold and seal it. At first light tomorrow morning, I shall send it off to France by Special Messenger. Already the tip of the sun's bright face is creeping over the horizon and filtering light spots onto the walls through my narrow window. I bring my night-light close to my bed and pick up a small book of poesy to help send me to sleep. I could not concentrate on Aurellus' Meditations in my present state of mind.

The following morning I awaken late, and decide I will have a bath. I shall not, of course, stay in the water for long, for it is well-known that bathing is bad both for your body and for your soul. I haven't had a bath since we arrived here at the Tower and sometimes, water on the body, can be a soothing sensation. I dress and speedily check on Isabella, and I'm glad to see that Margaret and Joan are attending to her. She barely speaks to me, nor does she answer when I say I am not well and wish to be excused from her company. So I take this as affirmation and depart, for I am in no temper for a scolding.

After presenting myself in the kitchen and arranging for servants to carry up a tub and several casks of warm water, I go back to my room to wait. It will take a while, for the fire has to be lit and the water warmed.

What's this? On my bed there is a letter and a tiny mound of dog-rose petals. I stir the petals with my finger and something else gleams through their soft-pinkness, something sparkling and coloured amethyst. It is a brooch, a beautiful brooch, round and large and I count the stones. A big one in the middle and, oh, at least ten smaller gems around the perimeter. It will look well at my slender throat.

With dawning realisation, my fingers break the seal of the letter.

'My dearest Love, my Lady, my Jewel, my Brightest Star in the Firmament…'

I let out a vile oath, for I am deeply cynical of such overweening drivel. As I continue to read, my incredulity increases.

'I am bereft. I am full of deepest, most dire, most anguished remorse. My Love, my Sweet, I crave, oh how I crave, your gentle forgiveness. For my heart is ever beating in sympathy with yours. I do not know how I shall live without your Love. A Love that has surpassed all my wildest dreams. A Love I have never known before. She meant nothing. She meant nothing but one night's shallow pleasure. I was lonely for you, I thought I would die. For, my Love, although not so beautiful as you, she reminded me a little of you. I had no idea you would return when you did.'

Holy Mother of God! Slowly, I shake my head in disbelief. There is just one true sentence in this letter, the last one. 'I had no idea you would return when you did.' And as for 'it meant nothing' such words are cheap. Does he really believe I am so gullible that I will go weak at the knees and then come running back into his arms? Well, I shall do no such thing. But there is more; another sheet behind this one.

'I beg you, please do not hold me responsible for what was an impetuous act, for the Lady, your sister, threw herself upon me, that to refuse was near-impossible.' 'You just wait, Mathilde,' I mutter under my breath. 'I repeat, dear Ellie, it was just one night and it meant nothing. Nothing, nothing, nothing. Nothing, nothing, nothing, nothing. I adore you and beg you to give me one last chance. I repeat, my dearest, she meant nothing.

'My heart beats wildly in anticipation of your reply, that it might be favourable to your sinning but remorseful Lover.
G'

Well! Well, well, well. I will have to think upon this, but there is one thing of which I am certain. Dear Guy is going to grovel more than a little before he creeps back into my bed. A few pretty words, a few lines of dressed-up sentimentality will not be enough to gain my forgiveness. An act of such tender fortitude must be earned.

After this, I am cool towards him and to my sister, Mathilde. I do not speak to either of them unless spoken to, and only then only to demonstrate civility but indifference. I set myself quite high above them. Both are clearly distraught by my demeanour, but I do not relent.

Each night, tiny mounds of dog-rose petals appear on my bed and I pounce upon them to find the delightful trinkets he hides there for me. When I have a fair pile of them, I send for a jeweller to attend me for the purpose of valuation. I am well-pleased. Guy is no cheapskate and rises a little in my estimation. Slowly, I forgive him, bestow upon him a nod or smile or a 'Thank you kindly my Lord'. I last as long as I can keep my urges in check and in this respect, I make a tremendous effort. For the precious pile grows larger daily.

One month has passed and how things have changed! My sisters depart today but I don't bother to see them off. Charlotte tries to find me, but I hide in my closet until she is gone. Isabella is still morose, but I'm gradually sneaking back into her confidence, for she needs me more than she knows. This is important, for it guarantees my security and first pick of all her discarded kirtles.

Guy de Clare is still hot for me. It's much in his favour that he refuses Mathilde's request to travel with her as far as the Port of Dover. A servant tells me she scolds much, but he is adamant.

I hear later that the Channel was extremely rough and take some satisfaction in imagining my ghastly sisters pewking into the sea. It's no more than they deserve.

Gently I stroke the pearl pendant which is Guy's latest offering of conciliation. The pearls are exquisite, large and lustrous and I am proud to own such a costly item. This time, I will do him the honour of wearing his gift in public. By this means, he will know that he is finally forgiven.

It's so long since I have had a man, I have stopped counting. I shan't hide in my closet when Guy comes to find me.

When he does, we are so happy that we fall into bed immediately, and we're all over each other, clutching and biting with wildest glee. But when our passion is spent, I see that something is troubling Guy.

'What is it, Guy?'

Guy's voice takes on a grave quality. 'Did you know that now that Gaveston has returned to England, he has been petitioning the Pope to revoke his excommunication? He writes letter after letter. He's also written to the French King, but wily Philip will have none of it. Even so, many believe he'll be successful with the Pope and the Barons are up in arms.'

'But the King…'

'King versus Church,' says Guy. 'It's the old, old story. You should know, Ellie, that there are stories that Gaveston has been seen nearby, at least, not far away, but I don't know if they're true.'

'D'you think he will ever come back to Court?'

'I think it's likely,' says Guy, gently stroking my bare buttocks, then easing his body over to cover mine. I push him away.

For once, I do not want to play with him.

After Guy has slunk away, a fair piece short of a groat, I need something to do that will allow me release for my rage. I command a manservant to fix a piece of hemp across my room. Over it I throw all my gowns, so they are caught at the waist over the hemp rope. This is something I like to do from time to time, for I'm particular in the extreme. Many Ladies don't bother about beating the dust out of their raiments, but there is nothing worse than grimy velvet. These sloppy Ladies smell just like the wall hangings before the castle is spring-cleaned. This activity is especially useful when I am in a condition of inner turmoil.

I take up my beater made of sturdy woven straw. It has a long, strong handle which I seize and I belt it against the material. A cloud of dust almost chokes me, but that doesn't stop me. Sometimes, when Guy is feeling submissive, he likes me to use my beater on him, and I do, but gently. For a little pain is sensuous, much pain is...painful. But now I'm not gentle. I beat as hard as I can, taking in a deep breath before I raise my arm. I'm imagining that Gaveston's writhing body is beneath the flat pan of my beater. With increasing frenzy, I lay into my gowns, into Gaveston, one, two, three. And harder, harder, harder. Over and over, my breath coming in short, mad gasps until moisture pours in streams from my brow.

'Ellie, whatever are you doing?' Irked at the interruption, I turn to see Margaret standing at my doorway.

'I am flaying Gaveston alive, what do you think?' I snap.

Lady Margaret has her hands over her mouth.

When she places them on her hips, an amused smile is playing around her reddened lips.

'What is it?' I'm abrupt with her for her impertinence.

'Lady Ellie. I thought you should know. Gaveston is back. It is official.'

I give the dark blue velvet a final frantic swipe, then sink to my knees, my hands covering my face.

'Shall I continue to beat your gowns for you, Lady Ellie?'

'Begone,' I say churlishly. 'I shall beat him myself.'

Indeed, Gaveston is back. In less than a year since his departure, he's back, be-jewelled, be-plumed, be-titled and arrogant. Gloucester, his brother-in-law, (who gave his own sister to Gaveston in marriage) has provided the favourite with every support. But Gloucester's efforts are not helped by the ostentation and display exhibited by the favourite.

How can the Earl speak for Gaveston when the favourite glories so in winning at jousting instead of being manly and modest? Furthermore, Gaveston crows about his victories, insulting all and sundry in a manner so wicked and so clever that he cannot be bested. This gets up the Barons' noses. Truly, I believe many are a little afraid of him, for he exposes their own inadequacies.

'Come, come, you mad hound,' I hear him

yell at the Earl of Warwick at the joust, which causes great hilarity amongst the elevated company. For the Earl of Warwick has an unfortunate habit of dribbling at the mouth, like a bloodhound. I feel sorry for the Earl, for it is cutting to be mocked for what you cannot help, especially when it is so disgusting. Little bubbles form at the corners of his mouth, then more and more, till a great swarm of them like tiny frog-spawn begins to slide down his chin. By which time his mouth is bubbling again. And so it continues. No one would dribble like that if they could help it.

Today, Gaveston is wearing black and red. Black for the devil and red for danger.

'Mad hound! Mad hound!' crows Gaveston.

'You snarling nincompoop!' retorts the Earl. 'You dare to mock me!'

It can be said for Gaveston that he dares anything, but I cannot understand how the King condones his behaviour, for it is juvenile and reflects badly on the jester. He shouldn't make enemies of such powerful nobles, even if they dribble frog-spawn at the mouth.

In the meantime, the war in Scotland continues, for the Scots are incensed that the English are still in possession of many of their major fortresses. The war is costing Edward dearly. He is so unnerved by the Barons that he contrives to prevent Parliament from meeting and thus loses taxes. The Royal Purse is empty. And now I have been asked to take a much smaller payment for my own services to the Crown. This is preposterous.

'How am I expected to live on this?' I squeak. 'Must I starve to death for the sake of a few essentials like wine and special treats?'

The Queen complains also about her household accounts, but eventually an arrangement is made for her to be compensated with payments from estates in Ponthieu. I'm glad to report she settles with me, including the omitted back payments. This improves my temper, for I cannot bear to be groatless.

Edward tries to bargain with the Barons in aid of Gaveston, but they are almost all sworn enemies of his lover. The atmosphere is strained. The Barons bicker amongst themselves and the feasting and fiddling and dancing once enjoyed by the Court is lost in the buzz of angry, complaining voices.

Now Edward has gone with Gaveston to fight at Berwick, but I think this is just a ploy to remove the favourite from the Barons' wrath. The Queen is furious. In any case, it will not come to anything. Edward's campaigns always fall into disarray.

CHAPTER 14

Gaveston is Undone

The Earl of Lincoln is dead. Poor old Burstbelly has burst the final buttons from his stupendous belly! I believe the King is relieved in one respect, as Lincoln has been a trial to him of late, but there is concern because his death has made Lancaster even more powerful. For the Earl of Lancaster, who's married to Lincoln's only child, a daughter, gobbles up all his father-in-law's estates and the Earldoms of Lincoln and Salisbury. Indisputably, Lancaster is now the most wealthy and important noble in the kingdom. He knows it and he shows it. This is dangerous.

So Lancaster is content. Although I hear his little wife weeps continuously, for she has been forced to marry a man much older than she and besides, she loves another. I shudder at the thought of being forced to share the bed of such a one as the repulsive Lancaster.

Berwick was a shambles. The King is good at hedging and ditching, but he is useless at war with the Scots. So, taking his responsibilities to heart, Lancaster sets off to take the King to task and entreat him to return to face the Barons, or, as they now describe themselves, (that little group of chosen stalwarts), the Ordainers. They have set themselves up to address all injustices. It is well-known that all men like to form themselves into Orders or Fraternities. This is because, unlike women, they can manage very little by themselves.

It is only second-speak, but we who wait at Court learn that when they meet, Lancaster overtly ignores Gaveston, which angers the King to the depths of his soul. However, Lancaster extracts a promise from the King to return. It takes him six months. During this time, the Queen grows increasingly fractious.

In August, the King is home and ready to face his foes at Westminster. True to form, he agrees to everything demanded by the Ordainers but he will not give up Gaveston.

'I agree to everything you ask,' he pronounces, 'except for the banishment of my dear brother, Gaveston.'

'It's a nightmare,' screams the Queen. 'I'm married to a madman.'

Finally, threatened by Civil War, the King complies and Gaveston is sent to Flanders, for the Gascons, too, have had enough of him. Almost immediately, we hear stories, similar to the ones we heard before, that he is back in England.

'It's hearsay,' says a knight.

'But I saw him with my own eyes,' says another.

At Christmas, we learn that the rumours are true, for Gaveston comes to Windsor, openly, boldly, caring not a goose for anyone. He strides up to the castle gates and demands to be admitted. His jaunty plumes bounce and his little purple doublet clings tight to his waist, revealing the taut lines of his impertinent bum. Edward is wild with joy, the Queen is mad with rage.

'Madame' says Gaveston insolently. 'Aren't you pleased to see me?'

'My brother,' fawns the King. 'My dear, dear brother! How are you? Did they treat you well? Come, my brother, kiss me. We shall never be apart again.'

The two of them embrace, right there before the Queen, who shrinks to see them so enamoured of each other. I try to persuade her to leave with me, but she turns her face to the wall, too stricken to stir herself. So I must stand there and witness the great reconciliation. I manage not to be sick, which is, in itself, a great feat of human will. Now the common people are becoming more involved than ever before and clamour against the instability of the Royal Household.

And the Queen is pregnant. The sun never shines but it burns us all to a frazzle.

'Ellie, I have something to tell you,' says Isabella. I turn to face her, raising my brows in a question. She takes a deep breath.

'My husband is at war with Lancaster. The Barons are plotting a strategy. I must flee to the north, forthwith, with my husband. And, of course, Gaveston will join us. The King wishes to negotiate with the Bruce.'

It does not take much thought to see what is really happening.

'I think I understand. The King is set on negotiating with the Scots for Gaveston's safety in Scotland? Is that the plan, my Lady?'

Isabella looks abashed.

'And you are going to aid them in this plan?' I continue. I can hear myself sounding impertinent, but I really cannot help it.

'You could describe it in such words,' says the Queen quietly.

'Then why?'

'It's not safe for any of us here.'

'But Madame, you are with child.'

'It's imperative that I use my diplomatic skills to gain support in order to suppress the uprising?'

The rehearsed manner with which Isabella says this convinces me it's been badgered into her. And she believes it.

'But, Madame, the child! You must refuse the King.'

'I don't refuse my husband. I'm his loyal wife. Perhaps, even now, something may be salvaged from our marriage.'

'Isabella!'

Isabella shows me her palm in a gesture of defiance. 'Whatever you say, Ellie, I'm going. But I'll leave it to you to decide if you'll accompany me.'

I stare at her silently, at the determination in her small chin, the hard light in her huge eyes, the way she now holds onto her stomach in symbolic, fearful protection of her unborn child. Fascinated, I watch the long, smooth fingers knead at the flesh of her belly, already a little stretched. I wait. She waits. Eventually, she speaks:

'Will you come, Ellie?'

'I'll come.'

'You may bring Guy de Clare if you wish, Ellie.'

My heart flutters in my breast at this concession. Oh, I will come. I'll come a hundred times over, if Guy is to be at my side. I clasp my hands together in delight.

'Thank you a thousand times, my kind Lady.'

There is something soft in her expression which emboldens me and I start towards her and am swiftly wrapped in her arms although, it's awkward straining over the budding mound of her stomach.

'I shall put the dogs into the care of Lady Despenser,' says Isabella, 'for she adores them.'

She is welcome to them, I think to myself, and although I do not dare to say so, I sincerely hope they pee on her sewing.

We travel first to York, then on to Newcastle. There's plenty of time on the way to Newcastle to look for small trophies, like little berries of a poisonous variety. Gaily, I sport through the woodlands while the company rests in the shade. In this art of identifying berries, I have been tutored by my lover, Guy, for the purpose of ensuring I do not accidentally eat some of the wrong variety and drop dead, thus leaving his bed empty.

I hide the berries in the folds of my kirtle, and then I crush them with a wooden tool made for the purpose, although I don't know its name.

Men have many names for the tools they use, but I concentrate on more important matters, like poison and politics. You don't need to know the names of tools if you're an intellectual. It won't be hard to slip the rich liquid into a mug of beer or wine for Gaveston without being seen.

Gaveston is to experience a stomach ache he will remember for the rest of his life. This outcome, I trust, will not be long. This knowledge, this power, aids my soul in rising above his bawdy insults and jibes, which continue despite his malady. Oh, how I enjoy myself.

He will pay for his sins, not least, for calling me Chief-Lady-in-Mating!

The following day, they take him off his horse and lay him in the cart containing our provisions. He looks ill enough, with the sacks of grain and cloth, bumping about and groaning and drooling like a little baby, all the while clutching his taut stomach.

'I'm dying. Help me, for I'm dying,' he whines. In this way he is like any other man, for it is the nature of their sex to make a loud drama out of a belly-ache.

'Stop,' I say from time to time. 'He's delirious. I must tend to him.' Then I jump in the cart and swish some water about his face, after which I pronounce him, 'a little unstable but comfortable.'

'What a sweet ministering angel you are, my love,' says Guy tenderly.

'Life's not just being alive, but being well,' I murmur.

'What say you?' asks Guy.

'Martial. Born in the Year 40. Epigrammata.'

'A sound mind in a sound body,' says Guy.

'What say you?' I ask amazed.

'Juvenal. Born the year 60. Satires.'

We laugh because we have just had our first learned exchange, for usually we're too eager, too fruity to give thought to such matters when we meet. Then I give him a hearty slap on the arm for upstaging me and he leans over and tweaks my nipple.

He looks so handsome on his fine black stallion, his shapely legs at home in the stirrups, his fine chin held high beneath his red and purple plumes. Uneasily, I notice Edward eyeing my lover. Guy is far more pleasing to the eye than the ailing favourite, so I ride close to him and glare defiantly at the King. Edward smiles, seeing my possessiveness and relinquishes his own inclinations with a sorrowful shrug. Even in lustful desire, there's something honourable about the King.

Later, he reins in his horse to a trot, to keep pace with mine.

'One day, Ellie,' he says, 'you'll make some good man a wife to be proud of.'

'I cannot imagine anything I'd more gladly decline, Sire.'

The King laughs and spurs his horse on to check on Gaveston, who is still moaning fit to wake the dead.

I'm disappointed the berries do not have time to do their work properly, for at the first opportunity, on reaching Newcastle, Edward summons a physician. We spend some time in that great city, at Tynemouth Castle, while Gaveston slowly regains his health, the King hovering anxiously at his side.

When the King is satisfied that Gaveston is out of danger, he summons Isabella. I accompany her, for she's weak from her pregnancy and needs a supporting shoulder.

'I am taking Piers to Scarborough, where he'll be safe,' says the King. 'You'll remains at Tynemouth, Isabella.'

'My Lord...'

'You will do as I command,' says the King assertively. 'Piers' life is in great danger and I must find a place of refuge for him. We'll take possession of Scarborough. It will be perfect for our purpose.'

Isabella is trembling, she clenches her fists, she darts rays of fire from her eyes and her skin is whiter than chalk. It is a moment before she can speak.

'May I remind you, Sire? I am your wife.'

'And my wife you remain, Isabella. I'm not divorcing you. I'm not even leaving you. I'm merely requesting that you remain here at Tynemouth, with your Ladies and your Escort, while I go about my business of state.'

The Queen begins to cry, not silently as she usually does, but vehemently, great, deafening vixen-like wails. Edward steps back, as though unsure how to behave towards his Royal spouse, who is behaving more like a fishwife than a fishwife.

'You cannot go and leave me all alone.'

'You're not alone, Isabella, you have me,' I soothe. For this, I receive a hearty blow to my ear, then another to the opposite ear, so it shall not feel neglected. Astonished, I rub my injured ears and gently shake my head to clear the mist.

Isabella, with a further theatrical wail, turns her back on her husband then falls into a dead faint at my feet. I open my palms to Edward in a gesture of appeal.

'It's no use, Ellie. I cannot be swayed by feminine temper. It is imperative that Piers is removed to Scarborough immediately. Attend to your Mistress and make her comfortable as you can.'

Edward turns on his heel and leaves me to it.

I have no choice but to call for two manservants to lift my Queen onto a stretcher and bear her back to her quarters, where she's deposited onto her lonely bed. I bathe her face, now sweating and blotchy, while the clamour inside my own battered head drives me fair to distraction.

After this, I go for a little walk and look at the magnificent views, which inspire a bright idea. I cannot wait to tell it to my mistress and get myself back into her good graces. It is a stroke of pure genius.

'We'll tell a story to persuade the people to be loyal to you,' I tell her. I give her a moment to overcome her cynicism.

'What's that?' She sighs as she asks the question, as though she has heard enough of my stories.

'We'll say you were captured. A pregnant Queen captured. Can you imagine it? Then the people will both pity and admire you and truly notice how badly your husband treats you. They'll see how brutally he abandons you for his favourite. Then they'll worship you above all others, for the English love a martyr.'

'We cannot say such a thing.'

'Indeed, my Lady, you can. You must see that this will bring pressure to bear on the King to improve his behaviour, not only from the Barons but from the common people.'

'I don't know if that will be for the best,' says Isabella doubtfully.

'Of course it will. You'll be a heroine,' I reply.

When the Earl of Lancaster arrives I take him into my confidence. But first I supply him with plenty of wine and compliment him on his fine moustache. Then I tell him my plan.

'But it's a lie, Lady Eleanora,' he says, for he has not much imagination.

'It won't matter if it's a lie if people believe

it,' I point out as reasonably as I can. 'And they will be sure to believe it, for it is such a very ambitious lie.' But Lancaster is not a logical man and shakes his head. How can I persuade him? Another glass of wine? Some ripe fruit? Then I have it.

'We can say that you rescued her,' I suggest. 'We can say you galloped up to the Queen on your fine steed and drove off the attacking Scots, parrying their blows with bravery far beyond expectation. The terrified Scots fell back in disarray and were vanquished. With tears in her eyes, the Queen fell to her knees in gratitude and admiration. Oh, can't you see it, my Lord? You'll be a hero!'

This is helpful. Lancaster ponders and twiddles the fat brown moustache of which he is so proud. All you need do to persuade a man to your point of view is to flatter his vanity. And suggest a way in which he can excel in the eyes of his peers and servants alike.

Lancaster's beady eyes are shining with excitement under the two hedges that are meant to be brows.

'It might help if the people believe I saved her from the unruly Scots. And it will bring to bear the unnatural way in which her husband abandons her, in a remote place, pregnant and unguarded. It will do the King no good at all and may help our poor, young Queen.'

'It's in the Queen's best interest. It's good of you to co-operate in this matter, my Lord.'

He's sometimes slow of thought, the worthy

Earl, and needs a little encouragement. Now he agrees it is a fine idea. As I have said before, sometimes I amaze myself with my own cleverness. Oh, I can manage people so easily, Royalty and Earls and Lovers. I think I am a Mistress of Diplomacy. If I were a man, I should be a Baron.

'Indeed,' says the Earl. 'I'm glad I thought of this excellent plan.'

By the time the Earl is ready to set off in pursuit of Edward and Gaveston, we have our story worked out to the finest detail. I do so enjoy making up stories, for it gives me the opportunity to use my vivid imagination. I am sure the Queen and the Earl are impressed with my ability.

This part of my story I cannot tell from personal experience, but my witnesses are reliable. I cannot reveal who they are, for I was told in strictest confidence and I never betray a confidence except for money or jewels or, perhaps, a particularly fine gown of Indian silk like the one the Queen has hidden in her chest. I think she sees that I covet that gown.

Edward and Gaveston are on their way to Scarborough and they take possession of the Castle. As soon as they arrive, they're told the news that fearsome Earl of Lancaster (and just about everyone else in the shires), is on his way to forestall them.

'You must stay here safely in Scarborough, Piers,' says the King, 'and I'll go to York to fetch reinforcements.'

The lovers are devastated at having to part, but after a dramatic farewell which has the entire escort in tears, the King sets off on his mission. He looks a lonely and pitiful figure, riding off into the darkness, his broad shoulders bent over with the burden of responsibility which never came easily to him. As he journeys, he plans what he'll say to promote his cause.

Of course, when he arrives in York, no one's interested in the discomfort of the favourite. They're more interested in being rid of him. However, in return for delivering Gaveston to the nobles, the King negotiates a legal, English trial for him. Gravely, the Earl of Pembroke, deemed a fair man, promises Edward justice. Because Pembroke is regarded as an honourable man, Edward is satisfied with this.

On May 19, Piers Gaveston, on Edward's recommendation, surrenders himself to the keeping of Pembroke. A month later, at Deddington, Piers Gaveston is imprisoned under guard in a house, while the Earl sets off, as Earls are prone to do, to spend the night in a local Castle. (Someone mentions he has soft spot for a lovely maiden, a virgin, about to be wed and needing to be broken in. I wonder if there are any young knights around, about to be wed and needing to be broken in especially if they are virgin. For what is good for the pig is equally good for the sow.)

But all is reckoned without the intervention of the unruly Earl of Warwick, who's still seething with hatred. Supported by his peers, the Earls of Lancaster, Hereford and Arundel, he seeks out Pier Gaveston and already he has murder on his mind. Gaveston is torn from his bed while still half asleep and stands naked before these angry men. Naturally, he is bewildered.

'I have been promised safe custody with Pembroke,' he protests, but his pleas fall as chaff upon the field.

Before they bear him away, they tear open his baggage and find all manner of incriminating evidence of his greed and corruption. Fine jewels. Precious silver. Money. A special ruby gem called The Cherry. Even a few Crown Jewels. (Not to mention some silver spoons that belong to me. I hope I shall recover them.)

The fury of the Barons can be imagined.

The ringleader is indisputably the Earl of Warwick, with Lancaster a close second. Incensed that the favourite has nicknamed him 'The Black Dog of Arden', Warwick retaliates with worse. 'If I am a dog, then I will show the ruffian how I can bite,' he howls, baring his yellow teeth.

He calls Gaveston Thief and Vagabond and Witch and Bender and Whore's Son. This last seems most unfair, for it blames his mother. But many of the cruel taunts men use towards other men blame women. 'You bastard,' they say. Or sometimes, 'Strumpet's spawn.' But the crime is nothing at all to do with the poor lady, regardless of whether she has conceived him in or out of wedlock. There is no sense to any of it.

Furthermore, the Barons don't give Gaveston a fair trial, or try to produce evidence for any of these accusations. It is as though he's no longer a man, with the ordinary rights of a noble, as fought for in the Magna Carta. I don't care for Gaveston, but it is a matter of concern when Earls behave in this fashion. They're a law unto themselves, which is dangerous for all.

Off they bear him, to Warwick Castle, clad only in a horsehair smock. Thereafter, to famous Blacklow Hill, shrouded by the cold night air, where one solitary oak stands against the skyline. And there, in that bleak place, forgotten by his God, he's impelled to kneel and lay his head against a large stone of black flint.

As the axe falls to sever his handsome, curly head from his torso, he cries out just five words.

'Edward, Edward. I am undone.'

He is indeed undone, for the heartless Barons abandon his headless corpse where it lies and Warwick kicks his head face-down into a ditch.

'Who's a bad dog now?' he laughs.

Eventually, the body is rescued by some simple tradesmen, who carry it to the Earl of Warwick, but he's no longer interested in Gaveston now he's a corpse and rendered harmless.

'Begone,' he says. 'I am busy.'

The men sew the head back on and wipe the mud off his eyes and mouth, an act of piety that I cannot imagine for the messiness of it. Then they bear the corpse to some Friars who, in humble charity accept it, but don't bury it. They cannot, because Gaveston is excommunicated.

Is he to decompose on the floor of the monastery cellars? The Holy Place will reek for months and will surely put them off their prayers. Perhaps they can apply for a special burial dispensation from the Pope.

When I hear this story, I feel pity for the favourite, but relief that the ordeal of opposing him is over for the Queen. In truth, it's all for the best.

Many say it is to the Earl of Pembroke's credit that he has gone mad with rage about the nobles' betrayal, for he had given his word that Gaveston would be safe in his keeping. It's strange how men's words are so much more highly regarded than their morals or their kindness.

As far as I'm concerned, he has had his fun with the young maiden and if he now has a guilty conscience because of his inability to separate the business of the king from the business of young maidens, then it is no more than he deserves.

CHAPTER 15

Placating the Pregnant Queen

Now she's seven months pregnant, Isabella moves with difficulty and needs much attention. And much patience! My feelings towards her are ambivalent, for sometimes she is so sharp of tongue. At other times she is affectionate and my heart warms towards her. When she's shrewish, my heart sinks, for I know I shall not receive any treats, like a free afternoon or a ride in the countryside. Or a new trinket, for little things mean so much.

We are staying at Windsor Castle. It's September in the year 1312 and here Isabella will give birth, an excellent choice of venue, for it is so peaceful here and the gentle hills stretch for miles around. Wild flowers bloom in the hedgerows and the lake shows the willows how lovely they are. It's a pity the tranquillity doesn't calm her more. Of course, I make allowances. She's pregnant for one thing.

So much has happened to her, apart from Gaveston's summary execution. It's true she always hated him. Nevertheless, the change is a shock and her husband has been overcome with grief, weeping and railing, which has been a trial to her throughout her confinement. Bearing brats is bad enough, but when your husband behaves like one, it's vexing.

But then, life hasn't been easy for any of us.

One small improvement is in her marriage. Edward is spending more time with her now that Gaveston has been removed, and sometimes I see small signs of affection between them. Today is not one of those times.

Odo is poorly. It's hardly surprising, for he's not young and has been hauled across the Channel, travelling hither and thither as the Court has moved from place to place. He lies across my Lady's knees, his bedraggled tail hanging down one side of her lap, his nose down the other between his limp paws. His ears dangle as though they have relinquished all joy in belonging to a dog.

'I cannot think what to do with him,' sniffs Isabella. 'Ellie, that physic you brought from the apothecary…it hasn't helped at all.'

Of course, I have to accept all the blame. Never mind that the little brute is old and ill and fair worn out with petting. It's still my fault. What's more, King Edward is in high dudgeon because all of the Queen's attention is on the listless Odo, and there's none left for him.

'You would think she would have more important matters to concern her than a stupid mongrel,' he mutters mutinously. 'What with the child and preparations for the birth. Someone should toss the brute from the top of the Tower and put an end to its misery.'

I'm irked by Isabella's mawkishness and think the dogs an unnecessary irritation. All the same, the King's solution seems a little drastic. It isn't like him to be cruel except to traitors.

'But my Lord,' I protest, 'my Lady has loved Odo from a puppy.'

'You have a great deal to say for yourself, my Lady,' chides the King.

Chidden, I stick out my lower lip, which is usually sufficient to exact a plea for forgiveness. Of course, I forget momentarily the King is not as other men.

'Such petulance, Ellie,' he murmurs.

'Leave her alone,' snaps Isabella. 'You whisper loudly, my Lord. I heard exactly what you said and you're cruel and heartless.'

'And you're the height of sweetness and light!'

'You expect a great deal when you treat me so badly.'

The King glares at her and she glares back. Oh dear! Now I have made them quarrel. 'Let me take Odo to the apothecary in the village. It'll be better for him to prescribe a cure if he can see how he suffers,' I implore Isabella.

'Ellie, you're an angel,' whispers the Queen.

So I wrap Odo in a soft blanket and carry him down the stairway, along the cloister and out to the bailey. His head hangs out one end, his tail out the other as if he's dead. I tug at his tail to see if he yelps. He doesn't. Frantic, I start to run. The guard lets me out, lowering the drawbridge especially for us. I know where the apothecary lives, so soon I am banging on his door. The apothecary is annoyed at being disturbed, but co-operates when I inform him icily that the dog belongs to the Queen. Entering his abode, I place Odo on his blanket on a table.

'I'll do what I can,' he says and disappears into the nether regions of his dwelling, where he keeps his stores of drugs and potions. He returns with a sprig of garlic and waves it over the dog's nose.

Immediately, the little dog gives a violent shudder and is rendered inert. He lies supine on the table before my eyes and wild panic grips me.

'You've killed him.'

'I haven't killed him.'

'But he's dead.'

'He's dead. But I haven't killed him. There's a difference.'

I don't like this man. He's too smart for his own good. With my head in my hands, I try to find a solution. I try so hard my head hurts.

'You will have to obtain another dog, exactly identical to this one.'

'The Queen will know the difference,' says the apothecary.

'On the contrary, these dogs all look the same. I cannot tell the difference between Gundulph and Odo.'

'I'm sure that the Queen can tell,' interrupts the man angrily. 'Don't even think of such a deception. If you want to keep your head attached to your shoulders, I suggest you tell her the truth.'

'Not if you get another the same. One brown ear and one black ear. Just like Odo. You have eight days. I shall tell the Queen you'll keep Odo and can cure him in eight days. That is when I shall return for the new Odo. You'll be well-rewarded for your trouble.'

I leave the man scratching his head in puzzlement. When I arrive back at the royal chambers, I explain that the apothecary will cure Odo in eight days.

'Are you sure it'll work?' says the Queen, doubtfully. I nod with vigour.

The King, who is sitting at the writing table, regards me suspiciously, but I won't catch his eye.

As promised, in eight days I return and sure enough, the apothecary has another Odo tethered outside his house. This Odo is very lively but does sport one black ear and one brown. I am well pleased and reward the man generously.

'May God have mercy on your soul,' mutters the man, which is not encouraging.

Proudly, I bear the precious bundle back to my Lady.

'That's not Odo,' she cries and my heart skips a beat.

'I told you he would be like a new dog,' I blurt. 'But you wouldn't believe me, would you, dear Isabella? If I didn't know the truth, I would never believe that it was the same little Odo. How happy Gundulph is to have him, see Isabella!' Gently, I bend to put the little dog down but he struggles wildly and leaps from my arms.

'Why, he looks much younger, almost like a

puppy again,' cries Isabella as Odo sets about Gundulph, who runs into a corner with his tail between his legs. 'See, even Gundulph does not recognise his brother.'

'But Gundulph has his tongue out and wags his tail. He's happy,' I insist, stepping between the Queen and the dogs so she shall not observe Odo's lips drawn back in a snarl while Gundulph cowers.

'It's very strange,' says Isabella.

'Come, Odo, come to Ellie,' I trill and Odo scurries beneath the King's table and tugs on the upturned end of his slipper. I fall to my knees at the King's feet and tug at the dog, then the King leans over and lifts my chin. His knowing eyes are twinkling with merriment. 'What a very clever girl you are, Ellie!' he chuckles and guiltily I smile back. I am relieved he's amused and know he will keep my secret. This is far more than I did for him, when I told Lancaster about the King and Gaveston's midnight love-making. From this small beginning, wheels were set in motion and I thank God that the King need never know the part I played in hastening his lover's execution.

'Ellie has done very well,' Edward pronounces to his wife. 'If it were not for her, your little pet would be dead.'

For a few days, I'm uneasy, for I have to explain why the new Odo has a habit of making large puddles in the middle of rugs. 'It's the physic,' I explain. 'The man warned me of this, but it was necessary to effect the cure. It will not last.'

'No matter,' says the King. 'He'll soon settle down. Ellie will train him. The rugs can be easily cleaned.'

If he continues to pee on the rugs, I suppose I must take him back to the apothecary and request that he finds me yet another Odo. But it would be tiresome in the extreme and my sanity would be sorely tried. Yes, everything and everyone is expendable, including me.

As I glance at my Lady, idly stroking Odo's ears, I notice the colours are reversed. The left one is black, the right one brown. Not like the original Odo. She hasn't noticed. Please God, she never will.

Expendable? Something inside me turns over and twists.

My Lady is delivered of a fine, healthy boy on 13 November, 1312 in the early hours of the morning. I can hear him yelling his head off and it is hard to believe such a tiny scrap of humanity can make such a loud and unpleasant noise. He is named Edward after his father.

The Ladies and I go to the Chapel and light candles before the effigy of the Holy Mother in thanks for her precious gift. Lady Despenser has a beatific look upon her face and genuflects with wild abandon as if to show the Holy Mother the enormous depths of her personal grace. It fair gets up my nose, the manner in which she carries on.

'The Holy Mother wept tears of happiness,'

she tells the Queen a little later. Lady Margaret and I exchange a glance and her eyes arrow ceiling-wards in response to mine. There's great rejoicing throughout the land, now there is an heir to the throne of England. Windsor is full of French nobleman, anxious about the outcome of the Queen's confinement. Isabella is tired, but proud. The celebrations are glorious, the people wild with elation. The entire Court drinks itself into oblivion that evening and messages of congratulation arrive in a never-ending stream.

But all this is not much use to me, for I have to be at Isabella's side constantly. The Ladies gawp and simper and make peculiar noises at the brat, but I really cannot understand it. Babies are such intolerably messy, uncivilised creatures, stinking of sick and shit. Royal babies are no exception.

I urge my Lady to call the wet-nurse with due haste. For, in my opinion, babies should be put to one side and left to the experts who are paid to deal with them until they have reached an age when they are interesting. Like around sixteen years!

'What a beautiful child!' croons Lady Mortimer.

'Oh, could I hold him, just for a tiny moment?' murmurs Lady Joan, looking ready to swoon.

'Don't you dare! You'll drop him,' admonishes Lady Mortimer.

'He looks just like his Mother,' trills Margaret, looking sidelong at Isabella to see if her flattery has taken effect.

The King hovers around, looking helpless and infatuated all at the same time. 'I'm the most fortunate of men,' he says repeatedly. 'The most fortunate of men. He's the finest baby boy that ever lived.'

Prince Edward looks identical to all the other babies I have been unfortunate enough to encounter. He has not even the distinction of having differently coloured ears, like Gundulph and Odo. Poor dogs! For now that Isabella has her new toy they are quite ignored. This fellow-feeling arouses within me a rush of sympathy for the little hounds and I offer to take them for a walk.

It's all so tiresome. The entire Court has lost its head, metaphorically speaking of course. All the same I'm glad the child is born, for England if not for myself. And glad that the King, who has been prostrate with grief over Gaveston, seems happy again.

I hurry outside with the dogs at my heels. 'Let's look for Guy,' I tell the dogs, but they each run off in a different direction. Heaven only knows how the Queen has not suspected the truth about the second Odo, who was born contrary. Yet somehow I like him better for that.

CHAPTER 16

Battles at Home and Abroad

Eventually, I find Guy, who stands with his falcon on his arm on the west side of the bailey. I watch him as he fondles the bird, talking to it gently as he strolls across the threadbare grass. Catching the dogs up, one under each arm, (for I don't trust the bird), I approach him gingerly.

'Guy! Guy!'

His face lights up when he sees me and I feel a rush of affection that is everything yet nothing to do with sexual appetite. When I see that he has the bird secured, I put down the dogs and timidly put out my hand to stroke the bird's back. The feathers are so soft, so smooth.

'I'm glad that you enjoy stroking my cock,' he says impudently.

'Indeed,' I reply, 'for it's such a fine, upstanding cock. I could stroke it all night.'

'Tonight, then in my chamber,' he says, 'if you can wait that long.'

How well my love knows me!

Suddenly, in the middle distance, I spot the King's golden head. He is casually dressed in working raiments, a loose smock of some rough grey material. Beside him, I recognise the tall figure of Hugh le Despenser the Younger, who has recently come to Windsor. They are talking not touching, but I sense although I don't see, a light of joy in the King's eyes. It's clear he likes this man and trusts him. I have a terrible sense of foreboding, of having been through this experience before. Hugh le Despenser is a forceful and greedy man, every bit as much as Piers Gaveston. I don't like him and I know he has little sympathy for the Queen, nor she for him.

Guy's eyes swivel in the direction of mine.

'So you see what I see, Ellie.'

'I'm sure it's nothing,' I parry.

'Ellie! What is it? Why so pensive?'

'Nothing. Nothing at all.'

Swiftly I raise my face for his kiss and, calling for the dogs, I hurry back to the security of the Castle, for this is a possibility I dread to confront. When I arrive back at the Queen's apartments, I find she has other matters on her mind besides her husband. She doesn't talk to me about these things any more, but she snaps at everybody so we are all creeping around as though on snail-shells, trying hard not to be noticed.

I wonder if she's not happy about Edward's friendship with Hugh le Despenser. Does she sense in the tall noble a potential enemy? She can hardly be blamed, for Despenser was a vehement champion of the Gascon.

It seems things cannot get worse, but they do. The Queen dismisses Lady Joan for dropping Baby Edward on his head. Although I think Isabella is being petty over such a little thing, for the Prince slips through Joan's small fingers before she can stop him. I'm sad for little Joan, who is so apologetic, weeping copiously and pleading piteously for forgiveness. But Isabella is implacable. If that is what being a mother makes you, irrational and mawkish, then I shall remain barren to my dying day.

Now Joan is a kitchen-maid. I must court my Lady's approval, for I shall die before I become a kitchen-maid.

A new Lady-in-Waiting is employed and her name is Lady Despenser. She's the wife of Hugh le Despenser the Elder who spoke for the King to the council and subsequently was dismissed. She's a Tartar with a long face mostly composed of chin. Lady Despenser and Lady Mortimer make a fine pair with their cross, crumpled faces and dowdy raiments. They're identical, dogmatic Old Boots, with laces tied tightly to keep out the weather. It is not so agreeable for the Queen to have Big Hugh's wife for her Lady-in-Waiting, but the King has commanded it and she must obey.

I torment the Ladies Mortimer and Despenser whenever I can and take pleasure in their displeasure.

I cannot guess how it will all end!

In the spring of this year, 1313, the King and Queen go to France for the knighting of Isabella's brothers. The Queen doesn't appear overly excited about seeing her family. It's not surprising, for it must be difficult to be the sister in such a family, to have so little control over what happens to you. Besides she looks exhausted and hardly up to such a strenuous journey. They're due to return home in July. I don't go. I could go with them, if I wanted to, but Guy's presence is required in England and I don't wish to leave without him. He's appointed to the Council in a small but important clerical capacity and Edward has promised to knight him if he proves himself able.

This is fine as matters stand, while the King and Queen are on fairly good terms with one another. Should there be discord between them, it will be awkward in the extreme for my lover and me if we have our feet in opposing camps.

I damn the Despensers. No good can come of their plotting.

In due course, a meeting takes place between King Edward and the Recalcitrant Earls. It is called The Reconciliation. It means they have all have a good, long debate and air their differences and agree like good children and now they're friends again.

Or they're pretending to be friends again. In my experience, there is no tongue more false than that of a Baron. I cannot imagine how any of them can possibly know who their real friends are. I suspect they have no real friends when shifts in power have such lasting repercussions.

I wonder how long it will last, this Reconciliation.

Tomorrow, at cock-crow, the army will depart once again, but tonight I swear there is more heaving and groaning and wailing and howling that on any battlefield. Even ladies seldom sought after in the game of love are blessed tonight. It's a Passion borne of Desperation.

For who knows how long before they return? Or, if they will return, for many will be killed or maimed for life. Of course, the nobles and men use this to their advantage.

'But Beatrice,' I overhear one young blood, earnestly in conversation with a comely kitchen-maid, 'if you don't, I might die a virgin.' And what can a maiden say to such a plea? How can she resist? For the guilt will be too much to bear. In nine months' time, the entire Court will resound with the cries of babies. It is enough to make one weep!

It is like a feast before a famine; as soon as there is a wink that something will be in short supply, everyone wants as much of it as they can get. A shortage of loaves? The baker is sold out in as many seconds as there are loaves. Guy comes to me, eager and panting, and our cries mingle with all the others, and the entire Castle heaves from its foundations with the activity it contains. If love were loaves, my belly would be as huge as a house.

When our passion is spent, I help Guy into his armour, for he wants to display it to me before we lie down to sleep. I have to admire it and tell him what a fine and brave fellow he looks, wearing it. It is, of course, the fine new armour plate, for the chain mail is now old-fashioned and no soldier worth his mettle would be seen dead in it. The armour is heavy and cumbersome, with its separate leg and ankle pieces, and makes more clanking sounds when the soldier moves than the chain mail.

'How do I look?' says Guy, clunking around so vigorously that I am afraid for my china and pots and knick-knacks. Something falls to the floor and shatters into pieces.

'It's fine, but too noisy. You'll waken the whole Court.'

'The whole Court is already awake, for the whole Court hasn't yet gone to sleep,' he laughs. 'Let us love a little more, for it may be a long, long time before fortune smiles again upon our pleasure.'

'Oh, yes, Guy, for it renders me fair wild with desire when you wear your armour.' And it is true. It is because he is so covered in his heavy suit of armour that I am inflamed and cannot wait to get at the warm flesh confined within that sturdy corselet.

It takes so long to undress him now, that by the time I have him naked, we are weak from wanting.

The following day, even Ladies Mortimer and Despenser have a peculiar bloom about them. Yet it's well known that Lady Despenser doesn't sleep with her husband. So why has his Lady such a dewy look about her? There will be plenty to gossip about in the next few months, which is just as well because there will be little else to do.

I'm anxious about Isabella and hope Edward has not left her alone last night, but when I hurry to attend to her she's in robust spirit, despite the prospect of enforced separation from her husband.

By the time the army is ready to depart, intent on collecting further reinforcements en route, most of the ladies who were moaning with pleasure last night are weeping. I see the bonny Beatrice clinging to her Thomas, who, (from the superior expression on his face) is no longer a virgin. That is, if he ever was, which I doubt.

'You will come back and marry me?' she cries.

'Of course I will.'

'You're my own true love,' she hurls after him, an adoring expression on her pretty face. As he gallops away, another young beauty rushes up and catches at his leg, bright red hair flying free, for her head-dress has come adrift. He smiles and she dimples.

'Don't forget your promise to me, Thomas.'

'Never,' he smiles. 'Soon I shall return to you.'

'And we shall be married,' she cries, clasping her hands.

'I shall be back for you.'

'You're my one true love.'

'Forever,' he cries, leaning over and slipping his palm around the back of her neck, pressing her face to his and covering her yielding mouth.

Well, I think, to myself. That young man was certainly busy last night. And now two young maids are going to be daggers-drawn, for they are bound to find out about each other, while he will be far away and free from their wrath. It is pitiable how, when a man deceives, innocent women fight each other instead of him.

Isabella, of course, retains her dignity as she says farewell to her Lord and she looks composed and queenlike. Edward reaches out his arms to her and they embrace. It's as though he's truly sorry to be leaving her.

And there's Hugh le Despenser the Elder with Lady Despenser. It seems to me there is little love lost between these two. Yet, they look as though they have much in common, for there is something hook-nosed and mealy-mouthed about the pair of them. Something sly. Their son hovers nearby and he is also called Hugh. All the Despensers regard themselves as much more highly-borne than their peers, a fact which does little to increase their popularity.

I run and skip, my skirts billowing in the light breeze, calling out to Guy, waving and crying with all the other squealing women. We drop back as the horses break from trot to canter, as though the female fuss is all too much for their grim-faced riders. For this is the nature of men. They cannot bear too much dramatic demonstration. And crying is quite the quickest way to be rid of men, for they run like rabbits pursued by a fox. They are now soldiers, not lovers and husbands and we must understand our importance has diminished. Soon the surge forward has served its purpose of increasing the distance between us and the army. Then they slow down, for they have far to go and must keep a sensible, steady pace so the horses will not tire.

The change in the Ladies is arresting. Shoulders droop and chins slacken and smiles fade and the bright voices are silenced.

We are stranded outside the Castle walls, staring after our men, wondering if we will ever see them again. Except for Beatrice and the red-haired maid, who are rolling over and over in the mud, tearing at each other's hair and scratching at each other's eyes and squealing fit to arouse all the ancestors in their tombs. By comparison, male brawls are like the gentle play of children. A mob of peasants and their children gather to enjoy the spectacle and to cheer them on and place bets on the outcome.

If Isabella sees these maids in that condition, they will be in serious trouble. All the same, it is excellent entertainment and takes one's mind off one's own troubles!

Later, Isabella, who is again pregnant, the Ladies of the Boot and I sit sewing quietly, when something hits me fair and square between the eyes like the piercing of a sharp lance.

'Isabella,' I murmur. 'I didn't see the Earl of Lancaster with your husband leading the army.'

'That's because he wasn't there, Ellie,' says Isabella. 'Nor did he provide any of his men as substitutes for his own illustrious self.'

'That's unpatriotic!'

'It is not only unpatriotic, it's an affront. I don't trust him. I wouldn't be surprised if he doesn't assemble an army against the King.'

At this, I am profoundly shocked, for it's treason and the Earl might lose his head. But, if he doesn't lose his head, if he's victorious, what will happen? Could his insurrection incite Civil War? Civil War is the worst kind of war imaginable, friend against friend, brother against brother, son against father. Widows and abandoned mistresses. (More mistresses than widows, I suspect.)

'Thank heavens for true Royalists, like your husband, Hugh,' I remark to Lady Despenser. 'At least the King has some people in high places he can trust.'

Lady Despenser simpers, modestly placing her hand on her heart. I smile upon her piously.

I don't like Lady Despenser, but my flattery has an ulterior motive. I don't have anything on her and one only obtains something on someone by first gaining their confidence. Of course, Margaret saw her with a man who was not her husband last night, but this is common knowledge. In any case, she was so careless, I suspect her husband does not mind what she does. So this information is of no use. To have something on someone, no one else must have it. The more people who have it, the less "on" it is.

I need to trap her into telling me something about herself, something she would not like anyone else to know, in order to have it on her.

This is politics.

Of course, I am bereft without Guy. I miss him desperately. His arms, his lips, his tongue, his long, luscious cock. While I am in my bed, my arms reach out for him. Even on the occasions that my reaching arms encounter some other substitute lover, it is Guy of whom I am thinking, for I'm intensely loyal by nature. And the substitute lovers are such a nuisance, for they think through possession of my body they are entitled to stay all night. One can hardly believe their presumption! And it is so difficult to be rid of them, for men find nothing undignified in pursuing a reluctant lover.

One of these gentlemen, a rather handsome noble excused from duty on the battlefield due to a missing foot, is particularly troublesome. Finally, in desperation I weep and plead with him to marry me, for I'm convinced this will scare him off. When he eagerly accepts, I have an even greater problem. I persuade Margaret to tell him I'm only after his money, believing that will do the trick. After that, he leaves me presents, little bags stuffed with full with coins.

Soon I have quite a collection.

I don't give them back. I hide them at the bottom of my chest, with the jewels bestowed upon me by sweet Guy. I decide it will be worth the tedium of his attentions to keep them, especially as my noble has a foot missing and cannot possibly catch me.

The year of 1315 will live in the hearts of all, royalty, aristocrats and commoners as a terrible, terrible year. First, we hear that Edward has made a Pig's Ear of accosting Robert the Bruce at

Bannockburn. Brave Bruce is cocky with triumph, while Edward is like a beaten dog, tail between his legs. Yet, his courage is not in dispute. There's much whispering at Court about his lack of planning, his inability to apply a strategy, his total disregard of the advice of his Generals.

Not only is the country laid low in spirit by the Bannockburn defeat, but it never ceases to rain. It rains and rains and rains. The fields are awash. Rivers burst their banks and livestock is drowned. One cannot go out without getting the hems of one's pretty gowns spoiled. Then there is widespread famine across the known world, for the rains have ruined the harvest and the wheat is not fit to be ground.

A man, woman or child might be murdered simply for a half-loaf of bread and one hears of cannibalism in Ireland! In one instance, seven little children from one family were carried off by desperadoes and never seen again. Even horses, which are naturally more valuable than mere children, are eaten.

In the autumn, even the Royal Household is unable to buy bread and the price of wheat is high as the heavens, even vegetables, oats, malt and barley are beyond most commoners' purses. I go to chapel and give thanks that I'm not a commoner.

And the Scots are still on the rampage, making turmoil while the rain keeps raining. We must all paddle our boats the best we can.

Eventually, winter passes and it is a miserable

time indeed, but then three major events occur.

My Mistress is delivered of another child, a son. It gives her something to think about, for she has been sad. Apart from her husband's absence during the Bannockburn catastrophe, the second event, the death of her father King Philip, was a shock. It's never pleasant when a family member dies, even one with whom you are not on good terms.

So a little baby is exactly what she needs. A summer baby. Prince John, born 15 August, 1316. Of course, we must go through the tedious candle ceremony yet again.

'Two fine boys,' says Lady Mortimer, when my Lady is sufficiently rested to request our company. 'How clever of you, my Lady.'

Everyone is pleased with the Queen. In such turbulent times, a spare prince must be a consolation to the Royal Couple.

'It's very small,' says the young Prince Edward disparagingly. 'And it smells.' My sentiments, precisely. His name is Prince John and he is like most babies, wrinkled as Methuselah, ugly as sin and with short spiked hair like a monkey. His face is red as beet, with snail-trails of sick running down his chin. Ugh!

'He looks exactly like you did, when you were born,' says Isabella, smiling fondly upon her first-born, who makes a face displaying such comical disgust that both the Queen and I are convulsed with laughter.

'Don't give such cause for merriment, my son,' huffs Isabella, clutching her belly. 'It hurts me so.'

'I didn't smell so bad,' sniffs little Edward.

'Indeed, you did.'

Mortally offended, the child trots off to torment the royal dogs. Smiling, I follow him, for I hate to see him with his little crown askew, (metaphorically speaking.) In truth I have come to like him well, for he's a jolly little fellow, lively and funny and full of grave confidences which it pleases him to share with me. We share a common dislike of the Ladies of the Boot, Mortimer and Despenser which further strengthens the bond between us.

'Ellie,' he says. 'I command you to catch that dog for me at once.'

'Sire,' I reply, 'I would if I could but I regret I cannot. He's too quick for me.'

'Oh,' he says dismissively. 'I suppose you're only a woman.'

I pay him back for this by tickling him till he screams for mercy. He must know he's not too fine a personage to stand upon his dignity with me. I have to stop when Isabella complains about the noise we're making. Then I pause and wonder where he heard that telling little phrase, 'You're only a woman,' for he did not dream it up by himself. In this way do men pass on their scorn of so-called female weakness to their offspring.

'Thought shall be the harder, heart the keener, courage the greater, as our might lessens.' I shall make a psalter of these words and place it in the Great Hall for all the fine nobles to see. I don't know if the words are those of a man or a woman, for 'Anonymous' has no gender.

But I think these must be the words of a woman.

The third event occurs a week or two later. Gundulph expires, but I see it coming, thanks be to God, and I manage to exchange him for a new, bouncy Gundulph, with ears coloured correctly. The new Gundulph scraps with the new Odo all around the Palace, much to the distress of the Queen. At least the new Gundulph is castle-trained, otherwise we would not have a dry rug to our names. It's fortunate the Queen is not excited by the art of counting, for at the present date, the little dogs should be twenty-one years old! To silence their incessant yapping, I spend much of my meagre allowance on Pigs' Ears and the butcher grows richer by the minute. It pains me but it is worth it.

CHAPTER 17

Charlotte's Wedding

Then my father visits. I receive no notice that he is coming, and it's a blessing that when his arrival is announced, I am alone and not cavorting in bed with Guy. Guy is very proud and I doubt he would submit to the humiliation of hiding naked under the bed or in the chest with all my kirtles. No, he would save his pride and proudly confront my father, while I, no doubt, would receive a beating for my sins.

Father doesn't say so in words, but I know he believes the death of the French King will release his country from many of the horrors she has suffered. He's distressed about the fate of the Templars, the pogroms on the Jews, the cruelty towards those falsely accused of witchcraft. He tells me the curse is endemic. Again I think of that first burning I saw, when we arrived in England after Isabella and Edward's marriage. Although I have seen further atrocities since, this one has stayed with me and still gives me nightmares. I see the face of the young girl as though it were yesterday, not six years ago. I feel her pain. It's like your first lover, whom you never forget, however much time passes.

Although these crimes happen in England too, King Edward is far less vengeful than the old French King was. Edward tries, as far as he can, to avoid the perpetration of cruel punishments unless truly necessary. But, sometimes he's weak and doesn't try hard enough. Or he's distracted by more enchanting pursuits.

Philip is succeeded by his eldest son, Louis.

'I truly hope he will be more merciful than his father,' says Father.

'The old King was a wicked old tyrant,' I reply.

My father nods slowly. 'Indeed, he was. A strong King, but he had no compassion. But, my Daughter, we will think no further on such matters. I have joyful news. A marriage!'

'So the Runt is to be married. No, not the Runt, I mean, Mathilde.'

'It's not Mathilde.'

'Not Mathilde?'

It's Charlotte! Charlotte is to be married. It is such a surprise, for she is surely the least comely of the three of us, even if one tries to be charitable. This, in her case, can strain even the most charitable of hearts, which mine is not.

'But what has happened to Mathilde's suitors?' I gasp.

'She will have none of them,' says Father. 'She says she does not love them. Such nonsense. I cannot imagine who's been filling her head with such notions and she has been scolded and threatened with the whip. But she will not relent.'

'And Charlotte?'

'It is a fair match under the circumstances.

He's well-thought-of and presentable. He's comely in appearance. I am told he enjoys a remote family tie with the Monarchy. Charlotte is anxious that you should attend her marriage and that is the reason for my visit, to persuade you. She felt a letter might not…persuade you.'

Well, nothing would keep me away, for my curiosity is aroused. How little my father knows me, he whom I thought knew every little virtue and fault I possess. Besides, it will be satisfactory to parade my fine jewels and wealth before the Ladies in the French Court. I shall bask in their envy.

'I shall be happy to come,' I tell him graciously. 'with the Queen's permission. I am sure she will be agreeable.'

I write down the date and dutifully kiss my father.

I'm a little concerned about Mathilde. It's distressing that my father has seen fit to threaten to beat her into submission and I feel a surge of pity for her as well as admiration for her spirited resistance. I never dreamed my sister had such dogged determination. And I feel this despite her dalliance with Guy. (To be truthful, I would have done the same in her position, had she an admirer I fancied.)

But a beating! I do not like to think on this. I suppose I have escaped from such a shaming event because I am not a drain upon Father's purse. It's a relief, for I am not yet ready for marriage. I'm having too much of a merry time. Everything changes for the worst when men and women become married.

Sometimes, I ruminate upon why this should be.

Even the Bible says, 'It is better to marry than to burn,' and this is what I find a cause for concern. It's as though marriage is perceived as a method of avoidance of deadly wrath rather than as a means to great joy and an abundance of lawful pleasuring. And the latter I have already without the trammels of marriage. I hope God will be merciful to me. Death is so far off and there is plenty of time to repent when I am old and no longer beddable.

Something unsettling has been gradually dawning on Isabella and me. The Two Despensers, father and son, are becoming increasingly powerful at Court. Most people call them Hugh the Elder and Hugh the Younger. I call them Big Hugh and Little Hugh, but more as a mark of disrespect than with any attempt at accuracy. For Little Hugh is as tall and ambitious and imposing as Big Hugh and makes quite as much noise as his father. Between them, they make a loud roar in the Court of King Edward II, but the King seems not to mind. One might say he even relishes their involvement.

It's a pity, because Isabella and Edward have been living together in harmony now for some years, allowing us all to enjoy our lives. But now the Dreaded Despensers have emerged, like a pair of Big Bass Drums amongst the fiddlers.

Big Hugh is the Earl of Winchester, a Marcher Baron, and he has land stretching far and wide. The other Barons, of course, despise him, because he sided with Edward over Gaveston, thus setting himself apart from them. They will not easily forgive him for this. Also, they fear him. They fear there may be reprisals because they opposed him over Gaveston, and then summarily dismissed him from office. He will not easily forgive them for that.

Little Hugh acquired barrels of money and land when he married Eleanor, daughter of Gilbert de Clare, (another of Guy's many distant relatives.) But, like his father, he still wants more. That is the trouble about wealth, the more you have the more you want. I must admit I am a little like that myself. Now Guy is more certain of me, I get fewer presents. And the one-footed noble is just as bad. He has given up trying to bribe me with bags of coins and instead, he glares at me whenever he sees me. One would think he would have forgotten all that by now. I'm afraid he will send in a spy to recoup his losses from my chest. So I hide the money and jewels in a safer place, a place known only to me. A secret is safest with just one person knowing.

Of course, the Baron complains to all and sundry and calls me unpleasant names. But I take no heed when men insult me. It is always so when a lady has rejected a suitor's advances, or refused to marry them. It's their way of taking revenge for their injured pride. So far, thank God, Guy doesn't suspect anything.

Now, Charlotte's wedding is upon me! My possessions have been placed into chests and loaded onto a cart for transportation to the Port of Dover.

'I have a surprise for you, Ellie,' says the Queen. 'I've had a word with the King and you may take Guy with you to your sister's wedding.'

It's as though she has dropped a castle turret on my head.

'But my Lady, he cannot be spared.'

'Ellie, aren't you listening? I've spoken with the King. Guy can be spared and he's happy to accompany you. I was reluctant to disappoint you, so I asked him before I told you.

'Thank you, my Lady,' I say meekly.

I'm not too sure I'm happy with this. For one thing, I am desolate at the thought he should meet again with my sister Charlotte, married or not. Charlotte might have the same birth parents as I, but she acts like a peasant with her rude manners and loose talk and I'm afraid of being judged by comparison.

And the Runt will be there. The Runt with whom he betrayed me and I'm not certain I can stomach seeing them together again. Their parting may have been no more than a lovers' tiff. I trust neither of them.

I cannot tell the Queen I don't wish for Guy's company. She'll want to know why and that I cannot tell her. She'll never understand. It's a *fait accompli*. With a small escort, Guy and I set sail for France and the marriage of Lady Charlotte to one Adam Langley. It's not a romantic trip; the Channel is as rough as it was on the marriage journey. The boat tips alarmingly from side to side and a hundred times

I think we will capsize. Of course I'm sick, and Guy is not much help, for he is sicker than I am. With green faces, we stare at each other but don't speak.

When we reach the French Coast, the weather is still hostile with heavy rains and a huge black cloud like a vast omen over our heads. At least we are still alive. I think, occasionally, of the rough man who took me on the crates at Dover. I never saw him since and I wonder how he fares.

Finally, the towers of the Palace come into view and I need to make contact again, to know everything will be fine. So, as we climb down from our horses, our clothes sodden, my hair falling in thin wet strands around my face, I clutch at Guy's hand. I sigh as his fingers close around mine and squeeze. If we can still be kind to each other under such conditions, we're not lost. I long to climb into some dry raiments.

We are given separate chambers, far apart from one another, which is fitting, for my father and sisters are here. I wish our quarters were not so far apart. It will be impossible to creep into the other's chamber without being noticed. A maidservant helps me to dry myself and hands me my night-gown. My father comes to say good night and explain about tomorrow's plans, but I am too tired to pay much attention and he doesn't stay long.

'My gown for tomorrow. It will crease,' I whisper to the maid as I fall into my bed.

'Where is it, my Lady?'

'In the brown chest. It's green silk.'

'Sleep well, my Lady. It will be taken care of.'

I adore the green silk gown. It is a present from Isabella, for consoling Prince Edward and keeping him from jealousy of his new little brother.

'I want you to have it, Ellie,' she said when she gave it to me. 'The colour doesn't flatter my pale skin, but it's perfect for your ruddy complexion.'

I was not impressed by this but bit my lip, for the gown was so lovely I swallowed the insult. Maybe it wasn't even an insult, for the Queen is not always tactful and I do have a sunny glow, which I like. Besides, the gown fits my figure better than hers, because I am still slim as a reed while her waist has thickened with childbirth.

I have my favourite head-dress with me and hope it is not spoiled by the journey and the damp.

Charlotte's wedding will take place tomorrow at noon at the little church in the village. I remember the church; it is modest but charming.

I wonder what the Runt will wear.

Next day, I am dressed, with the maid to help me, in all of my finery. My cheeks and lips are rosy, my head-dress is tall and grand and the rest has done my complexion good. I feel elegant as I make my way down to the Great Hall where the company is gathered. How Guy will admire my beauty! There can be no one to match me.

I hear Charlotte before I see her. Some things never change. It is her raucous laugh, which carries for furlongs around. I stand on the upper balcony and survey the scene. Charlotte is in scarlet and ermine and she's even larger than she was before. My eyes search the gathering for a glimpse of the groom, but all the young men are attired in such finery, it is difficult to see who it can be.

Then I see the Runt and there's suddenly a tight pain in my breast.

The Runt is in green silk. The bodice is lower than mine and her breasts rise plumply from its contours. Each sleeve has fourteen buttons compared to ten on mine. Emeralds sparkle at her throat and in her hair which has been woven into her head-dress. A ringlet drops over one eye. Such a hussy! And at her side is Guy. She gazes up at him and even from here I can see the adoration in her eyes.

In an instant, I realise why she has never agreed to take one of my father's choice of suitor. It is Guy she wants. And who can blame her for wanting? What I blame her for is trying to take. And she shall not. She shall not. I shall die before I permit it.

This is the worst decision I have ever had to make in all my life. I have two choices: to hurry immediately to be at Guy's side, to take possession of my mate, to stand between him and my flirtatious sister. Or fly back to my room and find a different gown, one not be in such poor competition with Mathilde's. The former action will expose me to ridicule, for wearing almost the same gown as my sister, only not quite so appealing. The latter course will allow Mathilde that much more time to work her charms on my lover.

It takes just a moment to think about it. What else do I have in my chest? After all, the green silk is attractive to me mainly for its newness. Most people here will not be familiar with my other gowns except, for Guy. And it is Guy I most need to impress.

A servant comes hurrying by, just at the right moment. I seize him by the arm. 'Do you see that Lady, the one by the arch, talking to the handsome man in a purple cloak? She's wearing a gown like mine. Go to her at once and tell her she's needed urgently in my chamber. It's just here.' Urgently I point towards my door. The servant hesitates. Perhaps he fears I intend Mathilde some harm, because she is wearing a gown like mine.

'Now, hurry. At once,' I command.

Pleased with myself, I return to my chamber and open my chest, spilling out the gowns. I pick over them and wait. Once the Runt is with me, helping me to adorn myself, my lover will be left alone.

I decide on another gown, which is gold brocade and which I wore for Guy a few months ago. It will do, for I was not in it for long; he was mad with desire for me at the time and the gown was merely an impediment and immediately discarded. He'll never remember it. It is fit he should now look at it properly. Quickly I whip off my clothes.

Then the Runt is there beside me. I try hard not to be dazzled by her.

'Dear Ellie,' she gushes. 'It is so wonderful to be together again. We have so much to talk about.'

'Help me put on this gown,' I say quickly. 'I shall be late.'

I've already kicked the green silk out of sight under the bed. She shall not have the satisfaction of knowing why I'm changing my gown.

It's a wedding. That's all. Weddings are always exactly the same. Some chanting and some singing, the bride with a silly grin on her face, the groom with a sick one. Father looking grave as befits the occasion but relieved to be rid of a daughter. Ladies remarking on the gown and the head-dress. The older Ladies weeping, because they have had their day and it was so long ago, they can barely remember, poor old things!

There's a sermon that leaves the congregation in no doubt as to what marriage is for and it's certainly not love and enjoyment and unbridled lust, which are the reasons most people marry. Too much praying. There's so much praying I think even God will be bored to distraction.

Charlotte looks like a bear with all the ermine around her wedding gown, but she is happy and her face is plump and bonny. She giggles a great deal, which causes my Father to cringe in embarrassment. When we exit the Church to gather in the graveyard, she pinches her husband's bottom so hard that he yells and the Ladies twitter in alarm.

Charlotte's husband is extraordinarily thin

and looks as though a light wind would bear him away, but he has a pleasant face, with clear, gentle eyes and an easy smile. I cannot help thinking that three of him would fit into Charlotte's wedding gown; even so she is looking well. Then I notice how he looks upon her. With true adoration! Really, there is no justice when I think back on the beautiful Queen, humiliated, ignored. Charlotte is indeed fortunate.

I try to get closer to Charlotte, to talk to her and wish her well. She's gracious towards me and her new husband kisses my hand, then both my cheeks.

'I'm so happy you were able to come, Ellie,' says Charlotte.

'I'm happy too. And happy you are…happy with your new husband.' I giggle at myself, for I sound gauche in the extreme but nobody seems to mind and I know it doesn't matter. For the sun is shining and in the sky there are tiny clouds, all floating independent of each other, like fat, fluffy tails of white kittens.

But Guy is beside me, all at once, and looking at me in such a strange manner.

'Perhaps I should speak to your father,' he says.

I have a feeling as strange as the way he is looking at me. I'm not sure what I'm feeling.

'Why must you?' I ask lightly. He does not answer, but gives me a broad wink. Maybe he has some business to discuss with Father that's nothing to do with what I'm thinking. If it is, if it could be to ask for my hand in marriage, then I should be flattered for I adore Guy. He's a good prospect, he has possibilities. For people admire him and that is most of the battle. In bed he's everything I need. And that is all of the battle. Yes, if I could bear to be married to anyone, then that noble would be Guy.

Then he says the most cruel thing anyone has ever said to me:

'Ellie, we may yet be brother and sister-in-law.'

'We may be brother and sister-in-law?' I repeat stupidly.

'Yes. I shall ask your father for Mathilde's hand in marriage.'

I cannot speak. My throat is so tight I fear I shall faint to the ground at his feet! The world moves in a mad whirl in front of my eyes and I'm swaying, so that I have to cling to him to keep myself from falling. Strange, choking sounds erupt from my throat.

'Ellie, what's the matter? Wouldn't you like it if we were to be related?'

'I shall murder you,' I burst out at last. He has the temerity to look surprised at this. 'But Ellie,' he says, and there's true wonderment in his voice. 'But Ellie, why should you mind? Why can't you be happy for me? It's time for me to settle down and marry and have children. This time must come for every man.'

'You could do that with me! Although I must

say, I wouldn't have you now, for I'm sorely insulted.'

Now his voice grows colder, harder. 'You have no cause to scold me, Ellie. Do you think I don't know about the many lovers you've taken since we have been lovers? Do you think I'm so foolish I don't know about the infatuated, one-footed Thomas?'

'That meant nothing.' Then I remember, with a sick lurch inside my stomach. This is what Guy said to me when he betrayed me with the Runt. Besides, I would never have married Thomas, however many presents he gave me. But Guy isn't finished, for guilt makes him cruel.

'Believe me, Ellie, you are the talk of the English Court and I will not be laughed at for a cuckold.'

'You're not without blame.'

'You were unfaithful first,' he retorts.

'No I was not. You were.'

'You may lie to me Ellie, but don't lie to yourself.'

We sound like children quarrelling, as adults often do when they are hurting. 'Then marry her, for I no longer care.'

I walk away from him and he follows me, trying to justify himself, trying to force me to admit responsibility. I will have none of him. Everything is a blur, but in some manner I manage to survive the trite conversations, the Wedding Feast, the forced jollity, turning my head away proudly as I see Guy in earnest conversation with my father.

    I long to hear what they are saying, but I will not demean myself by trying to eavesdrop.

CHAPTER 18

The Dreaded Despensers

The following day I set sail for England with my escort, but Guy is not with me. He's remained in France to pursue his suit with Mathilde.

I hear no further news. I despise him for his two-faced impertinence, but I'm certain Mathilde is hot as red kindling for him. I think she is so confident in her new-found seductive appeal that she will play hard-to-get and will brook no nonsense, and in this way she will gain the upper hand. She has the sense to know that men appreciate most what they have to fight for. In this respect, she is more sensible than I am.

I lean against an apple tree, watching a maidservant gathering poisonous toadstools, for the castle is buzzing with flies in this recent hot spell. The maidservant will mix the chopped toadstools with a little sweet goat's milk and, as bodies struck down by plague form into a burial mound, so the voracious flies will swarm to their multiple deaths. I must tell Prince John, for he enjoys watching the slaughter. I consider how satisfactory it would be to disguise this mixture in a pie and feed it to one's enemies. I am having such evil thoughts of late, but they're a consolation. Yet I'm almost too listless to put them into practice.

Before long, Guy is back in the English Court, sheepish and check-mated. I'll have nothing to do with him. He has hurt me too badly. He writes letters, which I tear up and throw away. He sends me expensive presents which, naturally, I put away in my chest, for I'm not stupid. However, I don't wear them. I'm implacable in my resolve, however much my heart and my body ache for him.

After this, I am too busy to feel sorry for myself. Isabella's latest pregnancy has run full term and she's on her bed suffering the pangs of childbirth. Lady Despenser mops the Queen's brow and the midwife peers up the Queen's birthing gown and Lady Mortimer bustles around with a duster, heaven knows why. She is not competent in a crisis, Lady Mortimer, and that's why she has a nice, comfortable duster in her hand.

I send Margaret to the kitchen to boil some water. I am not sure of the purpose of the copious amounts of boiled water needed, for I arranged not to be present at my Lady's previous birthings. But I heard somewhere that boiling water is a major requirement for successful birthing.

'I have arranged the boiling water,' I say importantly.

'I can see the head,' says the midwife. 'She's almost here. Already! Push, my Lady.'

The Queen heaves hard with a great, mournful wail which echoes back from the high ceilings. I shudder, wondering why women should allow themselves to suffer so, while men have all the pleasure and then go off fighting battles or hunting or playing chess or tennis.

'One more time,' says the midwife.

'I'm dying,' screams the Queen.

'It's a girl,' cries the midwife, 'a beautiful little girl.'

I think perhaps a girl will be better and I lean over to see the result of my Lady's latest effort, expecting big blue eyes and golden curls in a sweet, round face. The Queen blinks back a few tears, then gazes up at me proudly, awaiting my compliments.

My disappointment is therefore almost more than I can bear. Another little wizened-faced monkey with ears disproportionately large. Still, I console myself when I think of Prince Edward and I hope this one gets better-looking before she's much older, for I don't think I could bear to touch her in her present condition.

'She is sooo beautiful,' coos Lady Despenser. 'Coochie, coochie, chuck, chuck, chuck.'

Disgusted, I decide it is time to leave. No doubt the Ladies will know what to do with the boiling water when it arrives. Personally, I would make do with cold and drown the yowling little brat.

I sidle over to Prince Edward. 'Would you like me to take you to the piggery? You know what fun we have watching those fat brown pigs rolling in the swill. And the sow has a litter of piglets.'

'Not now, Ellie. I have my new little sister.'

Disappointed in Edward, I wander up to the battlements and stare over the country vista before me but Margaret appears and interrupts my necklace of thought. She's all of a flurry, her eyes shining.

'Lady Ellie,' she cries. 'You will never guess.'

'I shall not need to guess if you tell me,' I say.

'The new baby princess has been named. She is Princess Eleanor. The Queen has named her after you. I have the Proclamation right here. It says Princess Eleanor of Woodstock, born 18 June 1318.'

'My name is Eleanora,' I say, 'with an a on the end.'

'Oh, Ellie,' says Margaret. 'How can you be so…?'

'I am most particular about my name,' I tell her, 'and besides, she will not be the least like me.'

'Oh, I think she has a little of your look, Lady Ellie. And your expression! When she screws her face up to yell she looks exactly like you do at this very moment.'

'Lady Margaret!'

She giggles, drops a curtsey and off she goes. Impudent little wretch, how dare she! There was a time Lady Margaret was quite in awe of me and hurried to do my bidding and would not dream of turning her back on me when I am angry.

Sometimes I wonder what young ladies are coming to.

Little Hugh is a slippery serpent. You can tell he is, just by looking at his false, thin-lipped smile beneath the long, combed moustache, his dark, calculating squint. To begin with, he butters up the Earl of Lancaster, in direct opposition to his father, Big Hugh's allegiance to King Edward. As a result of this buttering up, Lancaster clearly thinks Little Hugh is out-of-favour with the King. Moreover, he is not averse to Little Hugh becoming Chamberlain of the Household. Upon which, Little Hugh promptly changes sides. Truly, Court politics are worse than a game of chess.

Isabella says it's all because Little Hugh affects to be such an amiable, easy-come, easy-go fellow that everyone trusts him including the King. I think she's right, for, despite the lips and eyes, he has a well-looking face and a strong, measured voice. Perhaps the Queen and I are the only ones who notice the artifice in his expression.

'I'm most displeased at the regard in which the King holds these plausible Despensers,' she says. 'It seems to me that the Barons are becoming lax and that is why the Despensers' influence with the King is increasing. They can do as they will in complete confidence.'

'It may not be as bad as it seems,' I reply.

'I fear your judgement is false, Ellie. I am certain that the Younger Despenser has taken Gaveston's place. The trouble is he is even more avaricious than Gaveston. With his connections and riches, he is therefore more dangerous.'

The only spider in the gruel for both Edward and the Barons is the Earl of Lancaster, who cannot get along with anybody.

I hear the King and Little Hugh talking together at a jousting. I'm lingering nearby, gazing around innocently, remarking that it looks like rain. I often linger and gaze and remark upon the weather, for it is amazing how much you hear when you look and sound innocent. 'He's a bully and a bombast,' says Little Hugh, which I note more or less describes himself, even though he covers his faults so well. But, no, he is talking of Lancaster.

'I know many of the Barons are up in arms due to his incompetence,' muses Edward.

'That's true. And I sense their loyalty is returning to you, dear Edward. Our advantage increases day-by-day.'

Now my ears really burn! Dear Edward! Such familiarity! It's unheard of. For, although Edward is a gentle soul, he is still King and expects to be treated as such. But he doesn't rebuke Little Hugh. On the contrary, he places his hand on Hugh's arm and squeezes it, almost timidly. There is a strange, plaintive expression on his comely face, and I am sorely discomfited by his self-effacement.

'Don't worry, Hugh. I think matters are beginning to turn to our advantage.'

'Dear Edward, at this point, may I mention that I'm interested in the Earldom of Gloucester? It would be so desirable, so fitting…'

'Dear Hugh, surely you must know I cannot bestow an important Earldom upon the son of a secondary Baron,' says Edward. 'It will be more than my life is worth. Come, come, dear Hugh. We must be realists. You must not pout so, for it's not my fault.'

'I understand, dear Edward, but, well, I wonder if I could, at least, raise with you the matter of the land you promised me? For I've set my heart upon it and cannot wait until we can go hunting there together. Among other delightful things, of course.' Little Hugh purses his mouth in a thoroughly revolting way.

'Soon, Hugh, soon. You must give me a little time. I cannot afford to upset the Barons now, when matters are improving by the minute.'

'But dear Edward,' wheedles Hugh. 'I cannot wait forever.'

This dialogue is beginning to swell my head with its implications. I listen carefully, for it must be repeated word-for-word to my Lady and is probably worth a handsome present. Isabella is fair in this way, appreciating useful information but never punishing the messenger for the message when it harbours bad tidings. I hurry to tell her. Isabella listens carefully.

'Hugh the Younger has aggrieved many of the great Barons,' she says. 'I heard Hereford and Arundel talking of him most bitterly. Of course, the powerful Mortimers are at odds with him and they are his brothers-in-law.'

The Queen broods upon this for some time. She also complains to the King that she struggles by on a pittance. But the King won't listen to her complaints.

'Ask Hugh,' he says.

'It's he who has brought me to this,' she cries piteously.

'It's not my affair. You must ask Hugh. The Treasury is his responsibility.'

And so it goes round and around.

We must wait and see what happens.

What happens is that the Mortimers go on a rampage, for they are vandals and scoundrels and they cause much destruction to Big and Little Hugh's' properties. The Despensers' great manors are pillaged and robbed, their game poached, their horses removed en masse in the dead of night, and much fresh meat appears in the Castle larders, whole carcasses of cow and pig, row upon row of them. We never ate so well. I have another spot and wonder if it is the pork crackling.

We hear later that the Earl of Lancaster was largely responsible for inciting the Barons, especially the Mortimers, to this act of vandalism.

'Good for the Earl,' says the Queen. 'Those Despensers deserve their punishment.'

Then King Edward appears and he's in a state and it's certainly not a Royal state. It's May 1321 and Parliament is sitting to deal with the Dreaded Dispenser Disaster. The Barons, again led by Lancaster, are of one mind while Edward is of another. To show their solidarity they wear white bands on their arms. As is usual, the King is outnumbered and the Despensers are exiled, their properties forfeited.

The King stamps around the Royal Apartments shouting vile oaths while the Queen tries to hush him because of the innocent children. He's in no mood to be hushed and eventually she ceases to chide him, for it's a futile exercise. I feel much pity for her, for she is again big with child. It's clear the King is still keen to perform his husbandly duties on occasion for the sake of the succession. Such is his commitment to the Royal Line.

Several times I have to admonish little Edward, who thinks he's a man because he can utter vile oaths exactly like his father.

'It's not clever to speak thus,' I tell him. 'It's rude and uncouth.'

'But my father…'

'It's permitted for your father. He's a man and he is angry, and angry men are permitted to be uncouth. But it is not permitted for little children like you.'

'That, Ellie, is not logical.'

Of course, he is right, for he is a clever little boy. But what else can I say? So I give him a huge hug and a few loud, wet kisses around his little red ears. This soon makes him forget the bad words, for he's too intent upon escaping from my clutches. At this age little boys do not care for such attentions.

Now Isabella has more pressing matters to ponder. It seems the Tower is falling apart, for rain keeps pouring in the roof and everything in the chamber is damp. There's not a dry chair to sit upon and some of the valuable wall hangings are spoiled, not to mention the fine rugs and my favourite slippers. This does not bode well for the Queen, for her latest confinement is soon upon her.

'How can he expect me to do my duty as the royal sow when he neglects my comfort so?' she bawls. We're all shocked by the vehemence of her rage.

'Oh, my Lady,' babbles Lady Margaret, 'I'm certain the King doesn't regard you as his sow, even though you are only kept to produce heirs.' This wasn't the most diplomatic way in which to console her. I swear Margaret only avoids kitchen duties because Isabella is distracted by sudden heartburn.

The King finally relents and has the constable of the Tower dismissed. Not only is it too late now, but it has solved nothing, for the constable cannot spend money on repairs if he has empty coffers. He is merely a convenient scapegoat, and anyway, the damage has been done.

'It's not the fault of John de Cromwell,' weeps Isabella. 'It's the fault of the Despensers and their false economies.'

Guy says there is truth in her words, for the two of them have total control in the management of the Treasury.

'Where do you think the money went, Ellie?' he points out, his noble forehead creased with worry. 'I shall tell you. It went straight into their coffers.

And, no doubt, it's still there. And will remain there, while the King has his way.'

I think back over the previous weeks. Many of our French servants have been despatched back to France, while Isabella's properties have been confiscated and she exists on a miserly pension.

And so it goes round and around.

The new baby is a girl, born on 5 July, 1321, and her name is Joan. She is a puny-looking brat, smaller than her siblings and does not cry much, which is a blessing. Eleanor is jealous of her and craves attention. She climbs all over her weary mother, her fat little knees pummelling and bruising, till Isabella commands that I take her away to her nurse. The nurse is equally miserable and I can see in her face she would like to send the little tyrant back to her mother.

When nobody is looking, Eleanor pinches the baby's skinny little legs and makes her cry. I have to watch her constantly, and prevent her from committing childish violence upon her sister. She pushes barley grain up Joan's nostrils and, on being reprimanded, throws a temper and lies on the floor kicking her fat little legs. I give her a light slap.

'You're too sharp with her, Ellie. She's just a small child,' Isabella complains.

It is no use explaining that I have just saved her youngest child from certain death. Edward supports me and tries to distract Eleanor, but Prince John is a solitary child, always off on his own and can never be found except at meal times.

Big Hugh goes abroad, some say to Lundy Island, which I am told is a delightful place, although a favourite haunt of pirates. He seizes two merchant ships to set himself up in comfort, which I suppose is all he can do, for he's not used to rough living.

Little Hugh is not so easily cast aside. Oh no. Not Hugh le Despenser the Younger. Greedy and confident, he thinks nothing can touch him. I think back on Gaveston and watch Hugh as he sets about preparing his own fate. Neither Isabella nor I can be sure just how close this relationship is between the King and Little Hugh. But we are deeply suspicious. The favouritism shown him by the King makes him her natural enemy, and therefore mine too.

It's a dangerous game he is playing, for the people also will regard him as the Queen's enemy. And the glorious Queen has never been more popular than she is now, for wherever she goes they clamour for her, for her beauty, for a kind word, for an act of charity. They're beginning, truly to trust her. (I don't trust her one bit.) Eventually, Little Hugh departs too, for even he cannot stand up against the united wrath of the Mighty Barons.

'We shall go to Canterbury to the shrine of St. Thomas,' the Queen tells me in October that year. 'We will stop off at Leeds Castle, for it is now part of my dower and I should like to see it.'

CHAPTER 19

Trouble with the Barons

I am excited by the prospect of the trip.

'Who is custodian of the Castle?' I enquire.

'It is one Bartholomew Badlesmere. I am told he is away, but his wife will welcome us.'

So we set off and it is a sunny morning, which is a change after the recent bad weather. It is not such a gruelling journey, for the sun is not as hot as it can be in midsummer and there's a light breeze to cool us. When we are in sight of the Castle, the Queen sends a marshal ahead of us to announce our arrival. She's clearly excited about this new addition to her dower and is longing to see it and gloat upon it.

As we reach the drawbridge, we see the marshal waiting for us, still on horseback. He doesn't jerk the horse aside and allow us to mount the bridge. Bewildered, we rein in our horses.

'My Lady,' he says in a sheepish voice to the Queen. 'My Lady, I'm sorry but...we're not permitted to enter the Castle.'

'Not permitted to enter!' echoed the Queen, aghast. 'Why not? Is there pestilence within? Or plague?'

'You could say that, my Lady,' replies the marshal.'The pestilence is in the form of

Badlesmere's wife. He's told her she must not permit anyone to enter the Castle in his absence. She's not to be swayed. I've implored her to my utmost ability. I beg pardon, my Lady.'

'Have you told her it is her Queen?'

'Yes my Lady.'

'And does she know I own the Castle?'

'I have acquainted her with that fact,' says the marshal, a little pompously. He is clearly most awkwardly placed and afraid the Queen will blame him.

'This I find difficult to believe,' says the Queen and I can only admire her patience, for she must be seething within. 'What exactly did the good lady say?'

'She says you must seek some other lodging forthwith. She says she must obey her husband, not the Queen. The woman is quite mad.'

This last statement is confirmed by what happens next.

To our amazement, there is a loud scream and we look up and there, above our heads, is a row of archers ready to let fly their arrows from the battlements. This they do, the arrows whizzing over our heads and all around us, making a most frightful whooshing sound that turns my knees to blubber. Some of our party fall dying or wounded. One man is directly at my horse's feet and the animal panics and shies away, almost unseating me. We are numbed with the shock, for it is a bloodbath.

We flee. There is no choice, for it will be

boiling oil next. The Queen is almost in tears as she finally jerks her horse to a halt and looks back over the bodies from her party as they lie amongst the grasses and bracken. One member of the soldier escort tries to move, apparently to help a fellow victim. He's seen and another arrow released. It finds its mark in his throat and quivers therein, as though in delight. In sympathy, I clutch my own throat tightly, so tightly I almost strangle myself.

We can hardly believe what has happened!

'Badlesmere and his wife will pay for this,' weeps the Queen. 'And so will their sponsor, the Earl of Lancaster. It's senseless slaughter. My poor, poor soldiers! They didn't know they were going to battle.'

We return home. Although we wait until nightfall, when we can safely gather up the wounded and the bodies of the dead, and round up the loose horses to bear them on the homeward journey. Everyone does what they can without complaint, including Isabella. Seven men have died and three are badly wounded. Isabella has no stomach now for visiting the Cathedral. It's a long trek back and it seems longer because we are all sick in our bellies and heavy in our hearts.

A sorry, pitiable sight we must look when we arrive.

It seems every single member of the Court, noble and servant alike, rushes out to see what has happened. I'm almost unseated from my horse, which bucks in panic at the sudden surge of bodies. I hang on grimly, gritting my teeth, for the effort is more than my poor body can bear and my arms are fair wrenched from their sockets.

Soon, Guy is at my side and with a cry of relief, I fall off my horse into his arms and cling to him with all my sapped strength. I have forgotten my anger with him; his is simply a friendly, familiar face. I am weak with hunger and fear and exhaustion. All I yearn for is peace and the security of familiar surroundings, far away from spilled blood and anguish and death.

'Someone,' says Guy, 'is going to pay for this atrocity, even if I have to kill him with my own bare hands.'

'It wasn't a him. It was a her,' I tell him weakly.

Needless to say, this is more kindling to light the angry fire already burning inside the King's heart. He is both horrified and infuriated by the lack of sympathy from the Barons, particularly from Lancaster. The following day a messenger arrives with a letter from the custodian, Badlesmere himself, which, in effect, is meant to vindicate the mad actions of his wife. As the King reads, I can see a pulse throbbing in his forehead as his anger increases. I've never seen him this angry before, and even Isabella trembles.

'Impudent wretch,' yells the King. 'While he lives, this land cannot be England.'

So Edward leads an expedition against Leeds

Castle. It seems the entire city of London is incensed by the treatment of its Queen and the rallying call brings forth a fine, avenging army from its inhabitants, all shouting for Badlesmere's blood in return for his insult to their Queen.

'Forward,' yells King Edward, mounted on his fine, much-decorated Iberian war-horse, his double-bladed sword held high in the air with more eagerness than I ever saw when he set off on previous campaigns. He's even more handsome when he's on fire. His shield looks well, with its fine coat of arms protecting his left flank.

We wonder how long before they return from their siege of Leeds Castle. I've never experienced a siege but have heard many colourful stories and they are deliciously exciting, unless, of course, one is a victim. For dreadful acts are perpetrated. Rancid animal carcasses, crawling with vermin, are ejected over walls by giant catapults to spread infection and reduce the besieged by disease. Foundations are undermined and cannon-balls let loose. Sieges are costly in life both to attackers and defenders. If those within the Castle walls surrender with little persuasion, they are treated leniently.

But, the consequences if resistance lasts long are terrible to recount. The anger of those attacking builds up beyond endurance and, once the Castle walls are breached, there is violence, pillage and rape which make mockery of the Code of Chivalry by which our knights are bound.

No person is spared the terrible onslaught,

and no vengeful act is too appalling to contemplate. It must be a painful dilemma for the defenders to decide whether they should fight or surrender.

Not long after, the army of soldiers and motley Londoners returns and when I hear the announcement, I rush out to the outer bailey where I find Guy. It's quite a story he tells me.

'The garrison surrendered after four days. It was a fine battle with little loss of life to our army. Twelve of the key members of the garrison were hanged from the battlements and we took the old carrion crow, Lady Badlesmere. You should have heard her screaming. She knows more oaths than any common soldier. We have her in custody now. But Badlesmere himself wasn't there. He has flown, like the poor coward that he is, to seek shelter elsewhere.'

'Did you rape and murder and pillage, Guy?' I ask breathlessly.

'What a strange question for a Lady to ask her lover,' says Guy, looking amused and tweaking my nose. I reassert my dignity.

'I am always interested in philosophical questions regarding violence in battle. For I know the ancient laws of chivalry do not always apply.'

'Ellie. I'm hungry,' says Guy. 'I want food and beer and then I want you.'

I'm peeved that Guy's priorities demand food and beer before me, but I suppose a lover must keep his strength up. By the time he has done with feasting, I'm more than ready for him. He lies down naked and lets me do things to him, for he's too exhausted to rise to anything excepting that which happens of its own accord. So I amuse myself exceedingly in diverse and imaginative ways until, at last, he pleads to be permitted to sleep.

'For we shall have a fine day out, tomorrow,' he promises.

Guy speaks the truth, for as a consequence of the successful coup, mad old Lady Badlesmere is sat upon an ancient nag and led, screeching loudly, through the streets of London to general mocking and jeering and pelting with rotten eggs. I throw quite a few myself, for Guy and I follow the procession, hurling insults with the rest of them.

We have a fine day out and feel much better for it. We have avenged the deaths of innocent men. Lady Badlesmere ends up in the White Tower and I think she will remain there for some time to think upon her crimes. It serves her right! Exhilarated, we return to a Great Feast and Guy and I dance rowdily, for the wine is flowing freely, the fiddlers are noisy and tuneful and everyone is merry.

Lady Badlesmere's husband may have flown to seek safety, leaving his wife to take the consequences, but a party sets off to recover him, for they have fine plans for him too. Perhaps when they find him, there will be another Great Feast like this one.

King Edward is very much admired, not least by the Queen, who pets him and spoils him till he looks as though he cannot take any more. It seems, for a brief while, they've never been more in harmony.

Little Edward insists that the King tells him the story of the siege each night before he goes to sleep. The Queen thinks this is inappropriate bedtime storytelling for a child, but in truth, little Edward sleeps like an angel in heaven. The King is clearly satisfied with the way he has conducted himself and there is about him some of the cockiness that puts me in mind of Gaveston. He's a King who has led his army to Victory, albeit in his own country and against his own wife's Castle. All the same, Isabella isn't satisfied merely with the hangings and the imprisonment of the Badlesmere woman. Isabella wants blood for blood. No woman truly forgives a humiliation, whatever its source.

'You cannot permit Badlesmere to go unpunished, my Lord,' she tells her husband. 'You owe it to my honour to make an example of him.'

Edward has other things on his mind.

'First we must rescue the unfortunate Despensers,' he says, shaking his golden head and spoiling everything for Queen Isabella. 'Their banishment was ill-conceived and they must be returned to their rightful place by my side forthwith.'

'My Lord!' cries Isabella, outraged, but he doesn't wait for her tirade. He simply removes himself from her presence with all due speed, and there's a spring to his step that was never there before as he strides from the room. King he might be, but he knows only one way to avoid a complaining wife and that's not to be present.

So it's thanks to the King and his cronies, the Bishops, that the Despensers are returned to their 'rightful place by his side,' on the grounds that their banishment was illegal.

The wind never blows without it knocks down all the trees and whips off Ladies' head-dresses. The King has to quell the Marcher Barons who gather along the Welsh borders. He seems highly confident about confronting the Marcher Barons, for the victory at Leeds has quite gone to his head.

Besides, he hates Roger Mortimer. It is not because Mortimer has wealth, for the King is not an unduly envious fellow. However, Mortimer had been eager to join the Ordainers and brusquely ordered the King to comply with many demands, which did not endear him to his sovereign. That is a difference in character between Mortimer and Despenser, for the former's confidence depends less upon approval from his peers.

So there he is, black-eyed Roger, tall and imposing in his fine, fluted helmet and body armour, with his father, Mortimer of Chirk, waiting on the Welsh border for Lancaster to join them and make pig-swill of Edward and his army.

Off gallops the King, with his faithful army, and when they arrives they find the two Mortimers quite beside themselves with pique, for the unreliable Earl of Lancaster fails to put in the promised appearance. So the King is able to demonstrate his courage and zeal in complete safety by taking them both prisoner then bringing them back to England and throwing them in the Tower.

'What d'you think?' I ask Isabella. 'The Mortimers are in the Tower.'

'You have too much to say for yourself, Ellie,' she says.

I'm indignant, for does my Lady expect me to be silent about such interesting news? What is it to her whether they live or die?

'But my Lady, aren't you pleased?'

She doesn't answer and assumes an expression that puts me in mind of the Old Boots. I pick up her comb and lift it above her head, but she dashes my hand away with a curse. Rejected, I withdraw.

The Mortimers are incarcerated for some time, but Isabella will not speak of their trials. Finally a sentence of death is passed on them. A traitors' death. I notice she's particularly melancholy upon hearing this news, but I control my urge to invite gossip.

All resistance from the Marchers ceases and Edward makes merry at feasts and jousts and plays and has a fine Christmas. But Edward, being Edward and too gentle for his own good, finally relents and cannot bring himself to have the two imprisoned nobles executed. He commutes their sentence to life imprisonment. Inexplicably, the Queen is cheered.

Early in February the following year, the King presents himself to the Queen and I can guess what's coming. For there's a look about him of defensiveness, like little Eleanor has when she has torn her prettiest kirtle on a state occasion and expects a scolding.

'Madame,' he says to his Queen. 'I've come to inform you that I've recalled the Despensers to Court by Royal Writ.'

He says this very hastily and withdraws equally as hastily, before Isabella's anger descends upon him. I can hear his scurrying footsteps growing fainter and think how very unkingly, like children who knock on a door and run away.

His act is most unfair, for Isabella, being Isabella, has no option but to turn her fury upon my innocent head. I listen, my own fair head bowed, till I can stand it no longer.

'I wouldn't fancy Lancaster's chances now,' I say, which may be salt to the wound but takes her mind away from tormenting me.

'I don't care, for I don't like him,' she says sullenly. 'He's turned against us.'

'Maybe you don't, but he's probably the most loyal ally we have among the Barons,' I say. 'He hasn't deliberately thwarted you, my Lady. His sins are those of incompetence and thoughtlessness. If he has any sense, he'll flee. He'll go abroad before it's too late. Should we warn him, do you think?'

'He's not a child. Let him fend for himself,' says Isabella, who sometimes displays an amazing detachment towards her former protectors.

But Lancaster takes his fate into his own

hands. In spite of the example of the Mortimers, he deliberately opposes Edward in a battle on the River Trent. This is, indeed, Civil War.

'He's a traitor. He shall pay,' screams Edward, for he is now a regular warmonger. At least, for a King as pacific as Edward.

And pay he does. For King Edward, floating on a wave of triumph, and with his soldiers fighting valiantly by his side, defeating the Earl of Lancaster is as easy as breaking wind.

Lancaster is tried at Pontefract, his own castle, for resisting and hindering the King in a hostile manner at the bridge of Burton-upon-Trent and feloniously slaying the king's soldiers. In addition to this, he'd corresponded with the Scottish King, signing himself King Arthur.

Everyone laughs at this, for his conceit it beyond belief. But Lancaster keeps his head down, humiliated at having his grand delusions so publicly exposed. The Barons jeer and mock and it is a fair rowdy trial and greatly enjoyed by all.

He's sentenced to be beheaded. In the light of the sentences passed upon his aides who are condemned to die by hanging, drawing and quartering, the Earl is fortunate indeed. So, one fine, sunny morning, he's taken to St. Thomas' Hill.

'Let's go,' says Guy. 'Let's see the traitor finished.'

We're staying at a Manor House not too far away with relatives of Guy's, for Isabella has granted me a short respite from the Court. It'll be an excellent outing.

I put on a new sky-blue kirtle given to me by the Queen in one of her rarer moments of generosity, and we set off to St. Thomas' Hill. It's a fair journey, but we allow ourselves plenty of time and pleasure each other frequently to lighten the nights. (And the days and the hours and the minutes!) It's a wonder we get there on time, but we do.

We stand amongst the jeering crowds, craning our necks to see.

'There he is,' cries a small boy, pointing gleefully. 'Look, there he is, Mother.'

And there he is indeed, on a tiny pony of nondescript colour, a pathetic, ridiculous man, disproportionately large on his little steed. People throw stones and rotten eggs and fruit and ancient lumps of animal offal. A peasant beside me has a pail containing some visceral-looking red substance. I shudder, for it looks like... something quite awful. I glance at his wife and sure enough, she is carrying a new-born baby. Shuddering, I think how deeply Lancaster arouses hatred among the masses. The man with the pail starts forward, his chin thrust out in determination. I'm annoyed we have nothing to throw, for it does detract from the excitement. I must be better-organised next time.

'Hail, King Arthur,' yells the crowd. 'What have you done with Guinevere? Has she run away?''

This is an allusion to Lancaster's unfortunate marriage, for his twelve-year-old wife lacked desire for him, (for which she can hardly be blamed.) She escaped from him and hid and he never managed to find her. When he's dead, she can marry whomever she likes and I hope she does. Though it is a pity she has lost her immense wealth to her husband and will not enjoy its benefits.

His body heaves and rolls as the pony jerks its way along the rutted path, picking its delicate hooves around the rocks and stones.

'Oh, God, have mercy!' he cries. 'Dear God, have mercy on my soul.'

'Dear God, have mercy on Great King Arthur,' mocks the crowd.

'And shower your blessings on his widow, the sweet Queen Guinevere,' cries a wag. Indeed, the long journey on the elderly pony is a punishment in itself.

They're ready for him when he reaches the top of the hill. We scurry along with the others to get a good view of the execution and there is much pushing and shoving. A few fights break out over positions. There is such a commotion, for it's an ebullient crowd of merrymakers. It's so inspiring when people are gathered together for a common aim.

Lancaster is lying down with his head on the block.

'Look towards the North, where your allies, the Scots, live out their miserable existence,' says the executioner.

The Earl twists his neck to obey and I can imagine hearing his bones creak. His eyes are tightly shut and his fat lips are moving as though in prayer. A sliver of saliva rolls from the corner of his mouth.

The crowds draw in their breath of one accord and hold it. The silence is total, no birds sing, no child whispers, not even the squeak of a tiny mouse.

And the axe-man chops off his head and everybody cheers fit to burst their guts.

Guy says we should not tell the Queen we've witnessed Lancaster's death. He feels she will be shocked and disturbed by the news, despite her previous tantrums after the Leeds Castle fiasco. Sometimes Isabella says outrageous things to vent her spleen and doesn't intend for them to be taken literally. I thank God for that, for if it were so, half the Court would have been done to death by now.

'Let someone else tell her,' says Guy. Her anger will be great if she discovers we have hid it from her.'

'You must say you desired to spare her grief at this difficult time.'

Eventually, someone blabs about the Earl's execution, but she shows little reaction. I find this unpredictability a worrisome quality in one who has power over my fortunes.

CHAPTER 20

Roger Mortimer Escapes

'My life is over,' says Isabella, shoving her breast into the child's mouth, for horrors! she's decided to feed this one herself. Not just for a short while, but indefinitely. It's disgusting to see the milk dripping over the grasping, sucking little face.

And dead Lancaster is practically a saint, for it's the current fashion to make pilgrimages to his tomb. The King has ranted but it does him no good, for the people swarm there in their hundreds, like hungry bees seeking succour. Inwardly, I am certain Isabella feels more threatened because of the absence of Lancaster's support. The King continues to pander to the Despensers' every whim, while keeping his wife desperately short of money.

Time passes. I spend much of my time with the children, for once they're grown and have stopped shitting and pissing and being sick all over everything, I find them fairly tolerable. Edward and John are fine boys and Eleanor is almost as much as a boy as they are and I enjoy her liveliness. Little Joanna is the Runt of the Litter and largely ignored, but I make a special effort for her and take her to the piggery, where she squeals with delight to see the fat sow with her many hungry babies.

Then we hear astounding news. Roger Mortimer has escaped from the White Tower. His old father has died while incarcerated, but not Roger Mortimer, the Invincible. I'm surprised to see how pleased Isabella looks when the news is broken to her, for her face lights up like a gypsy fire at midnight. Her energy returns. She calls for a fiddler to amuse us. I wonder if she's had a hand in his escape, but no, that cannot be possible. There have been rumours of late that she has visited him in his cell under cover of darkness, but I cannot believe even she would be so foolhardy. Yet, I look upon her face and cannot help but think there is more to her than she cares to reveal.

'Someone must have helped him,' I remark. 'He cannot have escaped without assistance.'

'I wouldn't know about that,' snaps Isabella.

'Perhaps someone drugged the guards.'

'He got away in a boat,' put in Lady Margaret.

Later, when I am in bed with Guy, in that pleasant stupor that follows passion, (when one lies back and congratulates oneself on one's prowess), he says, 'I know how it was, with Mortimer.'

'How? Please do tell.'

'It was Alspaye, Gerard de Alspaye, the sub-lieutenant. He was seen with Mortimer in the boat. It is said they are making for the Isle of Wight.'

But this turns out to be a false lead. Sometime later the news reaches us that they were taken by ship to Normandy. In the meantime, the King is already on his way to Wales, convinced that Mortimer is about to rob him of his own lands. I swear the King is obsessed.

The poor King! That period of unmitigated triumph has been reversed and he's reverted to his original, incompetent self. The trouble with the King is that he does not profit from his mistakes, he simply makes the same ones over and over again. Occasionally, it seems, circumstances may favour him, but the soundness of judgement which he lacks is the most vital quality for a King. There will always be bad times as well as good, and the true test of character is stability and strong action when the odds are against one.

The Queen is travelling to Paris to visit her brother Charles the Fair. He's her last, living brother, for Louis and Philip are now both dead. All of her brothers have enjoyed a chance to be King, but the first two did not last long, so I hold little hope for Charles.

I think it would be an excellent strategy if royal brothers and sisters took turns being Kings and Queens, say for periods of two years. One can endure almost anything if one knows that there will be respite for a while, at least until one's turn comes around again. This would lessen the individual responsibility and they might all live longer. It should also avoid their becoming too elevated for their own boots and throwing innocent people into Towers.

Isabella is acting as substitute for Edward. Charles insists that homage is paid for the English possessions of Aquitaine and Ponthieu. The

Despensers have told Edward that it's not in the best interests of his country that he should go at this time. It sorely vexes the Barons that Edward listens to Big and Little Hugh rather than to them.

It's been one disaster after another. First Pembroke was sent, but, on arrival, clutched at his middle and died on the spot. No one appears to suspect foul play, except for me. He is such an unpleasant man although he acts holier than the Pope. I have often wanted to stick a sharp object into his stomach to avenge the betrothed maiden he took against her will.

He was followed by Edmund of Kent, the King's half-brother. The French sent Edmund back forthwith, for they do not suffer fools and Edmund is undoubtedly a fool. It's not his fault. Some people cannot help being fools. Look at Charlotte!

That leaves Isabella. Her mission is to negotiate a delay, so her husband, has time to think. Putting the responsibility onto their Queen suits the Despensers very well, although I do not say so to Isabella. I believe the Despensers are afraid that if Edward is free from their influence, he might be persuaded to do something which is not in their highest interests. I suspect Isabella doesn't realise that she is merely being used by the Despensers for their own ends.

Then, the last obstacle is overcome, for Parliament is agreed. Isabella will go to France.
I don't know if I am accompanying her until the very latest moment, so I have little time to pack my things

and I forget my favourite brooches and the physic for my spots, which I keep in a blue velvet bag in the bottom of my chest. This displeases me and I'm annoyed with the Queen for not being more considerate, for all Ladies need time to decide what they need to take abroad with them.

As the manservants carry out my chest, I pray fervently I have not omitted any other essentials. All the same I am glad to be going. It will take my mind off other matters!

But I'm not prepared for what happens when we arrive at the French Court. We are greeted amiably enough by Charles and I think how lavish, how sumptuous, after the dreary English Court. I'd forgotten how much more agreeably we live in France. It seems one can become accustomed to almost any privation and, if exposed to it for long enough, can begin to consider it usual. Oh, beautiful France, where everything is done with such exquisite taste!

So far from acting the diplomat, she has quite the opposite effect. She whispers into the ear of her brother at every opportunity.

'My husband is a clumsy fool,' she says. 'I'm sick to the stomach of his mad schemes. He prefers the company of the greedy Despensers to mine.'

'Surely not, Sister,' says Charles.

'Indeed, it's so. His infatuation with the Younger borders on the perverse. I suspect the Younger is merely another Gaveston. They may, indeed, be lovers. Despenser is the most hateful man, devious and money-grabbing. People are talking and I'm sick with the humiliation. I tell you, my husband is not a normal man and I should not be exposed to such ridicule.'

'It's appalling that you suffer so, dear sister.'

'It's not a marriage,' says Isabella. 'It's a tragedy and a disgrace that a Queen should be so maligned and by her own husband.' Isabella closes her eyes and crosses her hands across her breast as though to compose herself.

'It is, indeed, disgraceful,' says Charles.

'And furthermore, he completely disregards the important matters of state and the Barons are whispering against him.'

'It is, indeed, a shame,' says Charles, patiently.

Poor Charles. He is in a muddy river up to his neck. I imagine he doesn't know what he can do about it all.

To be fair to the Queen, she persuades Charles to agree a truce between our two countries and not take back our possessions before Edward can manage to fulfil his duties of paying homage. Reluctantly, Charles agrees, although he looks confused that Edward is making such a bull out of a little mouse.

'These are valuable possessions,' he says, 'and no previous monarch has found it so difficult to pay homage for them. I would like to know what is so important to Cousin Edward that he is unable to spare the time to make the journey.'

Of course, I could tell him, as could all the other members of our party. Edward is unable to spare the time because Hugh le Despenser is unable to spare him. They are having far too much of a merry time together in England, playing tennis and jousting and drinking and jesting.

'The King is most disappointed,' murmurs Isabella, tactfully remembering why she is here. 'There are urgent matters that require his Royal Presence, indeed, matters so urgent that he finds it necessary to forgo the delights of the French Court.'

When she chooses to be, Isabella is a diplomat; in this the King is fortunate. Charles is understandably even more confused.

With me, she's both temperamental and unpredictable and it's a strain when one does not know what to expect. Sometimes she will talk to me in quiet confidence; other times it is as though I'm a bellyache to her. One evening, when we are alone in her chamber, she says to me:

'I've been thinking, Ellie. I have been thinking it might be fitting if my son were to pay homage for his father. I'm missing the little Prince so desperately. I shall write to my husband immediately and demand that he bestows a suitable title upon him. Then he may come to England to be with his mother and his Uncle King Charles. What do you think of that, Ellie?'

This suggestion cheers me considerably, for I too am missing the little Prince and can imagine nothing more delightful than showing him the sights and teasing him without mercy and coaxing him to kiss me even though he doesn't wish it. I hope tiny John will not be sad without him. At least he has his new little sister to distract him, my almost-namesake. John is still too small to know it is foppish to play with girls.

'Oh please,' I say. 'You must write immediately. You may dictate to me, for my calligraphy is very fine and it will save the strain on your gentle wrist. All you need sign is your name.'

In this way, I see exactly what she writes and can make suggestions which may sway the King to agree.

To our joy, the King does agree and even sooner than we'd expected, the little Prince, now created Duke of Aquitaine, is on his way to amuse us. I cannot wait to see him.

The Ceremony goes very well. Prince Edward is dignified and co-operative and I can see that King Charles and all his retinue are enormously impressed by his dignity as he pay homage. He looks just like one of the cherubs painted on the ceiling, still boyishly full-cheeked and round of chin. Yet he holds himself erect and speaks slowly and distinctly. I'm proud of him, as though he were my own flesh and blood.

A tall knight, whom I recognise instantly as does the Queen, approaches Edward after the ceremony and pats him on the head, an action which displeases Edward, for his eyes flash blue fire at the knight. Prince Edward draws himself up to his full height and glares witheringly.

'And who might you be, Sire?' he enquires, and the words come out awkwardly, for his voice is just breaking. In this respect, his maturity is a little late. The knight and several other nobles laugh at this little Prince, so conscious of his royal dignity and so proper.

'My name is Roger Mortimer,' says the knight. 'I'm admiring your fine robes and manly stature. Not to mention the magnificent crown.'

But Prince Edward is no fool and knows when he's being patronised; whereupon he lifts up his head and, as far as he is able from his reduced height, gazes with chilling scorn upon the knight. Unfortunately, this provokes yet more merriment. I can see a situation beginning to develop, for if they continue to bait him, he will stamp his foot and thus spoil the effect he has created.

Isabella has the same impression, for she says to me quickly, 'Go Ellie, and fetch the Prince.' So I slip between the nobles and grasp Edward's hand.

'I'm required to take the Prince to his mother,' I mutter.

Disgustedly, Edward shakes off my maternal hand-grip, but follows me meekly away from the nobles.

'I'm glad you rescued me, Ellie,' he says. 'I don't like that Mortimer fellow. He has hard eyes, and he's cunning.' Then he adds, almost as an afterthought, 'But I think my mother likes him very much.'

So he's noticed! Noticed how Isabella's clear blue eyes stray constantly in the direction of the big, dark-haired knight with the chilling black eyes. Aware he has made a conquest, Mortimer returns her interest with sardonic satisfaction.

'Nonsense. You're imagining things,' I reply lightly.

'Ellie, you know I don't imagine things.'

No, he's not imagining things, for in the weeks and months which follow, it is clear the relationship between Queen Isabella and Roger Mortimer is growing more intimate, more unsuitable. He is wily enough to maintain an attitude of control. Never does he defer to Isabella, but treats her as an equal. I think she finds this attractive, for it is irksome for a passionate woman to be constantly deferred to. This I can understand.

But it's not so simple. For the balance of power between them shifts so subtly over the days, it's scarcely noticeable. It's Prince Edward who points this out to me.

'Mortimer treats my mother as if she is just his woman,' says Edward. 'He acts as if he is nobler than she.'

And, indeed, he does. They're no longer equals, for he controls her and she acquiesces and does his bidding. How he's achieved this power over her, I cannot tell, but she's besotted with him. Nor does she make any attempt to hide her infatuation from others and I feel I must urge her to be cautious, even at the risk of being sent back to England.

'Dear Isabella, people are saying that you are allowing Mortimer too much freedom with your person. They say you have allowed him to become your master.'

'Oh, Ellie, you must know how people talk about a Queen, whatever she does. And all of it cannot be flattering.'

'I'm urging you to take precautions to preserve your dignity and royal prerogative.' I can hear that my own voice has gone high with irritation.

'Are you scolding me, Ellie?' There is an edge to her voice and I know I must be careful. Placing my hands behind my back, I lower my chin in an attitude of submission.

'I apologise, my Lady. I don't mean to be impudent. I'm merely concerned for your welfare and continued power and prosperity.'

'I am happy, Ellie. Gentle Mortimer makes me very happy. He's amusing and clever and… and everything my husband is not.'

Now I find it difficult to suppress my frustration with Isabella and I begin to bang about, slamming down the china washing bowl upon the little table, lifting it up and slamming it down again. If I continue like this it will crack, then Isabella will be furious.

'Ellie!' There is unmistakeable warning in her tone. I close my eyes and count to fifty-three. I pick up the water jug and fill up the bowl for her toilette.

'At least my brother has agreed to withdraw his forces from Gascony,' she remarks.

There follows a protracted period of correspondence between the Queen and her husband, and between King Edward and King Charles, and the subject discussed is Hugh le Despenser.

'The man is a villain and I fear him. What will you do to allay my fears?' says Isabella's letters to her husband.

'Your unprovoked attacks on my dear brother, Despenser, are unfounded. He honours you with all of his heart,' writes Edward to his wife.

I don't know what the two Kings say to each other, although from snatches of news I glean from the Court grapevine, Edward continues to insist that the Queen is irrational and his dear Hugh is blameless. He has no intention of acting against him or his father.

The Queen frets and fumes, her face pinched and pale. While her husband, no doubt, continues to enjoy his peasant pursuits with his favourite at his side.

'I have a letter here from my cousin in Wiltshire,' says Isabella one day. 'She says England is in a state of anarchy. The laws are flouted and there are not enough sheriffs. Where sheriffs exist, they're corrupt. There's an epidemic of robberies and murders all over the countryside. Nor are taxes being collected. She doesn't know what will become of England if I do not return and talk sense into my husband.'

Isabella gives a short bark of a laugh. 'Huh! As if anyone has ever been able to make the King see sense!'

Then the Pope pokes his big nose into the mess and makes a bigger one. Edward has been bombarding him with letter and pleas. Now Charles has been instructed by the Pontiff to return the adulterous Queen to her abandoned husband. To refuse will bring about his excommunication.

Even I can see that the French King's has no choice, however badly he feels for his sister. Excommunication is bad enough for a commoner or noble. For a King it is a disaster. Charles and his advisors remain closeted in close discussion for several hours, and although I listen avidly at their door, I hear nothing, for their voices are hushed.

Warned in advance of the turn in events by a kindly ally, a cousin at the French Court, Isabella decides to take matters into her own hands. It's through Guy that I discover exactly what she intends to do.

'I cannot be with you tonight, my love,' says Guy. 'I have important matters to attend to.'

'What can be more important than our love?' I say, for I'm in one of my romantic moods and I try to embroider every base passion with a higher quality. It's a weakness of my sex to which I seldom succumb, but now I do succumb, for I don't wish to spend the night alone.

'Nothing is more important than our love', says Guy soothingly. 'It will still be there. You can sleep without me for one night.'

'I shall be lonely. And I shall be cold, for my room is miserable and draughty. And I'm hot for you, my love.'

'You're a spoiled brat.'

'I'm not. You're mean to say so. I do everything for you that a woman can do for a man.'

I stick out my lower lip, for usually that serves to break down Guy's resolve. But he slams his hand down on the table which startles me, for he is generally mild of temper.

'Ellie, I will tell you and then you will understand. The Queen plans to raise an army and invade England in order to overthrow the King and establish order. It is a bold plan, so bold that I'm on fire with the very idea of it and I have much to do.'

'But Guy, she cannot… she cannot…' I'm overcome with the enormity of such an enterprise.

'The Queen has no choice. Her brother will not risk supporting her against the express wishes of her husband.'

'She hasn't mentioned a word of it to me.' I'm peeved that such important plans have been bandied about without reference to me. Even more so, that Guy has the news before me. And, he's full of himself, full of his important knowledge and his important plans and I have to suppress a desire to slap him.

'I've been entrusted to handling the

diplomatic negotiations, and I have a list here of people I must talk to, to see how such an undertaking might be effected with as much speed as possible. The Queen is impatient to proceed. Then I have to meet with Mortimer to discuss the findings… But, Ellie, you must speak of this to no one, for to do so might send me to my death.'

I sink my head into my hands. Guy is sounding more like a waffling politician every moment. Where is my carefree lover? He is gone inside his head and forgotten all about his cock.

'It can wait until tomorrow.'

'Ellie, it cannot wait until tomorrow. It cannot wait at all. Don't you see the possibilities?

It's clear there is no swaying him, for he believes himself indispensable. Nothing can sway a man who is fanatical about his own importance. Therefore, I must subjugate my baser human urges and sacrifice them for England.

Or must I?

There's always an alternative.

The alternative is broad of shoulder and has more muscles than a French fisherman. There's a look in his eye of devilment and one corner of his mouth curls up to one side when he winks one of those devilish eyes. If the left eye winks, the left side of the mouth curls and vice versa. It is almost impossible to wink your left eye and curl the right side of your mouth. After Guy has left me, I practise in my mirror for many minutes, but I cannot do it without making an ugly face.

213

What trivialities we find to distract ourselves with, when deprived of our deepest desires!

CHAPTER 21

Vengeance in Mind

My mind is a whirlwind, in sympathy with my life. We're off again.

It's not unexpected in light of recent events, but it's so sudden I've no time to prepare myself.

'Am I to lose you so soon after I have found you?' murmurs my winking French fisherman. 'Come to my chambers. I have a present for you.'

There's just enough time to collect the present, although I'm almost left behind as the French fisherman wants to give me something more to remember him by. Urging him to haste, I allow him to fix the clasp around my neck, give him a peck on the cheek and I'm off, my feet hardly touching the floor, back to my own quarters and Guy.

We're leaving almost immediately. At least, I trust it shall be we and not just them, for Mortimer asks: 'Is the Lady Eleanora to accompany us?'

Isabella regards me slowly, considering. It's a worry to me that she needs to consider at all. Would they think of sending me back to my father and sisters? Licking my lower lip, I allow it to droop and open my eyes wide at Mortimer. I don't like pandering to him, but the consequences if he's not pandered to are dire to contemplate. That I should be left behind! That I should miss this new adventure!

And that Guy would be leaving without me and God only knows what temptations he may find. He may swear on his life; he may believe every promise he makes to me, but the mind of man is fickle and plays tricks in a lover's absence. Of course, I know I am not above reproach, for I'm frequently unfaithful to Guy, but that's different. I know what I'm doing. And I always keep a special part of myself for Guy, even when I am pleasuring another man. I'm faithful in my heart, if not my body.

I don't much like Isabella's expression. Sensing I have little support there, I concentrate my energies on Mortimer.

A tiny smile lifts the corners of Mortimer's mouth. He's a handsome man despite his cruel face, and also red-blooded, not impervious to female wiles. I try to squeeze out a tear, but cannot. I must ask Lady Margaret how she does it. However, this doesn't matter, for Mortimer says, 'It would be an unkindness to leave the Lady Eleanora behind, for there may be repercussions.'

'Humph,' says Isabella, raising her eyebrows at me and I wonder if she suspects that Mortimer looks upon me with an approving eye.

'Repercussions! What nonsense! She's not in England now; she's in her native France. And I suspect she has much to amuse her here at the French Court, what say you, Eleanora?'

'Yes, my Lady,' I gabble. 'There may be repercussions. For our enemies are everywhere, even here, and I'll be unprotected. Everyone knows I'm your loyal friend and that I have your ear and serve you loyally, and I may be tortured or racked or strappadoed or burnt on a great fire, and I cannot bear great pain, my Lady, and although I'm loyal and brave, the torments are beyond belief and I may be forced to speak, even though every thought in my head tells me not to, and...'

Isabella waves her hand at me, very fast, up and down from a limp wrist, a wave that says, 'Oh, do be quiet, you're splitting my head.'

'She shall come,' says Roger Mortimer, 'so long as she behaves herself.' He shows his authority by placing his be-ringed right hand on the nape of her neck. 'Do you understand, Ellie?'

'Yes,' says Isabella heavily. 'So long as she behaves herself.' She glares at me, hard and long.

Somewhere, along the way, I seem to have lost my Isabella's adoration and I cannot imagine why this is. But then, she has never been constant. It's not in her nature. I promise them, with my hand on my heart, that I shall behave myself and be the epitome of utter decorum. My necklace sparkles delightfully at my throat.

First we set sail for the Netherlands. I decide I'm not a sailor, for yet again, I spend almost the entire voyage bent double, spewing into the foam. I prefer Guy to stay away from me at these time for I feel wretched. I'm certain by now he must be full of derision for me, for there is nothing My Ladyish about spilling your guts out until your stomach is empty. If I were a man, I would have nothing to do with me at such times.

We're sailing in response to an invitation of Sir John of Hainaut. I've never been to the Netherlands before and it's very flat and very green. The scenery is uninteresting if one loves hills and valleys. However, it's good for fast travelling and soon we are at the Castle of Count William of Hainaut.

Everything is smart and bright here. Everything is in excellent repair. There are one hundred different kinds of floor and wall tiles in glowing colours and beautiful patterns. The tapestries and draperies are heavily embroidered and the furnishings are the height of fashionable comfort. How I envy the Ladies who live here in such luxury! It's not fair. Everywhere servants are striving to maintain cleanliness and beauty. The Castles of England are mere shadows in grey and black by comparison, with plenty of vermin thrown in for good measure.

And it's here Prince Edward meets the daughters of Sir William. I glance at Edward and see he's stirred by these four nubile maidens. This is a relief, for he's meant to be stirred. They are all gowned-up in their very best and giggle a little, as young maidens are wont to do. I think they look a jolly crowd of maidens and I cannot help but compare their sisterly togetherness with the fraught relations between Charlotte, the Runt and me. I feel a stab of envy for their sibling happiness.

'Oh, Ellie'! whispers Edward to me. 'Oh Ellie!'

'Do you like them, Edward?'

'Indeed,' he says with considerable relish. 'I like them well.'

It's clear he likes Joanna most of all. But the next day, he changes his allegiance to Isabel, then Margaret, then Philippa. I feel a little sad that the fickle nature of man is formed at such an early age. Then I remind myself that he's only just matured, that this may be his first experience of maidens viewed as something very different from himself. I say a special prayer that he makes the right choice.

If this is what the Queen has in mind, then King Edward is going to be tearing out his golden curls. For already he's negotiating the marriage of Edward with Eleanor of Aragon. I'm struck, all at once, by the extent of Isabella's cunning. She plans to trade-off her son to one of Sir William's daughters in return for an army to supplement our meagre forces.

How she has changed, for now she will stop at nothing to achieve her ambitions. Yet I hardly see her now. She's here, there and everywhere, and so is Mortimer and so is Guy. United, they campaign to muster support.

'She's a fine and proud Lady,' I hear Sir John, who is Sir William's older brother, say to his wife. 'We should assist her, for her situation is unconscionable.' Isabella is giving an excellent impression. She's serious, speaks with careful reserve and wears sombre clothing in dark colours like a widow. And that is how the Dutch Court sees her, as a widow, alone, defenceless, trying her best to salvage what she can in spite of her condition.

Who could resist her? They gather around her in their zeal, fired by notions of chivalry. They travel from far and wide just for a sight of her. She is all Charm and Innocent Grace. Once they have seen her, their loyalty is sealed. Eventually, her retinue numbers almost 3,000.

'It's done,' she announces on September 23rd, as she returns from her walk around the battlements with Mortimer. 'We're ready and we shall sail tomorrow.' She's satisfied with her decision and there is a spring in her step I haven't seen for a long time.

'When shall I see these fine maidens again?' asks Edward. He avoids my gaze as he waits for an answer.

'Soon. And you shall be married to one of them.'

'That's what I am not certain about, Ellie. They're pretty and I like them well. But I'm young and I'm not sure what's right.'

'At least you can choose from four,' I remind him. 'Most princes have to take what they get, whether they like it or not.' Then I add, 'And remember, they don't get to choose either, for there is only one of you.'

He looks a little alarmed at this, but decides I'm joking and gives me a playful shove.

'Whoever I choose shall consider herself most fortunate among women,' he says.

'Indeed, you consider yourself a fine fellow!'

'Indeed, Ellie, I do. Surely you must agree.'

I do agree, but I shall certainly not tell him so, for his head is swollen enough already. I make a dash at him, but he side-steps to avoid me and then he's gone, laughing and whooping. It's impossible to catch him, for now he's tall and fleet of foot and can out-run me easily. My only weapon is cunning, so I bide my time, for I shall catch him out in a practical joke. He is not yet as cunning as me, but he will learn.

We're escorted in fine style by the fleet of Dutch ships into the Port of Harwich. All looks quiet and serene, and there is no sign of hostility along the coastline of England, although the archers are ready, just in case.

I'm so excited, straining my eyes to see, taking in the sights of golden English beaches, white English cliffs and behind them, stately English trees, thatched English houses.

They are all there, on deck, staring at England as though she were holding her skirts up. Prince Edward stands close to the Queen, too close, for he's now a young man. Is he going to be a Mummy's boy? On Isabella's other side stands Mortimer, in his fine red surcoat and you can see how well he thinks of himself by his manner of standing. One hand on his hip, his chin raised so he can regard the scene down his long, cunning nose.

And the effusive Jean de Hainaut, who dotes upon the Queen, causing more than a sour look from Mortimer. He's talking to a Dutch Lord and the Earl of Kent. I bless the soul of the Earl of Kent, for he's the sweetest creature you could meet. Not particularly handsome, but he has a kind face and a soft smile.

Everyone except Mortimer looks haggard from the onerous journey we've undertaken, for the storm rendered the entire company sick since leaving the Dutch coast. Except for Mortimer. The horses on board are whinnying and stamping about their stalls, for they have sensed the fear. For the three-day duration of the crossing, I have had to hold my nose to avoid the stink of the horses and the spew that makes the deck too slippery to walk on safely.

I'm so glad to have my feet on firm ground at last. At last, we're en route to our first stopping place, Walton Abbey. Isabella sits on her palfrey with her son beside her and I see how she clutches at his hand as they jolt along the narrow streets. I'm uncomfortable, for my horse is skittish, but soon Harwich is behind us and we are in the open countryside. I give the horse a good kick and he settles down. Men and horses need to know who is in charge of them.

Yet, I see nothing has changed. We pass a village where five elderly women have been hanged for witches. They're all displayed in a tidy line from a large oak branch, their ragged raiments around the spindles of their legs stirring in the wind like so many old cloths put out to dry. Their swollen tongues protrude from their toothless mouths like huge, pus-filled boils. Three younger women are weeping at their feet, probably daughters or granddaughters. I pity these relations. Perhaps the old women were a burden on the purses of the young women's husbands. In such cases, accusations of witchcraft lighten the demands on the family budget. Old women are little use to anyone.

Further on, we see a closed cart, rumbling behind two stout black mares and I'm intrigued. There's a tiny window at the side with just one bar and I peer through it as I pass. The taut face of a young man stares back at me and I long to ask him who he is and what he's done, but I'm intimidated by that bleak stare. The driver doesn't look at me and I won't demean myself by addressing him.

'It's a highwayman who's been captured for the bounty on his head,' hisses Mortimer in my ear. Mortimer enjoys airing his knowledge.

'I know. I've seen many such rogues on my travels.'

When we arrive at Walton, the men enquire about various lodgings and people are sent off in all directions. Isabella's party is shown into the Abbey, where we can hope for a peaceful night's rest.

After I have directed the servants about the stowing of my belongings, I go to seek out Isabella, to offer any services she may need. Although she seems to need me less than ever, preferring the attentions of the clumsy Lady Margaret, which fair gets up my nose. As I reach her room, a figure is approaching in the opposite direction, his familiar coat of arms stretched across his chest. I slink back against the wall so he shall not see me there. He enters my Lady's chamber and I tiptoe up to the door and listen carefully.

'You seem not yourself, my sweet Mortimer,' says Isabella.

'I shall not be sleeping with you tonight, Isabella,' he says brutally and without any further explanation, he exits the chamber, almost knocking me to the floor. 'Lady Ellie,' he barks, 'Were you listening at the door?'

'Of course not, my Lord. I was about to enter to see to my Lady.'

'See to her, then,' growls Mortimer. 'I shall not be seeing to her tonight.'

Reluctantly, I enter the chamber. Isabella is crying. When women get older, they shouldn't cry; it's not becoming. They should scold and rage and get their own way and brook no resistance. I hope my dear Isabella is not losing her spirit as quickly as she is losing her looks.

'He's jealous,' whimpers Isabella. 'Ellie, he's jealous of that funny, little round Jean de Hainaut. Did you ever hear anything so ridiculous?'

'Never, my Lady, but don't mind him. A little jealousy never did a man any harm. It will keep him eager for you, but for now you must allow him his little tantrum.'

'Do you really think so, Ellie?'

'I do not think. I know. You see, my Lady, when you are very beautiful, men are bound by their natures to be jealous. Why, I myself have experienced this difficulty and it's truly exasperating. Certain of my admirers have been so jealous of me that I have been fair beside myself.'

'Really, Ellie! *You*?' says Isabella with such innocent incredulity that I am grossly insulted. I stifle the urge to slap her. Instead, I begin to breathe deeply and she fixes her eyes upon my heaving breasts.

'Are you quite well, Ellie?'

'Quite well,' I snap. 'In fact, I feel much better than I look.'

'I'm glad, Ellie, for your good health is very important to me.'

I sigh with resignation. Perhaps she doesn't mean to offend me.

'Now come, Isabella, you need your rest. You've had a gruelling journey. It is best that tonight you sleep alone and untroubled.' I try not to add, 'The strain is beginning to show on your face,' but I'm afraid I do. She looks suitably startled, but I smile sweetly to confuse her. Then I put my hand on the top of her head to steady her, and begin to comb her hair. This pacifies her.

She allows me to help her prepare her for bed and I send Margaret and Joan packing with a cursory wave. As I lay her down I sing her a gentle lullaby, something I have not done for a long time. Her fair lashes rest upon her cheek and she looks once more like the untouched young girl she once was.

'Again, Ellie, for that was so beautiful.'

At least, Isabella thinks my voice beautiful. I oblige her because she's my Queen, but I wonder who will sing me a lullaby to send me to sleep, for my head is buzzing so. I shall have to sing myself to sleep. So I do, and surprisingly my head empties and the next thing I know it is daylight and I'm wide awake and ready for anything.

Yet, in spite of my loyalty to Isabella and the support I owe my lover, I have just one heartfelt wish. I wish it were possible for me to warn the King of the danger that threatens him. What chance has he when betrayal comes from where he least expects it?

Isabella is proud of her achievement. Proud of her Kingly son, proud of her dark-eyed escort, proud of the deep-hearted approval and love that surrounds her. She looks stunning in her new Parisian gown, purple velvet with a tight bodice and delicious full skirt. It's the latest fashion. She has a dozen more packed away in her chest.

Sometimes I cannot resist taking them out and looking at them, then carefully folding and replacing them. I'm thrilled at the thought that one or two might come my way in due course. Much time and effort have I spent thinking of ways to induce her to give me one. But they are so finely made it will be an eternity before one is sufficiently imperfect to pass on. I could, of course, arrange a small accident, for it might be difficult to replace a lost button or two.

'What are you doing with my gowns, Ellie?' she says, surprising me in the guilty act one day.

'I was looking to see if all the buttons on the sleeves are secure,' I reply quickly, for I have already rehearsed the answer for such an occasion. 'I'm sorry.'

'Why are you sorry, Ellie, if you are only looking for badly-sewn buttons?' she asks.

'I think Lady Ellie is envious of your fine clothes, Isabella,' says Mortimer, who, as usual, is close behind her.

At this I blush to the roots of my skin. Guiltily, I drop the red gown I am holding to the floor, quickly take it up again before the dust clings. At these times, one never knows what's going to happen next. Fortunately, Isabella is in a good mood.

'You like that gown you're holding, Ellie? I can see you do. You may have it.'

It's still a mystery to me why she's so gracious. It may be she has merely had a good day, or wants to make an impression on Mortimer by showing her generosity. Either way, I don't care. I manage not to throw myself at her in an unseemly demonstration of gratitude, for she wouldn't like that. We're no longer maidenly confidantes as once we were, when she would simply have laughed and hugged me and told me not to be so silly.

'I don't know what to say, dear Isabella,' I murmur and I am almost genuflecting in front of her.

'Then say nothing,' she says lightly. 'Come,

sweet Mortimer, we have much to discuss.'

As she speaks, she's already removing her bodice. Clearly the discussions are more fruitful without raiments. I grab my gown with one hand and Margaret with the other and leave them to it.

'Oh, Lady Ellie, Lady Ellie.'

'Yes, Margaret.'

'May I have it when you tire of it.'

'I shall never tire of it.'

'May I borrow it? Just once.'

'You may not, Margaret. You've been ungracious to me of late.'

'I shall be gracious. I shall be most gracious, forever and ever.'

I beam at her, clutching my gown to my breast, feeling the smoothness of the fine material against my skin.

'We shall see, Margaret,' I reply and I feel a little of the power that Isabella feels when I'm slavering for one of her cast-offs and I swear it is the best feeling in the world.

I send Margaret off on some errand and I wend my way stealthily to my Lady's chamber and listen outside her door. I have sharp ears and can detect conversation easily, even on the other side of heavy doors. It's another of my talents, finely honed with frequent practice.

I have to wait until their huffing and puffing diminishes and I appreciate Guy more by the minute, for it sounds an exhausting business rather than a joyful one. Then Mortimer's breath explodes in a series of grunts like the snufflings of a wild boar.

'Your husband has been busy trying to rally support to raise an army against you. But his efforts have been in vain. It might be a different story if he was done with the Despensers, but he'll never see sense. Isn't it strange that our enemies are our greatest strength at this moment?'

'I've also heard he has started to neglect himself. He's not as proud and handsome as once he was,' replies Isabella.

'Handsome!' says Mortimer. 'I don't remember ever thinking your husband handsome.'

'Not as handsome as you, of course,' says Isabella. She's always conciliatory when she is with the pompous jackass. She should let him wonder a little, for then he would be more anxious to please. It always amazes me how some people make pleasure, then the moment they are done, fall to talking of the war, the weather or some other tedious, practical matter.

Then they begin again, with the huffing and puffing. I cannot believe it was so good the first time that they care to repeat it. All the same, their carnal activities awaken a desire in me and I go in search of Guy.

I feel a rush of excitement deep inside me. Half the delight of an assignation such as this is the delicious expectation. I hope Guy will be in a lighthearted mood so that I can ignite his passion.
I start to run, and I can feel my cheeks glowing hot as my hair starts to tumble down around my

shoulders. How lucky I am to have such delightful distractions. I hope Guy will always appreciate his good fortune in having me!

CHAPTER 22

Death to the Traitors

It takes a while, but eventually I find him with his hawk. It's a goshawk, I learn, and it sits as regally upon Guy's arm as King Philip once did upon the French throne. Its face is equally cruel. I have never seen a bird that looks so fierce, but I am no longer afraid of it.

'Ellie!' Guy cries. 'Are you after my cock again?' The bird gives a derisory squawk and I laugh and stroke him. Then Guy's gentle face turns grave. 'There's a serious matter I must tell you about,' he says. 'Even the Queen knows nothing of this yet. I do not know how to break the news to her.'

'What is it?'

'The King has sent out a proclamation. Death to the traitors who took part in the invasion of England. That's us, Ellie, you and me.'

A traitor's death! Me! But I was only following orders.

'But Guy, he cannot. He cannot put his wife and son to death.'

'They are the exceptions,' says Guy.

'You mean, a *traitor's* death to all who took part in the invasion except for Queen Isabella and Prince Edward?' I have to repeat it to absorb the true, terrible meaning. 'Precisely.'

'But she's the one who started it. Her and her obnoxious lover!'

Already I can feel the noose around my slender neck, its grip tightening as the cruel point of the butcher's knife hovers at my naked belly and the mob howls for my blood. I've never before imagined myself a victim of this grisly practice and the picture in my head moves me sorely. I clutch at Guy's arm so I shall not crumple to the ground.

'And Mortimer?' I ask, confused.

'Mortimer most of all for he's the Black Traitor.'

'Does the King mean it?'

'He may regret it later, but he certainly means it now.'

'It's outrageous!'

I'm feeling faint so I turn away from him and stumble to the shoemaker's trestle table and lay myself across it, face forward, with my legs splayed out, toes brushing the ground. I feel Guy's hand on my shoulder to reassure me. Then I realise he is not bent on reassurance, for I can feel the wind where the wind seldom ventures. He has pulled up my kirtle, the knave! Startled I twist my head around. The hawk is gone and Guy has exposed his own nakedness in all its potent glory.

'We cannot!' I yell. 'Not now! We may be hanged, drawn and quartered tomorrow.'

'Exactly so,' says Guy and proceeds, with stallion thrusts, to make me forget all about it. I am so lost in abandonment to my own pleasure that, for all I know, half the Court might be watching us. Such is the nature of carnal pleasure that when in its grip, we care little who looks on.

Later, I worry about this unexpected coupling, for I was not protected and it is my fertile time. So now I have two things to be anxious about.

Nothing happens, for we are both still here, unhanged, undrawn and unquartered. Nor I am with child, for the little red message arrives this very morning. Thanks to God. The next we hear is that Edward is gone to Bristol. For a while, we begin to feel a little safer. The constancy of the masses is with Isabella. In deference to their Queen, a mob strikes against the King's stalwart ally and spy, Bishop Stapledon, cutting off his head, thus proving their loyalty.

She's touched to receive the severed head of the unhappy Bishop via the Earl of Gloucester, as a present. I'm surprised she does not have it stuffed and mounted on her bedroom wall.

Immediately, she sets about raising more troops, enough men to confront the army of the King. Many Barons support her, including Henry of Lancaster, plus a few Bishops for good measure. Then Isabella makes a list of the King's mistakes. I help her. I feel less pity for the King since I learned he's happy to sacrifice me for a traitor, and throw myself into inventing many items for the list.

'You mustn't take it personally, Ellie,' Guy told me last night. 'You're merely one of several thousand.'

But I don't understand his argument. If you're hanged, drawn and quartered, how does it help to know two thousand, nine hundred and ninety nine others are suffering the same fate? It doesn't help one bit. It's one's own neck and one's own guts and one's own quarters which one holds in most affectionate regard. I value all my quarters exceedingly.

The Queen also offers a reward for the head of Hugh le Despenser.

'One thousand pounds, do you think Ellie?' she asks.

'Double it, my Lady. Make certain. You would not spoil a gown by going short of a button.'

'Well argued, Ellie,' says the Queen. 'Two thousand pounds for the head of Hugh le Despenser the Younger and cheap at the price.'

The Queen's army sets off for Bristol and the Castle is surrendered without bloodshed. All the people in Bristol are loyal to the Queen and they are vehement in their support. It's a wonderful sight to see, as they wave and call and throw flowers at her feet. Guy is up front with the men, but I follow behind, proud and erect on my piebald mare. I get the left over flowers. The moment she enters the Castle boundary, the Queen dismounts and, forgetting her dignity, runs calling for her daughters.

Little Eleanor and Joan, whom Edward had left in the care of a Lady, rush into their mother's arms and it's a touching sight. Eleanor's knees are bruised and scratched and her face grubby, for she should have been a boy. Joan is Mistress Perfect, clean and tidy in her little grown-up kirtle with her fair hair combed smooth.

What's not so touching a sight occurs some time later, when the Queen comes face to face with Big Hugh. He's old now and has lost weight. His spine is shortened and he has spindly legs. He asks for a fair trial in a proud but plaintive voice.

'I ask for justice,' he says, 'and a sentence befitting the position of a noble.'

But Isabella's patience has been too sorely tried. I feel a lump in my throat when he's immediately sent to the gallows, helpless and bewildered by events. But Isabella is right, even this bandy-legged old man is dangerous. To be a Despenser is sufficient unto itself. She shows no reticence in her eagerness for his death.

'Come Eleanor, come Joan,' she takes each daughter by the hand. 'We may watch from the window. See what happens to your mother's enemies. Watch him dance, my daughters, watch him dance.'

Joan squeals and covers her face with her little hands, not wanting to see yet peeping through her fingers. I understand her compulsion, her fascination with a sight too dreadful to contemplate but impossible to ignore. Eleanor has no such qualms and she jumps up and down in excitement, her cheeks round and rosy.

'I can see him dance! Oh, Mother, I can see him dance! Is it a jig, Mother?'

Isabella chortles and ruffles Eleanor's hair. 'Indeed. It's a Marcher Jig.'

Meanwhile, we know the King has attempted to take Little Hugh and Chancellor Baldock and a small retinue to Lundy Island. A few days later, news arrives that a storm forced them back to the mainland. So it goes on... Edward is here, Edward is there, Edward is everywhere.

He's not at large for long. In November he's captured and taken to Llantrissant. As for Little Hugh and Baldock, their time is come.

Isabella rubs her palms together and glows with satisfaction, for her plans have borne their sweetest cherries. I've never known her in such fine spirit and receive some pretty buttons to sew on the sleeves of my best gown. Buttons! It's a sad reflection on my position that I must be grateful for buttons, especially as Lady Margaret gets a jade pendant. The miscreants are surrendered to her and stand before her in all their abject misery, are finally at her mercy.

And God knows, she has little mercy left in her.

Of course, we join the procession. It's cosmopolitan. There are English and French and Dutch and a few Germans. All the Barons, all the Bishops, all the tradesmen, all their wives and children and aunts and uncles and cousins, all the servants, all the beggars, all the common people. Guy and me. We're all present to see justice done most thoroughly.

I remember the Channel crossing when Isabella's army sailed to invade England and we all were heartily sick, except for Mortimer. Well now, we all are merry, except for Little Hugh. Little Hugh who's now Big Hugh, for he has inherited his title from his father, much use it will be to him now. I cannot wait to see the Black Traitor receive his comeuppance.

Like Lancaster before him, he rides on a worn-out pony. Truly, it looks half-dead, carrying the immense weight of the tall, broad-shouldered man. But Hugh is growing more poorly by the moment. His skin has taken on a hue of palest green and sweat pours down his forehead and cheeks, moistening the drooping black moustache.

'Give him some water,' yells someone. 'He won't live to face his punishment.'

'Give him some water,' echoes the crowd, afraid that their entertainment will be withheld.

'It would best to give him water and leave him to die of typhoid,' says a woman. 'For his suffering would last longer.'

'It would be less interesting to behold,' says another.

Hugh le Despenser shakes his head, refusing the water, so a burly soldier pinches his nose and jerks back his head, while another pours filthy water into his open mouth. He makes the most horrid noises in his throat and I think he'll choke if they don't stop. He swallows. Finally they release him and the little pony struggles on. They will slaughter it for meat when the journey is done, but there will not be much to eat for he is a scrawny fellow.

Hugh receives a trial of sorts. There's no defence. There's no point in a defence, for we all know what he has done and that's enough to execute him ten times over. Although in truth, he's blamed for almost everything, including the defeat at Bannockburn, which I think is stretching credulity a little far.

It's all most satisfactory. He'll be hanged for a thief, drawn and quartered for a traitor and beheaded. I don't know what the beheading is for, but I make that up myself. Beheaded for me. For Lady Eleanora, who frequently took the whiplash from Isabella's tongue on account of the Dreaded Despensers.

It's the Day of Judgement for Despenser. Big Hugh is going straight to Hell! The idea sends a delicious shiver down my spine.

They dress him in black, for he is, after all, the Black Traitor. This looks well on him, for it matches his black eyes and black beard. He has his escutcheon reversed and sharp thorns pierce his skull and nettles are placed on his head. I see Isabella waiting at the place of execution and excitedly I wave to her and she waves back eagerly.

'Is my Lady in fine spirit?' I cry.

'Indeed, I am, Ellie.'

This is a relief to me, for she will be in a

generous mood after the execution and may feel inclined to reward me in some little matter. At least, she may forget our differences for a while, so that I may, again, take a few small liberties.

They make Hugh le Despenser climb a ladder and tie him up to face outward so the crowd can pelt him with foul-smelling muck. Then, they gather kindling to light a fire at the bottom. They cut off his... (I really do not like to say this, for it makes me shudder and even Guy turns away his face!) Anyway, these parts that were so precious to him and his lover are severed with one slice of a sharp knife and cast into the flames. His head lolls forward, and the noose tightens around his neck. I think by this time, he's unconscious and I think this is well. But the Queen isn't satisfied.

'Throw some water on his face,' she cries. 'He'll die before his punishment is ended.' Her face is florid and contorted as she cries out and it is the first time I have seen her look truly ugly, like a red demon with a sword in its belly.

'Throw water on his face,' echoes a soldier.

Some water is thrown on his face and his head jerks sideways with the impact, then topples forward again. I cannot tell whether he is alive or dead, for not an eyelid flickers, not a muscle twitches.

Then - the *drawing*. I cannot describe this for I cannot look. But when it is over, it's a bloody mess that hangs there, a mess of entrails and blood from the gouged cavity that was once his taut belly. My own belly heaves. A revolting pile of Little Hugh's guts sizzles in the fire below with his other parts. I turn away my face, but there is a slow drip, drip, drip of blood on the rungs of the ladder which I cannot block out. Even though I block my ears, I can still hear it.

'I've seen enough for now,' I remark lightly to Guy, for I don't wish to sound lily-livered. 'Let's go.'

'We'll miss the quartering and the beheading. That's the best part.'

'Oh, it will just be more of the same and it is beginning to rain. My head-dress will start to droop.'

We've almost completed our political campaign. One matter remains to be dealt with. The King's deposition.

King Edward is presently held at Kenilworth. On 20 January, 1327, I am told, a deputation goes to Kenilworth and confronts the King, who's appropriately dressed in black serge, for this is a grim day for him.

Most of the Barons are after his blood, for only the shedding of blood, they say, will protect the Queen. One or two speak up for him, including the Earl of Rochester, till he realises his support of the King will endanger his own life. A good man and brave, but even he is no match for the might of the ruthless Barons.

Just one young person has the courage to resist the powerful Barons, for Prince Edward states he will refuse the Crown if his father is harmed or forced to stand down. Nor will he be swayed by their rhetoric or their accusations. He lifts his chin very high as he states his position. Isabella is furious at her recalcitrant son.

'But, Edward, in this you must take the advice of your Mother.'

'I've told you what I have decided. I've nothing else to say.'

'I shall ask Mortimer to speak to you.'

Edward responds with a vile oath which turns Isabella pale. 'And I shall say the same to him,' announces Edward. His defiance is impressive.

Isabella sighs, but Edward is too big to be beaten. He is too young and idealistic not to be determined where justice is concerned.

'Ellie,' he whispers to me later. 'I must stand by my father. You do understand?'

'I understand. You're right.' I smile at him gently and squeeze his hand and he gives me an unexpected hug which brings a lump to my throat.

'Thank you, Ellie. For I am certain you are the only one who does understand.'

Isabella instructs the Earl of Leicester and the Bishop of Winchester to bully the King into agreeing to stand down. The King, by now, is severely browbeaten and no match for the strong-arm tactics of these ambitious men. Under their relentless badgering, he succumbs.

Some says this is weakness and cowardice, but I think these are unfair accusations. It would be difficult enough for a strong, man, experienced in law and politics to resist these belligerent Barons. The King is sensitive and gentle and nothing has prepared him for such a confrontation. He's stripped of his Crown, his titles, his rights and his precious royal dignity.

Humbled and miserable, he waits anxiously to see what fate the Queen has in store for him.

So, the Queen and her Consort rule. The people are behind them. For our loyalty, Guy receives a knighthood and I am officially Chief-Lady-in-Waiting to the Queen. I wish I'd never lied that I was Chief-Lady-in-Waiting before, for now I truly am, no one believes me and should I travel to France to visit my father and sisters, they will not believe me either.
I wonder if I can persuade Isabella to issue an Official Proclamation on the matter.

'I wish we could be rid of Mortimer,' says Edward.

'Hush, Sire,' says Guy. 'To speak so will cause you danger. Mortimer is a strong influence, both with your Mother and with the Barons. You must listen to me. You must bide your time and keep good counsel until you are ready.'

'When will I be ready?' frets Edward. 'How long before I'm strong enough to overthrow him?'

'In good time,' says Guy. 'Trust me, Edward, I'll be there for you when the time's right. Now, how about another jousting lesson?' Guy ruffles the young Prince's tousled hair, then takes his arm and strides off with him.

Guy has taken to tutoring the King in manly pursuits, as much as he can without raising undue suspicion. Sometimes I watch them wrestle and Guy pushes Edward as far as possible. Edward's confidence is growing and his body is responding. There are small but well-defined muscles in his arms and chest and his thighs have thickened so that he looks well on his horse. Besides building up his strength, these pursuits help to channel his boyish energy and take his mind away from dangerous plotting. With Guy's encouragement, he takes parts in tilts and tournaments and acquits himself well for one of his tender years. It's fine training for a military career.

But, always it comes back to the same thing.

'When I kill Mortimer, my father can be released from that terrible place.'

'One day,' says Guy.

Indeed, Guy and I have changed sides. For although I'm still loyal to Isabella, I despise her avaricious Consort and I'm furious that the little King is treated so badly, for he's no more than a pawn in their convoluted games. Although the deposed King has his many faults, none of them justify his incarceration. I thank God he's fairly treated at Kenilworth by Henry of Lancaster.

Even so, daily letters are received from him by the Queen complaining about this and that, especially his separation from his precious children. I know they miss him too, especially Edward. The Queen sends her husband presents to assuage her guilt, or, rather, orders me to send them. Then she forgets about him. She has eyes only for black-hearted Mortimer.

I cannot help but remember the good qualities possessed by the deposed King. Although I have not quite forgiven him for threatening me with a traitor's death, however impersonal that threat may have been.

On 1 February 1327, little King Edward III is crowned by Walter Reynolds. He is just fourteen years old. Henry of Lancaster is Chief of the Council of Regency. My Lord Mortimer is not on the Council, but it represented by other knights who are loyal to his cause. In this way he can arrange matters to his satisfaction without having to take the consequences if the plans misfire. For Mortimer must never be wrong!

Henry of Lancaster is highly ambitious and wants to be Earl of Lancaster, in the stead of his executed brother. This suits Roger Mortimer. I hear them discussing it.

'He's our man,' says Mortimer. 'It would be well to humour him, for he can carry much of the responsibility. He will be an adequate scapegoat to our cause.' Thus, he confirms my earlier judgement.

Even so, these words send a shiver of fear up my spine. I would not be Henry of Lancaster for the world.

CHAPTER 23

The Execution

Things never stay the same. There have been whispers, and I've always found whispers to be far more dangerous than roars. We've heard of a conspiracy to rescue the King, and two brothers, one a friar, are suspected of its provenance. Their name is Dunhead, but I've never heard of them before this day. They possess much property in the region of Kenilworth Castle and that's enough to send the Queen and her sycophants' into a state of shock and fear.

As a result of this, the deposed King Edward is speedily removed to Berkeley Castle for security purposes. Unfortunately, the worthy brothers then try to help him escape, but they're foiled.

It's enough for Mortimer. He glowers, glares, breaks vases and whips innocent servants, while the children run and hide.

'Who are these miscreants that they dare to oppose me?' he bawls.

One would think he was himself the King and not merely the Queen's Consort. I'm so afraid that I seek out Guy and tell him of Mortimer's fury.

'Be calm, Ellie,' he says. 'There is nothing to be done about it. We must wait. The King's not ready yet. His father wouldn't wish us to make a bad decision for his son because of this.'

Dropping my forehead forward onto his chest I take a deep breath, wanting him to put his arms around me and to feel like a small child in the safe embrace of my father. He senses my need and holds me close and I think how I like the manly smell of him.

'He cannot take over the reins of power for some time yet. We must wait.'

'Guy, what about…deadly nightshade? Once I tried it and it almost worked. I think, perhaps, the brew wasn't strong enough.'

'Ellie, don't even think of such a thing. Imagine what might happen to you. What might happen to both of us. We must endure it, Ellie.'

'It's not we who must endure, but Edward's poor father.'

'Edward will have to be told.'

'Indeed, he will have to be told. But who's to tell him? For I doubt the Queen will dare to breathe a word. It will be dreadful indeed should he hear it from some other source.'

'I shall tell him,' says Guy.

For three days the King shuts himself in his chambers and will not grant audience to anyone, not even me. My heart aches for him. I hear him crying softly, alone and uncomforted, without hope or illusion. His mother doesn't venture near him and I can only surmise she is too ashamed.

'Mistress Ellie,' says Mortimer.

'Lady Eleanora,' I correct him.

'This is no time for jest, my Lady.'

'I'm not jesting. My Lady will suffice.'

Mortimer heaves an enormous sigh and regards me in that way men have when trying to make a woman feel like a woman, in other words, something much less than a man. I return his gaze with equal severity.

'The King is ailing fast,' says Mortimer.

'I'm not surprised, shut up as he is in that awful place. We have all heard of his agonies.' Mortimer begins to pace the room and I sense his discomfort.

'He couldn't expect to be confined at Kenilworth forever, being waited upon and cosseted. In any case, he did nothing but complain, despite his kindly treatment by Henry of Lancaster.' Mortimer stops his pacing and stretches himself to his full height, all the more to look down upon me.

But I'm not impressed, nor am I finished with him:

'So he was sent to Berkeley Castle, where he now languishes under the eye of his enemy Thomas of Berkeley. A fine thing, to expose him to a host who has a grudge against him,' I point out. There's much truth in my words, for some time ago, Berkeley had committed a political offence and Edward had him confined to Berkeley Castle. The Queen had Thomas released on her return to England. What's more, this gentleman is married to Mortimer's whining daughter.

'I think it's outrageous to give Thomas of Berkeley authority over the King.'

'The *deposed* King!'

'Deposed or not, it's unjust.'

I cannot help but feel concerned about the King. Although I try not to think about his plight, it plays on my mind and I feel a pang in my heart that I'm unable to suppress. I ask myself why I'm bothered. He's a man and not even an ex-lover. What is more, he is not even a woman's man. He is not strong in character and most people regard him with a degree of contempt.

Yet… I like him, even though he takes a great deal of understanding. I remember his many kindnesses towards me and others. For Edward has been kind even when there was no need. Even when kindness didn't offer promise of reward, which is surely the most genuine kindness there can be. I would like to do something to help ease his pain.

News of the deposed King's fate reaches us in dribs and drabs from many quarters, from servants' gossip (which travels as though it had wings) to information exchanged at banquets and other gatherings across the land.

He's in a tiny cell in Berkeley Castle, and has only rats and cockroaches and big hairy spiders for company. And ugly furry bats that flap their wings in his face at night.' I shiver, for these are the spectres of my own nightmares. Surely the King's condition cannot be so dismal.

I do not know if he has any consolation in these dire hours, someone to pray for him, to pray with him. How rank must Death smell in the dark, odorous air inside those stone walls. I can imagine, and it chokes me deep in my throat so that I awaken at night, gasping for air. I dream incessantly of travelling down endless corridors, descending long flights of narrow stone steps that lead to the oppressive inner recesses of this hellish place. My stomach churns, and I know fear full well.

The smells must beggar belief.

They say he has a small nightlight burning just outside the cell but apart from that, he can see little. It is small, so very small. A tiny window, high up, which overlooks a bleak courtyard. The stones beneath his feet are thick with slippery substance, maybe congealed food and bodily wastes, slopped out of barrels and pots carried by careless guards.

He slumps in a corner on a stone bench, ragged and dirty and panting with short, shallow gasps. He is thin, almost skeletal. His face is emaciated, yellow. The once golden curls are lank and lustreless like dried glass. Filthy matter on the floor covers his ankles and feet.

How can he bear it? I am sure I would expire from the putrid air.

At first he would plead for mercy, for the Queen to be told what was being done to him. She would not have him so mistreated. He is shaved with muddy water from a ditch and is ashamed to be seen thus.

There's a deep well in the floor; if you look closely you can see it. That is where the smell comes from, for they fill it with putrid matter, the corpses of slaughtered animals and other disgusting things, even the rotting corpses of human bodies. They hope he might die from the stench.'

I know one thing. I'm helpless. I cannot even think of a pithy Bible quotation to comfort myself, and my pity is of no use to him. There's nothing I can do. A feeling of faintness overcomes me.

He asks after his son, wondering if he is safe or if Mortimer has harmed him.

No one can help him now. We can only pray for him, and pray that death will come speedily for him.

Then, one day, a messenger comes. Screaming had been heard from the castle; loud, unearthly, ear-splitting, heart-cleaving screaming. Screaming like no screaming anyone had ever heard before, nor would ever wish to. But there was no shutting out its piercing urgency. It continued, long and loudly. People clutched at each other, fear seeping from their pores in a ghastly steam, almost tangible.

The screams continue. Would they never stop? This was what was so unbearable. How could such pain continue unabated? What manner of agony is it that endures for so long, and resists God's merciful blessing of unconsciousness or death?

Someone said 'It's a vixen for they scream most viciously.'

It was no vixen. The appalling cries were those of a living human, undergoing a tortuous death. Guy told me, as gently as he could tell such a terrible story.

They fashioned a horn to assist perfect penetration.

In a blinding flash of horror, I know. His jailors had devised a punishment, a death, that they considered would fit the crime. They have shoved the red-hot-spit into the very place where Gaveston and, more recently, Hugh Dispenser, so passionately plunged their own Weapons of Love.

Poetic justice. They describe it as poetic justice!

I'm trembling. 'But Guy, that is not even justice, let alone poetic justice. No one deserves such an end. No one. Not even Robert the Bruce.' I stare at him, willing him to tell me he is joking and that it's not true. For it cannot be true. I cannot let it be true.

Guy holds me close to him because I'm shivering violently and my knees threaten to give way.

'What's this?'

I recognise that loud voice immediately. I turn to stare at Mortimer who has, in his insolence, invaded my private quarters. At the sight of my ravaged face, realisation dawns on his own swarthy features.

'In heaven's name, you fool,' he yells. 'You've already told her! I said to wait for me to deal with her.'

'Get out,' snarls Guy.

I cannot take any more and I run, ducking out of Guy's embrace and slipping past Mortimer, who clutches at me as I pass. I run from their sight, from Mortimer's searching glare. Burying my face into the folds of my cloak, I run as fast as I can, till my heart seems fit to burst from my chest. I look back over my shoulder. No one is pursuing me. Indeed, if Mortimer has given chase, he would catch me easily, for he's lithe and strong. The two of them are probably engaged in combat but I can no longer concern myself with that.

My pity is so great that I feel I'm personally bereaved. I think of Edward frolicking with Gaveston in the wood, his bright blonde hair glowing in the moonlight, his lithe body twisting this way and that. There was something almost innocent in their games. Great Virgil said, 'Everyone is dragged on by their favourite pleasure.' If only the warring barons were as wise as Virgil.

Then I think of Edward at his Coronation, so proud, so promising. How his eyes met so meaningfully with those of his peacock-plumed lover. I think of the gentle way he spoke with the poor, how he enjoyed a jest with a friend, how he cared even for his beasts. I remember how he kept my secret, when I exchanged the deceased Odo for the new Odo. How he never did anything truly mean except what he couldn't help because of his nature. Were he not a King, he need never have married.

Fate and Mother Nature played many cruel tricks on the dead King.

He wasn't a bad man.

It's only some time later, as I huddle under a great oak somewhere in this strange and suddenly hostile countryside, that I fully understand my predicament. My loyalty to the dead King makes me vulnerable.

Yes, Mortimer knows I know he's implicated in Edward's appalling execution. And that makes Mortimer my most dangerous enemy. This means I'm in the gravest danger I have ever encountered in all of my life. By now he may even have killed Guy.

How I long for Guy. I long for his strong, sturdy arms around me, promising protection, his soft voice whispering words of love. And if he says these words to have his way with me, that's fine too. I long for the rowdy happiness we shared together, a happiness that overcomes everything, even betrayal.

For some people, the bond goes beyond that of the ordinary cut and thrust of human mating. For some people, nothing changes that bond, for possession does not enter into it except, maybe, on a physical level which doesn't endure. For people who feel this, it doesn't need to be said; it's simply there and they know it. I don't need to forgive Guy anything. It's enough that Guy is Guy and I am myself.

I finger Guy's pearl pendant around my neck and I'm comforted. Softly I begin to recite The Lord's Prayer.

253

I must return to my Queen, for only in her will I find protection from her violent lover.

CHAPTER 24

The Trials of Being King

The new young King is waiting for me on my return. He tries to be brave, valiantly brushing the moistness from his cheeks with his knuckles.

'Ellie,' he cries.

I hold out my arms and he rushes into them, pressing his face into my neck and he's shaking, trying, but failing to swallow the enormous grief he's had to suppress till this moment. I search in my heart for the words that will ease his pain.

'I know it's hard, sweet Edward. But you'll find the strength,' I murmur. The words seem trite and pointless. So I say no more, but hold him close to me, as though to crush the blinding pain out of him. I feel desolate that I'm so useless to him in his sorrow; that I cannot bear his grief for him.

'I shall give him the finest funeral any King ever had. He shall have a tomb as large and as fine as money can buy. No one shall ever forget him.'

'No one ever will, with or without your tomb. But it would be a fine gesture and the people will be glad of a special place to pay homage.'

'But Mortimer must pay.'

'He must,' I agree. 'But not yet. I've told you before. You must wait till you are older. You must bide your time. That would be the bravest, most mature thing to do. For now, Edward, you're not only the King, but a politician too. To be a good politician, you must be patient and wait for the best opportunity, for the right action at the right time. It's the only way.'

Tremulously, he tries to smile at me through his tears and in that moment I know he'll be a force to be reckoned.

Little King Edward III. heir to the throne and to its enemies, both here and abroad. What a legacy to leave your child!

'But, Edward, you must remember one very important thing.' I pause to make certain he listens. 'Whatever you decide to do about Mortimer, you must always take care of your Mother. For it's been… it's been unbearably difficult for her. This is something you must always remember.'

'I'll remember, Ellie. But I shall never, ever forgive her. For Ellie, I suspect… it is so hard to say what I suspect.'

I can say nothing to comfort him. He adores his mother. He has adored her throughout the duration of her affair with Mortimer and their mutual enterprises which have resulted in his father's torture and death. It is enough to send anyone to the madhouse, this conflict between love and hate. Can they exist, side-by-side, in the heart of one inexperienced youth? It seems so, and I'm anxious that this should not sour his future judgement.

'If you wait here, I'll go to the kitchen and mix you something to help you sleep. I have a special recipe. But don't tell anyone about it or they'll say I'm a witch!'

He manages a small smile at my jest. 'Will you bring it to my bedchamber?'

'I'll be a few minutes, that's all.'

As my feet skim the stone steps to the kitchens, I feel numb with fear for him. For a moment, I stand silently, looking upon the hefty sides of beef and venison that hang from hooks in the larder; at the blood congealing in puddles on the floor. Idly I wonder if more blood is shed from animals slaughtered to feed us, or from infidels slaughtered to protect us. And how many of these so-called infidels are as innocent as the beasts in this larder? As innocent as the murdered King Edward? As innocent as that precious youth, his son?

I've watched him grow from helpless baby to friendly child to almost-man. But how will he fare, this gentle boy, with his ambitious, beautiful mother and her grasping, power-crazed consort? It's an ugly, uneven match. He'll need wise counsel and great fortune to overcome such obstacles.

Edward absorbs himself in the important task of the King's great tomb, which he is erecting at Gloucester Abbey. Out of respect, Guy and I visit the tomb, as yet still in its early stages of construction. The masons are dedicated workers and show us plans of the design. It fair takes our breath away. It will be of marble, with canopies and recesses of intricate complexity.

'It'll be like the shrine of a saint,' I gasp, 'and people will make pilgrimages to Gloucester for its sake.'

The young King takes my advice and conducts himself with dignity despite the appalling circumstances of his limited power. Often I see Mortimer regarding him with a quizzical eye. It perturbs Roger Mortimer that he cannot tell what the boy is thinking. But the King is consistently civil towards him and Mortimer has no cause to complain about him to Isabella.

It's a dilemma for Edward, for he adores his mother still and it must pain him to see her at the side of the man he despises, the man responsible for his beloved father's death. As a result, their relationship is strained. Edward speaks to his mother in clipped tones and she, feeling his disapproval, tends to a sharpness which is usually reserved for me.

We all rally around him, even, to their credit, the Old Boots. Even Lady Despenser is gentle to the King, which is surprising, for although it seemed there was little love between her and her husband, he was still her husband. This sudden softness of hers concerns me. I must watch her closely, lest she be two-faced. I'm heartily sick of the Ladies of the Boot, for they're always gossiping about me.

Sometimes, when I enter my Lady's chamber I heard snatches of conversation before they realise I am present.

'She's a strumpet? Do you see the way she moves her body whenever there is a half-fair knight in sight? And she's with him at every opportunity and they are tearing at each other like a pair of wild animals.'

'Indeed! And they make such an unholy noise about it all as if they are intent on demonstrating their wickedness to the entire Court.'

'I cannot imagine why the Queen condones her sinful ways.'

'Perhaps the dear Queen needs a little wise counsel in that matter.'

They both almost fall off their chairs with surprise when I suddenly announce clearly in a cathedral-singing voice:

'Love your enemies, do good to them which hate you, the Gospel according to St. Luke.'

'Ellie, dearest,' cries Lady Despenser. Lady Mortimer has her mouth open like a dying fish and her crumpled cheeks almost fall into it.

'I shall pray for you both,' I announce piously. 'For jealousy and envy show on your faces and do you no service. That is why I shall pray for you.' Then I put my hands together and softly intone, 'Amen.'

'Save your prayers, Mistress,' grated Mortimer. 'We don't need them.'

'Indeed, you do,' I reply sweetly. 'Indeed, Lady Mortimer, you do.'

'There's a letter from your father,' adds Lady Despenser. 'He's to visit you, I expect. We will certainly take pleasure from a little conversation with your dear father.' She grins at me with evil intent then she stretches out her arm and, carefully avoiding contact with her flesh, I take the parchment from her.

I have no choice but to scurry away to read my letter, for my face is crimson with frustration.

I've been so very lax. I've been so busy with Guy and the plotting and the pleasuring, that I have completely forgotten how desperately I need something on both of them. Clearly, I must acquire this something on before the Ladies of the Boot talk to my father.

The letter from my father says that I must return to France immediately. He does not say why. He just says, 'Come quickly, Ellie, for I need you at once. It is of vital importance.'

This is so confusing, to be recalled home without a reason given, not knowing whether or not it is truly urgent. It could be he is concerned for my safety, what with all the strange goings-on in England, which are probably exaggerated when recounted in France. But then, I cannot be sure and if his need is dire, I cannot waste time writing to ask him for reasons. What should I do?

My mind in turmoil, I take the dogs out in the fresh air for a walk so I can think. My Lady is feasting with Mortimer and the Barons, so I have a little time to myself.

That evening, I am desperate for Guy, for I shall be away for some time. '

You wouldn't believe we have agreed a truce with the treacherous Scots,' he complains. 'There have been many infractions and now they've advanced over the border. They cannot be trusted. At present, they're causing mayhem in

Northumberland.'

'Come, Guy,' I coax. 'Come, for I am off to England tomorrow.' I put my hand behind my head and run my finger up the nape of my neck, lifting my huge mane of hair so it tousles forward over my forehead and cheeks. I pull a ringlet out from my forehead and allow it to coil back into place. I stretch out my leg and push my bare foot into his groin.

'And I'm away to Northumberland,' says Guy. 'The devils shall be routed.'

I pull up my skirts and caress myself in a ploy to seduce him from his pre-occupations. But amusing me is the last thing on his mind and he doesn't even look at me, although I gasp and pant most convincingly.

I don't try to dissuade him from the new Scots campaign, for rather he were locked in bloody combat than finding other amusement at Court while I am in France. So I don't scold, but continue to employ my female tricks to divert his mind from the impending battle in Scotland and pay homage to the more ardent action I'm planning for the present. My strategy is, in due course, successful and we disport ourselves with abandon on the midnight blue opulence of my velvet coverlet. In the morning, I must scrub it thoroughly lest the maidservant carries tales to the Ladies of the Boot.

Next day, I set off for France, wondering what has befallen my father to make my return necessary. I hardly need relate the account of the journey. I'm sick on the ship. I reflect that I have not been pleasured for eleven hours and twenty minutes. That's the trouble with journeys; one has far too much time to reflect. The passage is unpleasant, for two men brawl over some trifle and one falls overboard and drowns. Fortunately, although one of the men is my escort, it's the other who is drowned. I upbraid my escort in strong terms for risking leaving me unprotected.

One unusual event occurs. On arrival in France I flirt with a man at the docks and am sorely tempted at his invitation, but refrain from indulging myself. This, I immediately regret, for I may not be pleasured again for months and weeks and days.

My escort collects the horses and we set off across the countryside at a steady pace. This time I have a small likeness of Guy, which he gave me as a present, so I comfort myself before I sleep by looking upon it. It reminds me of that pretty likeness of the now-dead King, possessed by Isabella when she was young and still hoping for love. The memory wrenches my heart.

Some things change constantly. Most things change at some time. Everything fluctuates, begins and ends, lives and dies. Jeremiah said, 'Can the Ethiopian change his skin, or the leopard his spots?' It sounds like a simple question, but I think it's more profound. Tonight I shall look in my little Bible to see if Jeremiah answers the question. I hope he does. For sometimes questions are rhetorical, says my father. I think this means that the question sounds impressive, but is meaningless. Jeremiah would not ask a meaningless question. For then there would only be a meaningless answer.

Then I think it is, perhaps, the same meaning as the saying, 'Each to his own nature be true.'

Suddenly, I feel free and alive. The French Court is more tolerant than the English and it's easier to find privacy. If I'm discreet, I don't see why I shouldn't do as I please. I take out the pearl pendant, Guy's peace-offering to me when he betrayed me with Mathilde and pensively I fondle it. I have many good memories.

CHAPTER 25

Sisterly Concerns

'Your sister, Charlotte, is distraught,' says my father.

I stifle a desire to bellow from the depths of my soul. Have I come all this way for a trifle?

Abandoned my lover to resist the delights of the French Court far away from my watchful eye? Have I done all this only to find that Charlotte is distraught? What is it to me whether Charlotte is distraught or gloriously happy?

'It is more serious than you think,' says my father quickly, trying to avert my wrath. 'You must attend to her Ellie, for I no longer know what to do.'

Swishing my skirts about to show how tiresome I think it all is, I throw myself onto a stool.

'What's wrong with my sister? Has her husband found another to delight him?'

My father cringes and draws his robe tightly around him. 'Your intuition is sharp, my Daughter.

'Well, I thought she'd aimed a little high.'

'The marriage seemed substantial in the beginning.'

'All marriages seem substantial in the beginning except, of course, the Queen's. But now, poor Charlotte's marriage is beginning to fall apart?'

'It has been fair rent asunder amidst the

storms of great adversity,' says my father mournfully.

'Indeed, indeed,' I say for I have no stomach for such precious language.

'The other woman,' says my father heavily, 'is your sister Mathilde.'

It is so tragic it is pure comedy and I cannot help but laugh. 'Father, surely you jest.'

'Indeed I do not. They are shameless. They are living together openly and Adam Langley is petitioning to have his marriage annulled on the grounds of non-consummation. Charlotte denies that he has evidence for this indictment. She has been examined and is not a virgin.'

I can barely contain my astonishment. 'It may be she's not a virgin, but that does not mean Adam Langley deflowered her.'

'Ellie! How dare you!'

I shrug my shoulders. 'Sometimes these things must be faced.'

'What is more,' continues Father, 'your demented sister stole my sword and attempted to sever the arteries in her wrist.'

My interest quickens. This story has the elements of real dramatic tragedy. It would make an agreeable play at the English Court. Even so, Charlotte runs true to her nature. She can never get anything right, not even killing herself.

'What can I do?'

'You must talk to Mathilde. You must make her send Adam back to his lawful wife.'

'How can I if he doesn't wish to return?'

'It is his duty,' says Father, who sees only good and evil and nothing in between.

I sigh deeply, for I see if I don't agree to his bidding, I shall not hear the last of it.

'Where can I find them, the Runt and her lover?'

'I shall give you a map, for they are in hiding in a nearby village. You must take Charlotte with you.

'This isn't a good idea, Father. How can I have a reasonable discussion with them with Charlotte at my heels in a state of love-madness?'

'She will not be left behind. I fear for her sanity. We must humour her. And if the attempt fails, at least she will be forewarned and maybe she will accept her fate.'

When I recall Charlotte's protracted pursuit of the unobtainable Gaveston, it is hard to accept my father's logic. Against my best judgement, I agree.

'Come with me,' says Father. 'I shall escort you to Charlotte's quarters.' He takes me there, and then leaves us to talk alone. Resigned, I stare at my sister.

Charlotte's eyes are swollen and red with weeping and her gown is soiled and her fingernails are grimy with thick dirt. Because I pity her, I allow her to embrace me, but find the close contact almost more than I can bear.

'He has left me,' she sobs.

'I'm not surprised he's left you. Just see the

condition of you.'

'I've only neglected myself since I was forsaken. How can you be so cruel Ellie?'

'You'll have to clean yourself and put on a fresh gown. I'll not be seen with you looking like that. I have my own dignity to consider.'

Charlotte plumps herself down on a stool. The stool almost disappears, for her rump spills over its edges.

'Did Father tell you?'

'He told me.'

'It was Mathilde. It was her. She did it on purpose, to spite me, just like she did the same to you. She has many admirers and even proposals of marriage, so I don't understand why she takes away my own true love. Only in your case, it's worse, for she took him to prove her power. Fortunately for you, she tossed her unfortunate victim aside. I don't know how you have managed to forgive her, for you must always feel second-choice when you are with Guy.'

This comment cuts me to the very core of my being, for it is true. No woman likes to think she is tolerated because another was not willing. I begin to feel more and more furious with the Runt.

'It happened the other way around, Charlotte. Guy cast Mathilde aside, for me!' I say in defence of my dignity, although I am not at all sure of my facts. But Charlotte isn't listening.

In a great heave of self-pity Charlotte's body doubles over, her plump chest squashing onto her plump lap and her hair hanging down over her thighs. She begins to sob noisily, her rounded shoulders jerking with each inward gasp of air. I'm quite at a loss what to do. I wait till she recovers sufficient to continue.

'She boasts, you know,' mumbles Charlotte. 'She says she can get any woman's man for herself. None can resist her great beauty and charm.'

'She's deluded,' I say, but Charlotte shakes her head so vigorously her eyeballs roll around in their sockets.

'That's the trouble, Ellie. What she says is true. No man is safe from temptation when Mathilde has him marked for herself.'

If I did not despise her so, I would almost have a sneaking admiration for the Runt. Considering the disadvantages she suffered as a child, she's more than made her mark. Probably her motive is revenge.

'So you want me to go with you to talk to them?'

'Yes,' says Charlotte. 'You're my sister. It's your duty.'

'Then that is what we shall do. But, Charlotte, you must consider what will happen if he's not willing to return to you.

'That is easy,' says Charlotte. 'We shall kill them both. You and I. Devoted sisters united in seeking retribution for damage done.'

Of course, she's quite mad, for how will murdering the pair of them help get her husband back? I think long on this. Even if we merely murder Mathilde, it is unlikely to endear Charlotte to Adam Langley. We could both end up minus our heads.

Gently, I point out this simple truth.

'I shall feel better,' says Charlotte. 'And so will you. It's worth the risk.'

Perhaps she's not so mad after all. I should no longer fear crossing the Channel to France with my lover and that would be such joy. It would lay the ghost of my occasional black moods when I think how my youngest sister abused my trust. Charlotte is right. It's a mean act to steal your sister's man and then cast him aside, as though he's no more than a used kerchief.

'They will know it's us,' I say. 'Our father knows we go to visit. If they are found murdered, he'll know. His grief will be so great, he won't keep our secret.'

'I've thought of that,' says Charlotte. Charlotte is beginning to rise in my estimation. She may look a fair fright, but she has a brain in that clumsy head. 'Let's go now, Ellie, and I shall explain on the way.'

'We shall go after you have put on a clean gown and scrubbed your nails and washed your face. While you do that I must call a servant to fetch me wine, for I'm thirsty and need something to lift my spirit.'

Charlotte is inconsiderate, for I have only recently arrived, tired and hungry from my journey, and now I must gather myself and set off to confront a pair of lovers in a situation which may well end in bloodshed. How much of the damage I must inflict, she has not yet explained. Only Charlotte could expect as much of a sister.

The people in this village seem backward to our sophisticated Court tastes. Even Charlotte turns her nose up. Although dusk is falling, there are people going about their business. Rough men cast bawdy comments at us, remarking upon our raiments, our breasts and our other bits which we keep hidden. If Guy was here, he would run them through for their insolence.

'If our business were of a lawful nature, I should report these people to the sheriff,' I remark.

Anxiously, I caress the pearl pendant at my neck, which I have put on for luck. An idiot boy points and sticks out his tongue. His mother cuffs him and he runs off yowling. A ragged old man scolds us. A child throws a stone and it hits me on the ankle, but I don't respond although it hurts me.

'What revolting peasants!' says Charlotte. 'But it's not their fault. They don't have the advantage of our fine breeding and education, so they must live like rats.

Charlotte has a manner of stating the obvious while missing the point.

'Wait, Charlotte. Let me look again at the map.'

'Is this it?' ask Charlotte.

I study my father's map, which is as precise as I would expect, and I locate the landmarks, the oaks, the elms, the rough path, the tumbledown church.

'I fear so, sister.'

We're shocked at how low our sister has sunk. The house is a mere timber-framed shack, low and poorly constructed, with a door that doesn't fit properly and must let in a terrible draught. One of the windows is broken. The other window is missing altogether.

'I'm growing less angry by the minute, for it is a hovel,' says Charlotte. 'and I cannot imagine my husband living in such a humble abode.'

'It can only be from lack of choice,' I remark. 'Does he have no land or property? For I thought he was a prize acquisition.'

Charlotte is insulted. 'Of course he has. He has land and property the length and breadth of England, Gascony and Aquitaine.'

I cannot help but wonder how Charlotte has managed to snare such a prize. There is just no accounting for taste. And yet... and yet... I suppose she has a cheap kind of buxom comeliness about her. She exudes an earthiness which some men might find irresistible.

'Then why? Why has Adam sunk so low?'

'I know not.'

'Have his properties been confiscated by some powerful noble?'

'I think not.'

'Are his properties too far to travel to, for he does have business at Court?'

'That's possible.'

We're both confused.

'Let's go in and face what fate awaits us,' I suggest. 'I'll go first, for Mathilde may well bar the door and refuse us entry if she sees you.'

Charlotte shrinks back, just out of sight, which is difficult for a woman of her proportions. I lift up my chin and square up my shoulders and march up to the door. I knock with my knuckles, for there's no other means to gain attention. The door is opened by Adam Langley, who doesn't recognise me but smiles anyway, as though I am a welcome stranger.

'Sir, I am Mathilde's sister, Ellie.'

'Ellie,' beams Adam. 'Come in. Mathilde will be so pleased to see her beloved sister. She never stops talking of your talent and beauty.'

Feeling shy of entering the house, I hover on the doorstep, but Adam takes me gently by the arm and guides me inside. The interior of the house has a rustic charm about it, for the furniture is comfortable and there is clean, bright matting on the floor. Awkwardly, I wait as Adam calls for Mathilde. She glows into the room, unselfconscious and golden like a ray of spring sunshine that has found its path through the storm-clouds.

'Ellie!'

She sounds glad to see me. This isn't proceeding as I expected. There's no defensiveness here, no aggression, no recriminations and no apologies. They both look happy beyond belief.

Mathilde is quite changed.

She takes me in her arms, then holds me away from her as though she hasn't seen me for twenty years, and studies me. It's how a man might look at me, as though he cannot feast enough on my beauty.

'Ellie, I hope you're not too angry with your sister. I'm an outcast and I'm sure my father will disown me. The entire Court is appalled at our behaviour. But, you see, we love each other. I cannot make excuses, for I have made my sister so unhappy. But, she was unhappy before. I've never known Charlotte when she was not miserable, except when she had food in her mouth or a man to pursue.'

'Now, Mathilda,' chides Adam. 'That's unkind.'

'Indeed, but it's true.'

'It's not so bad, Ellie,' says Adam. 'For Charlotte doesn't love me.'

'She says she does.'

'She does not. I don't care to contradict you, Ellie, but you're in error if you believe this. Besides, I never loved her. I mistook pity for love.' Adam adopts a hangdog expression and I feel a great surge of deep contempt for him, deep in my gut.

'Charlotte's here and you must tell her this yourselves.' Before they can object, I step back and thrust open the door and Charlotte bursts into the room so fast she almost trips over a huge blue earthenware pot.

'Do come in,' says Mathilde with biting sarcasm.

Charlotte stands with her feet planted widely apart. What a transformation she has made from the pathetic creature of a day ago. I cannot help but think she looks magnificent in her indignation. She looks even larger in her wide-skirted kirtle, the colour of the Dover cliffs.

Even so, I want to be released from my promise to Charlotte. I cannot maintain the deep anger I once felt for the Runt.

'I cannot believe,' says Charlotte, 'that you have come to this!' The scorn she injects into her voice is fit to shrivel the boldest knight. 'It pains me sorely to see your degradation.'

'We're happy, Charlotte,' says the Runt. 'We're here because we choose to be. We want to live the simple life for a while, to be with common people and gentle animals and to commune with nature. You must understand that neither of us wishes to hurt you.'

'Holy Mother of God,' heaves Charlotte. 'Then what would you do to me if you were my enemy? Can you really think of anything worse than stealing my husband and leaving me bereft and groatless?'

'I'm a man, Charlotte. Not a puppy or kitten,' says Adam mildly.

'Shut your mouth! Or I will chop off your balls. This is nothing to do with you. It is between the Runt and me.'

Like a scalded puppy, Adam retreats behind the table, unconsciously holding his folded hands in front of his private parts.

Then everything happens very fast. Charlotte hurls herself at the Runt, clawing and screaming oaths that sound much viler than any I've ever heard before. For a moment, I'm too stunned to move or speak and stand motionless, clutching my joined hands to my breast. I must stop this or our plans will be ruined.

'Charlotte!' I cry. 'Wait. Remember what we said.' Anxiously I put my hand inside the special pocket on my kirtle, in which the poison is hidden. The poison is for the Runt, if she does not return Charlotte's husband. For, at the last moment, just as we tied up our horses, Charlotte had said she could not bring herself to murder her husband.

Now, after agreeing a plan to slip poison into Mathilde's beer, (a convenient way to murder her) Charlotte has spoilt it all and has the Runt pinned to the floor, unable to move with the great rolling weight on top of her and fair crushing the breath from her.

'Do something,' I cry to Adam Langley.

'I cannot. She's too strong.'

I grab Charlotte's hair and yank, but it is greasy and slips through my fingers. Again, I grab, clinging hard, yanking and twisting. A clump comes off in my hand and stupidly I stare at it.

Then I pick up the big, blue pot. I place each of my feet either side of Charlotte's legs and then I soft-shuffle towards her head. As I progress, the great bulge of her hips forces my legs wide apart and a shooting pain seizes my groin. I pray she won't suddenly leap to her feet, for I shall be tossed through the roof. I raise the pot high above me and crash it down onto her head. It breaks into a shower of jagged pieces.

Charlotte collapses onto the Runt like a monstrous creature from the bottom of the ocean. Adam comes to life, leaps forward. Together we roll Charlotte off the Runt and Adam falls to his feet beside Mathilde, feeling for her pulse. She doesn't look well. A tiny trickle of blood seeps from her slack lips and runs down the side of her mouth and her nose is swollen to twice its size. Her eyes stare, the pupils dilate. Adam cannot find a whisper in her wrist, so he tries her throat and a few other places' which I do not think actually pulse.

'She's dead,' he says, his voice thick with grief. 'You've killed her. When you hit my wife, she crushed the sweet breath out of my own precious darling. Oh, Mathilde my sweetheart, my life. How shall I live without you?' He collapses into spasms of agonised sobbing.'

I cannot help but think his language is somewhat picturesque for a man overcome with grief. People talk so in books, making great speeches while they fall dying with swords in their bellies. But it doesn't generally happen so in real life.

'I was trying to help her,' I protest. 'You know I was trying to help her.'

'You hit your sister too fiercely with that pot. They say you are a vixen and it's true,' he rasps between sobs. 'Now she's landed on my only precious love and killed her.'

Charlotte is also lying very still.

This is not happening to me. I'm dreaming it. Soon, I shall awaken.

'Charlotte,' I whisper. I pick up one plump wrist and drop it. It falls like a lump of cold pig fat, plop, onto the floor. I put my finger pad on her pulse. It is still beating, quite robustly under the circumstances.

'She's alive,' I whisper.

'But you've killed my precious love,' repeats Adam. 'Madame, you shall be beheaded for this.'

CHAPTER 26

A Well-Deserved Death

I slip out into the sharp air, which catches in my throat. Night enfolds me like dark velvet, soothing the thick red mist before my eyes. I untether the horses, mount and with Charlotte's riderless steed trotting along behind, I retrace my steps back home, my head buzzing with the story I shall tell.

By the time I reach Court, I shall have my story worked out. I shall have to explain it carefully. This is how it happened. It is not my fault. What else could I do? What could anyone do?

Besides, how would Charlotte know who slammed that pot on her head. She was first mad with rage then she was unconscious. Her eyeballs had disappeared into her head and her body was slack like a marionette.

It would be Adam's word again mine which of us attacked Charlotte from behind. Yes, I could make my story stick. I'll weep and ring my hands in anguish at the death of my youngest sister.

I know I have the courage. I must keep my head now if I aim to preserve it later. For the first time in my life I know what it means to have nothing to lose.

I am glad to be home in my chamber. Now I can feel the bile rising in my throat so I pour myself some beer from the jug to calm my spirit. It's no doubt for the best. For the Bible says, 'Saul and Jonathan were lovely and pleasant in their lives, and in their death they were not divided.' At least the second part is true, for now my sweet sister will be with our mother. My act has been one of kindness.

Here is my story:

I waited outside the whole time and allowed Charlotte to enter first, for that was how she wanted it. From the open doorway, I heard cries and screams and dreadful curses and crashes and more screaming although I couldn't see much past my sister. Finally, I leaned forward. I did not go in, for my sensibilities were badly affected by the sight I saw. It's clear what happened.

Adam was in the act of raising the enormous pot above Charlotte's head, and as it crashed down onto her, she fell on the Runt and crushed her to death. Terrified that I might be next, I made my escape.

Yes it will be his word against mine. I'm pleased with this. As I have said before, my own inventiveness amazes me. But, I must not be too specific about how it happened if I'm to convince my enemies that I was not actually *in* the room. I must merely explain the sounds I heard and what little I saw from the doorway, so the action can be filled in by those cleverer than I am.

It could happen that way. It could!

I shall start by telling my father. For if I make

any mistakes, he'll spot them but will be unlikely to mark them as incriminating. Then I can make my story perfect for when it really matters.

The conversation with my father is encouraging. I weep a lot and beat my breast with a limp wrist. I tell him how I am beside myself with anguish, even though Charlotte was a vulgar and badly behaved, and Mathilde took my lover only to cast him aside like a used toy.

'You are in error, Ellie,' says Father. 'Mathilde did no such thing. It was Guy de Clare who changed his mind. He asked for her hand in marriage, but he seemed unsure. I told him to wait, to think upon it, for I knew you were pained at his defection. Then he came to me and said, 'I must marry soon. But Ellie is unfaithful to me and I fear she does not love me. Mathilde is like her in many ways. I thought I could love her instead. But it is no use. I cannot change my affections. It is Ellie whom I love.'

This news pleases me exceedingly.

It's a pity I am left with just one sister. Does that make us twins now that we are no longer triplets? Although Mathilde was a trial to me, I'm not without sensitivity and I shall miss her. Apart from that, everything is magnificent. Adam doesn't return, no doubt he knows he will not stand a chance of incriminating me. I am completely exonerated of any blame and as I glide gracefully around the Court in my mourning raiments, people lower their heads and treat me carefully. A Lady bereaved of her sister is constantly deferred to. Flowers are left at my door. Isabella gives me a new gown and a sapphire ring. The Ladies of the Boot curtsey! Guy consoles me as much as he can and this consolation is of a most passionate nature and I am magnificently consoled.

One other thing happens of great satisfaction to me. I have something on the Ladies Despenser and Mortimer.

I'm walking silently through the upper passages, thinking upon this pleasant thought and hugging it to me like a precious jewel. Creeping around the Castle unnoticed is something I often do, for I gain much useful information in this manner. But, this time it is by accident that I stumble upon a whispered conversation in a tiny ante-room. I freeze where I stand.

'Sire, you must strike the first blow before you, yourself, are struck down.

I am not certain whose voice this is. Then, a familiar voice, which quavers slightly, names the conspirator.

'But, Montagu, it's a most dangerous plan,' says Edward. 'Are you certain the time is right?'

I can hear in the young King's tone a mixture of youthful inexperience and a desire to rise to his kingly stature. I wonder who this Montagu is, and I feel a sense of loss that Edward has grave secrets he chooses not to share with me. Suddenly, my breath explodes like a gasp of rushing water in my body and

I dread that they might hear me. By force of will I try to slow my heartbeat, struggle for control of my breath, strain my ears to hear Montagu's response.

'Tomorrow might be too late, Sire,' mutters Montagu. 'The Queen and Mortimer have locked themselves away and are protected by guards, for I think they smell our eagerness as a rat smells a lady's fear.'

'Then, what's to be done?'

'There's a secret way into their apartments and we may take them by surprise before they can arm themselves or call their guards. The Constable will show us this secret entrance.' I can see Montagu's shadow cast against the far wall by the flickering of a candle. It is a determined-looking shadow, legs wide apart, long forefinger wagging.

'If you're certain he can be trusted,' says Edward. I don't blame him for his suspicions. There have been few people in the young King's life who have been worthy of his trust.

'We have to trust him,' says Montagu, shortly. 'For you cannot trust the other one.'

By this remark, I assume he means Mortimer and there is wisdom in his words. I've been increasingly worried for Edward's safety, especially since I've observed with what cunning Mortimer's hard, black eyes appraise his Mistress's son. It is almost as though they stalk their youthful prey.

'The Queen must not be harmed.'

'The Queen will not be harmed.'

'I must consult first…with someone.'

'With whom?'

'I cannot say.'

'Sire, I urge you…'

'With El…with Lady Eleanora.' Then, indignantly, his voice rising to a higher pitch, 'Don't regard me thus, Montagu!'

Then I hear a strange sort of wheezing sound, which I'm sure must be Montagu trying to stifle his laughter.

'Consult with a woman! For shame, Sire! You are the King. The King doesn't consult with women. He may pretend to consult with his Queen, and then do what he must and from what I hear, the Lady Eleanor is little more than the Court Strumpet. Chief-Lady-in-Mating, they call her. It is said she has been ridden more than the old King's favourite war-horse.'

I'm almost beside myself, as I hear Gaveston's old, mean insult bandied about in jest. For no one has dared say it to my face except Gaveston himself and it's outrageous that this slur is still breeding on careless lips. I can hardly prevent myself for screaming out my presence. Somehow, I manage to stifle the impulse. Hard it is to be accused and yet deprived of defence.

I'm an object of jealousy and envy. Yet, although I know I am vain and selfish, in all of my adventures, I have been respectful of my lovers and have harmed no one except in self-defence, which is more than one can say for many married couples. I fight long and hard against the need to reveal myself, to upbraid Montagu for his disgraceful slander, demand from Edward that the conspirator die a traitor's death. But I dare not. I dare not. For maybe it is I who will have to die. Edward is talking now and I draw closer, to hear his defence of me.

'Lady Eleanora has great wisdom in matters pertaining to my welfare,' he states bravely. But, he doesn't defend my honour, which disappoints me, for I've been his most faithful ally.

'Then, Sire, give her the dagger and let her do it,' says Montagu, nastily. I am shocked he speaks thus to the King, but Edward doesn't answer and there's a long silence. It's time for me to slip away before my urges get the better of me.

Then, in the early hours of the next morning, Edward sends for me. I'm not sure whether I'm surprised or pleased or irked.

'Ellie,' he says, 'Mortimer is dead.'

I'm rubbing the sleep from my eyes and it is difficult to absorb the words, for I've been dreaming of Guy, and we're in a woodland glade, naked and aroused, surrounded only by the soft drone of hover-flies and the heady scent of forest flowers.

'Mortimer... *dead!*'

'Ellie, hush! Your voice is loud. Everything will be well now and I'll take care of you. But my mother needs you; she laments the death of her lover in a most disturbing manner. I'm at a loss what to do with her.'

'What did you expect, Edward?'

'It's justice. She's guilty of my father's death

and therefore, to be committed to trial. But she is permitted to lament her lover's death. She didn't allow me this privilege when my tormented father was murdered.

'How did you manage it, Edward?' I ask, stupidly. 'I hope you watched your back, for Mortimer has... I mean, had, powerful friends.'

'Surely, Ellie, you must realise I was not present at the assassination.'

Already the King is learning a vital truth about Kingship; one arranges for someone else to do one's dirty work. Courage is paramount, but only deserving of effort if the undertaking bestows honour on the noble hero. There is little prestige in a dagger to the heart in the dead of night. Will he have the paid assassins murdered to silence them? I wonder. I could dream a fitting end for Montagu. Court strumpet, indeed!

'Had you nothing to do with it, Edward?'

'Of course not,' he says, tugging on his earlobe and looking anxious, just as he did as a small boy when I asked if he were responsible for making his sisters cry.

Then he adds, 'Actually, Ellie, I was there. I'm only telling you this so you will not think me a coward. But you must keep my presence at the death of the Consort a secret to your dying day.'

So I'm wrong and have underestimated Edward, judging him by other's standards. This King is prepared to do his own dirty work and take his own terrible risks. It's a revelation! And I would truly like to know how it happened. For no story is of any consequence without details.

'Was it awful, Edward? Was there much blood and did he scream?'

'Not much. And no, he didn't scream. It was very quick,' says Edward, adding cautiously, 'So I'm told, for I was not in the forefront of the attack.'

'Did your men creep up on him, likes thieves in the night, their daggers drawn in readiness?' I'm picturing the scene in my head, relishing the moment when a dagger plunges and twists into Mortimer's black heart. I imagine his agony, however brief. I hope that, for just one moment, he knew the reason for his persecution.

'That's so, Ellie. But you should know that my mother repeats constantly that she pleaded for him. She says she begged for gentle Mortimer to be spared. But my mother mis-remembers. What actually happened was she threatened to... she threatened me... and her threats put me in fear of my life. Were it not for that, I might merely have had him thrown into the Tower.'

'Yes, Edward. But what did the Queen say?'

'I cannot tell you, Ellie. It's not for a gentle Lady's ears like yours. But don't believe everything you hear, for my mother is deranged. So you see, after her trial, I must send my mother into retirement, but she'll be paid a generous pension and all her needs will be met. You may stay with her, if you like, but I hope you will come to see me.'

It's always the same. The male gender is

useless at supplying all the fascinating, shocking, disgusting, delicious details that make a gripping tale. Yet, I have noticed, they delight in telling you all the tedious chapter and verse of bloody battles or tournaments or hunting trips or other such pastimes. This is mostly to do with what would have happened if something else had not happened first, or if they only had ten extra men, or if it were not pelting down with rain.

All the same, I beam and hug him. As we are alone, his dignity is not compromised. I feel a special bond with the young King as though we are brother and sister, for now we both have blood on our hands that is hardly of our own making. If you murder because you have no choice, it cannot be of your making. The victims of murder are, more often than not, responsible for their own fate.

'You must pray for guidance, sweet Edward,' I say. 'And, remember, you can count upon my loyalty and devotion.'

CHAPTER 27

Queen Isabella in Exile

Slowly, I walk along the upper stairway of Castle Rising to see my Queen in exile. When I enter the gloomy chamber which now belongs to Isabella, she is sitting on the bed, gazing at the cold, stone wall which is unsoftened by hangings or drapery. She's missing her gentle Mortimer. I wonder how she feels about her son. I'm soon told.

Hearing me enter, she turns and fixes me with a long, cold stare. I'm shocked at her appearance; she's a mere shadow of her former self.

'I gave him life,' she mutters, 'I bore him in great agony and I ministered to his smallest want, his tiniest whim. Now he's betrayed me, for he's deprived me of the one whom I've loved the most.' Her face is dirty and tears have made white channels down her cheeks and chin. Her hair falls in a great, unruly cloud around her face and shoulders.

'You won't leave me, Ellie. Promise you won't leave me.'

'I promise.' Again I feel the guilt. I hate to lie to Isabella, but what else can I do when she's so besieged by dread of the unknown?

'I don't know how I would manage without you.'

'You won't need to.'

This guilt, product of my hypocrisy, sinks deep in my stomach like a cannon-ball. I shall allow it to rest there for the moment, for I cannot shake it off. Isabella is desperate for comforting words yet all the while I know I cannot remain with her in this God-forsaken place. It's her punishment, not mine. I didn't run off with Mortimer and gather armies to besiege my monarch. I didn't kill the King, or arrange for someone to do it. I didn't compromise the love of my son. I've given all of my life to Isabella's service. Even now that I am older, I still feel young and eager for excitement and have no intention of burying my cleverness and talents in this remote prison of a castle.

'I feel so much better when I have you as my mentor, dear Ellie. I fear my son has cut me from his heart and will soon forget he has a mother.'

'Surely not, Isabella.'

The way to attack guilt is to allow it time, and not to make hurried decisions because of it. I excuse myself from Isabella, for the more promises I make, the more I listen to her pleas, the longer it will take for me to overcome my guilt. I remind myself that guilt will do me no lasting harm; it is simply an uncomfortable companion that may, with exertion of will, be despatched.

Free! Now I long to be free from the shackles of my Lady's needs. Never again to empty her piss-pot. To say what I think and think what I say. It's possible, for what can she do if I simply disappear? She cannot pursue me. She has no power. But I should do the right thing. I should tell her first.

As I ponder in my lonely chamber, a strange

thought suddenly strikes me. A thought I have never entertained before. It floods me like a sunbright, naked light.

I shall do the right thing. I shall not lie. I shall tell Isabella the truth face to face, eye to eye, bosom to bosom, and face the anguish in her eyes. Elated by this insight, I hurry back to her chamber.

'I've something to tell you, Isabella,' I say.

She puts down the psalter she is sewing. She puts her finger to her lips to silence me and regards me with a strange, mystical sadness, her eyes huge in her pale face, her hair, now almost white with all the distress she has endured so that she looks like a ghost of herself. When she speaks, her answer is so unexpected that I step back three paces.

'It is fine, Ellie. Really, I understand. You want your freedom. I shall miss you, but you may have it with my blessing.'

'Dear Isabella!' I'm overcome by her generosity. And relieved it has been so easy. She's come full circle. She's grown from tender pliancy, to vicious she-wolf and now back again to the gentle Lady I once knew.

'I shall visit you often, Isabella,' I gush and in that moment, I mean it. Overcome with gratitude, I fall at her feet to pay my respects and I gaze straight into her eyes so that she may see the truth.

I almost fly out of the chamber, brushing past the dry tapestries, down the stairway and back out into the open. Mounting my horse, I shout at the gatekeeper to let me out of this oppressive place. He seems anxious that I have no escort, but I brook no argument and soon we are running free, my steed and me, across the springy grass. I cannot help but sing with the birds as we trot peacefully over the hill. Never in my life have I felt more vibrant, more alive. On the way, I see in the distance a lone horseman and as he approaches, my heart lifts with amazement.

'Guy!'

As he comes closer, he looks at me with a confident smile. I confess my heart does a little leap at the sight of that rugged, handsome face, that jaunty brown beard. I drink in his beauty, and then close my eyes to commit the sight of him to my memory. Then I open them again and come to my senses. It's time for a change, a complete change. I have promised myself that and nothing must divert me from my conviction.

'I've come for you as I promised, Ellie.'

I laugh. How everything has changed! He thinks all he need do is bestow that crooked smile upon me and I'll be a quivering wreck at his feet. It is true, because I am smitten, but I shall not let him know it. First, he shall squirm a little.

'Come,' he says. 'We shall ride back to the Windsor together.'

'My dear Guy, I cannot.'

'You cannot?'

'I cannot.'

'Why not?'

My Mistress has granted me my freedom. Maybe I shall marry at last.' I am teasing him because he deserves to be teased. I want to hear him protest. I want him to convince me of his commitment. I want him to be jealous.

'But Ellie. You can marry *me*!'

I put on a sad, sad face, turning the corners of my mouth down soulfully. 'Dear Guy, you will never be true to me.'

Guy is almost beside himself by now, and posterity might consider me cruel, but although it is brutal, it is, after all, the truth. From now, I shall always tell the truth. I know that whatever happens, Guy will still be there. For that's how it is with us. He is so mad for me that he'll take me back whatever I do and I'm so mad for him I will do the same.

'Ellie,' says Guy. 'I have some news. I don't know if it's important.'

'News?' I have a sudden feeling of doom deep in my gut. I stare hard at Guy, and my discomfort increases for he looks severe.

'A sheriff came to the Court. A sheriff I had never seen before and he had your pearl pendant, the one I gave you. He asked me if I recognised it and I said it was yours and I'd return it to you. But he said no, it was needed for evidence.'

I feel a strange shiver inside my chest. 'Evidence for what? Did he say?'

'No. He was most evasive. I think there had been a murder, but obviously there has been some mistake. I dare say there is more than just one pendant like yours.

My mind is racing. The pendant must have

fallen from my throat in the little love-nest my sister Mathilde had shared with Adam Langley. After the tussle, Adam must have picked it up and handed it to the sheriff. In this way, he has managed to tell his story ahead of mine. What has he said? I need to think. It's still his word against mine.

'I have to go, my darling. I will try to contact you again soon.' Without waiting for a reply, I blow Guy a kiss and dig in my spurs and soon my horse is at a gallop and my mind is galloping faster than my horse.

As I reach the woods, I rein in my horse and look for the path, where we can pass between trees and bushes unobserved. I hadn't missed my pearl pendant, but I think I was wearing it when Charlotte and I went to visit the Runt and Adam Langley. It's my favourite jewel and I feel I can draw on Guy's courage when I wear his gift.

The trouble is that I swore to my father I had not been inside the house. It would seem that if I lied about that, I could have lied that I killed my sister. Will my father cover up for me in a lie. I am not that sure. He is a pedantic man. He is religious. Adam will be exonerated. I have to think of something. I could say it was an accident, not a murder. How can I convince the sheriff of my innocence.

Then I have it! Charlotte admired my fine necklace and out of the generosity of my heart, I insisted she should have it. For that's the kind of thing sisters do for one another. It was near the body because Charlotte was wearing it.

I have not lost my cunning. They will believe it so long as I can intimidate Charlotte into silence, once she is well enough to speak. She is unlikely to remember much about the occasion so it should not be difficult.

What happens next is a total shock.

'There she is,' yells a course voice. 'There she is, murdering little vixen.' Terrified, I try to turn my horse about so we may flee in the opposite direction, for two big, rough men on two big black horses block my path. Their faces are hard and determined and I know they will give me no quarter. But, there's no room to turn, the path is too narrow. My horse whinnies in fright and bucks as I urge him, pulling his great head to the side, jerking the reins, pushing in my spurs. Rough branches tear across my face and arms and rip my gown. It's such a shambles, that I hardly know what's happening. And all the time, my heart is pounding in my breast and something twists hard inside my belly.

Then, one man leans over, grabs me around the waist, cursing as I kick and scream and sink my teeth into the flesh of his arm. But I know I'm no match for him. Still, I fight, still I struggle and curse and spit at his face.

'Leave me be, you filthy cur. I'm not she you seek.'

He curses me back, loudly. 'Stay, vixen. Stay or I swear I shall separate your head from your body.'

'You'll do no such thing. Unhand me, for I am of noble blood. I shall have you whipped for this outrage.'

He strikes me a savage blow across the head and renders me senseless.

I sit here on the filthy floor in the White Tower in the cold and damp. There's a mouse in the corner, nibbling at some rubbish. Probably, she wants it for her nest, to keep her babies warm. I talk to her, for there's no one else to hear me. But I don't think she listens. She's preoccupied with providing for her little family. She has six babies. You would think one at a time was enough.

Young Prince Edward hasn't replied to my letters and now my writing things have been confiscated, except for this journal. I screamed so shrilly when they tried to take it away, they relented and let me have it back. I think Edward doesn't dare to communicate with me, for Charlotte's husband was a man of some importance in the French Court. In fact, he was a Man of Very Great Importance. Much more importance than I ever imagined. This is something I only discovered yesterday. At least, I think it was yesterday, for sometimes it's difficult to separate day from night.

How could I have guessed that from that pokey, sleazy little hideaway he had set up with my sister, Mathilde?

Charlotte's husband Adam was the murdered King's half-brother. Something no one acknowledged was that the old King had a Bastard Son. What a momentous discovery! I might have died not knowing, were it not for a kind note from the Ladies Despenser and Mortimer. This makes me sick.

I have killed the mistress of the half-brother of the deceased King, and uncle to the present young King. But how was I to know? Even Charlotte didn't know, for she could never have kept such a secret to herself. Could she?

Even so, in spite of his birth out-of-wedlock, Adam Langley is held in good standing by the Court and the Barons.

My word is useless against his.

CHAPTER 28

Ellie's Fate

So I shall never be free. Never, never, never.

I try not to panic, for that will do me no good.

I think about Guy. I think about his lovely cock.

I think about the beautiful red dress the Queen gave me with the buttons on the sleeves. I think about my pearl pendant. The pearl pendant that fell to the floor in that little tumbledown shack where I said I never was.

I think about the children and poor little dead Gundulph and Odo, both original and reincarnated, and I love them without exception.

I think about King Edward frolicking with his lover, Gaveston, in a forest not far from here and I think how they never knew I was there.

I think about the little bags of money and the one-footed noble who couldn't catch me.

I think about how I applauded when Gaveston got his comeuppance.

I think about how I clapped hands when Despenser got his comeuppance.

I think about the suffering King's dying screams.

I think about the man who raised my kirtle on the crates.

I think about all the other men who have loved me in their way.

I think about how I have not been pleasured by a man for seven months, four days and five hours. I make a tally with a stone upon the wall. It helps to pass the time until they come for me.

No, I mustn't think like that. I know that Guy will soon be coming for me. He sent me a letter. He will come, I know he will. I have every faith in my lover. He is steadfast. He adores me. Why shouldn't he adore me?

I am hoping he will have prepared an escape plan and a secret love-nest somewhere beautiful by the sea.

ABOUT THE AUTHOR:

Thank you for reading my book *The Minx*. I hope you enjoyed it.

Janet Cameron holds a BA (hons) 2.1 in Literature and Philosophy, and an MA in Modern Poetry with the University of Kent, which incorporates the philosophical manifestos of major poets and the work of controversial founding father of deconstruction in philosophy, Jacques Derrida.

Janet is a retired lecturer at the University of Kent, and an award-winning writer. She is also the author of thirteen books, mostly regional history publications, numerous articles on history, philosophy, poetry, feminism and human rights, novels and short literary fiction. She writes a monthly magazine column for Writers Forum.

Printed in Great Britain
by Amazon